THE GOOD TEACHER

BRIAN R. O'ROURKE

Published by Inkubator Books
www.inkubatorbooks.com

ISBN (eBook): 978-1-83756-371-5
ISBN (Paperback): 978-1-83756-372-2
ISBN (Hardback): 978-1-83756-373-9

PROLOGUE

NOW

Nelly slowly came to.

She didn't know where she was.

Feeling groggy, she tried to make sense of her surroundings. Ahead of her was an unadorned wall made of old cement that was crumbling in places. There was a naked bulb on overhead that bathed the room in a harsh light. The space had the look and feel of a basement.

She was sat in a chair. Nelly waited a moment for her head to clear more, then tried to stand up. She could barely move. She got a few inches off the seat, but that was it.

Then she looked down.

She was *tied* to the chair.

Panicked, she tried to reach for the rope but found she could not bring her hands forward. Something metallic was painfully digging into her wrists. With mounting horror, she realized she was also handcuffed.

Nelly let out an involuntary shriek. She tried again to stand but could only manage the same few inches. When she tried to move her feet around, she discovered her ankles were duct-taped together.

No, no, no...

She couldn't move, and she was trapped in a strange basement.

What is happening?

At that moment, her mental fog lifted, and everything came back to her. She recalled where she'd been and what had happened. She was in terrible danger.

Nelly began to tremble.

Six days ago, she had come to this new town to restart her life. But now she was going to die. And there was nothing she could do about it.

A door behind her opened. Light poured in from another room. A moment later she came face-to-face with her captor.

"Hello, Nelly."

1

SIX DAYS AGO – SUNDAY

Nelly was glad she'd allowed herself extra time to make it to the charity run early, because every person in the small town of Overland, apparently, had turned out for the event, creating a traffic snarl on what seemed to be the only artery leading to St. Peter's Church. Even though the race was set to begin in half an hour, the parking lot and overflow lot were already full, and teenaged boys in bright yellow vests waved orange-tipped batons, directing drivers to park on the shoulder of the road. By the time Nelly found a place, she was nearly a quarter of a mile from the starting line. She didn't relish the thought of having to walk such a distance before she ran (okay, jogged) a 5K, but there was nothing to be done about it now.

Showing up at the last minute and looking frazzled was not the first impression Nelly wanted to make, so she was glad she still had some time to register, collect her bib, and meet her new boss and colleagues. Taking a moment in her car, Nelly checked what little makeup she'd put on in the rearview mirror. She hadn't slept well last evening, her first night in a new place, and despite her best efforts, it showed.

You're not young anymore.

Nelly would never have pictured herself here at the age of thirty-seven: divorced, living in small-town Pennsylvania, about to start at a new school, where she'd have to prove herself all over again. But those were the uncomfortable facts. There was nothing else to do but make the best of the situation. After being out of work for longer than expected, and starting to wonder if her reputation had been permanently damaged, Nelly *needed* to make this work.

And why shouldn't it? The last year had been nothing but heartache and bad luck. She was due for some good.

Though Overland was part of a small school district, Nelly had gotten a good feeling during her job interview. The principal, Miguel Cuevas, seemed a decent sort, and she'd been especially happy to hear that he wouldn't ask much of her in terms of non-instructional duties at first. He wanted her focused on teaching and getting adjusted.

She got the jitters as she hurried from her car to the registration desk for the charity run. The attendant there directed her toward a navy blue canopy on the near side of the church parking lot, close to the starting line, with the words Overland Middle School stenciled in gold. Pinning her bib to the front of her wicking shirt, Nelly combatted her growing nerves by remembering this was exactly what she'd been waiting for. The chance at a fresh start.

Putting a smile on her face, Nelly approached the canopy.

2

"Nelly! Over here!"

Her new boss, Miguel Cuevas, spotted her from across the way despite the crowded parking lot. The principal waved excitedly and hurried over to meet her. He was shorter and smaller than she was expecting. Over Zoom, he'd seemed like a bigger man. His gray hair was turning white at the temples, and in person he looked a little older than he had during their online interview.

"Hi, Miguel," she said. "It's so nice to meet you."

He pumped her hand.

"I'm so glad you could make it!" he said, practically glowing. "How was your trip out?"

Few things were more boring than listening to someone else's travel pains, so Nelly gave him the abridged version. Her uneventful trip driving from California to Pennsylvania had taken three days. Her body wasn't on Pacific time still, but it hadn't caught up to Eastern time yet either.

"We have twenty minutes until race time," Miguel said. "Come meet the troops."

Nelly followed him back to the Overland Middle School canopy, where her new boss made introductions. Though she was used to standing in front of a roomful of thirty children and teaching, Nelly did not enjoy being the center of attention. After a whirlwind of names and small talk, Nelly found herself a little overwhelmed.

"You doing okay?"

The woman was young, looked barely out of college. Nelly thought her name was—

"Beck, right?" she said.

Beck smiled. "I'm amazed you remembered my name after meeting all these people."

"I'm a teacher," Nelly said. "Half the job is memorizing names."

The other woman nodded. "The other half is classroom management."

She brought her thumb and forefinger almost together. "And about one percent is actual teaching."

They shared a laugh. "We're happy to have you."

"Thanks," Nelly said. "So, is this everybody?"

"A few people couldn't make the race," Beck said. "And Emmett is busy running around, like always."

Beck was short and not exactly dressed for a charity run, sporting an oversized tie-dye T-shirt and khaki shorts over white leggings. She wore two different colored eye shadows. Nelly was willing to bet her life savings that Beck was the art teacher.

"I have to say this," Beck said. "Thank God you're here."

Nelly didn't understand why the woman sounded so relieved by her presence.

Beck gave her a knowing look. "Now I'm no longer the New Girl." She winked at Nelly.

"You make it sound so undesirable," Nelly said.

"It's not that bad," Beck said, teasing her. "We keep the hazing to a minimum."

"Wonderful."

"And strictly legal," Beck said. "Well, *mostly* legal."

The ribbing was good-natured. Nelly found herself relaxing and warming to the other woman. Beck caught Nelly playfully scrutinizing her outfit. She tugged at the neck of the much-too-large T-shirt.

"I woke up in a strange man's apartment and couldn't find my dress from last night," Beck said. "I grabbed the first garments I saw."

Nelly got the sense this was not the first time Beck had made an off-color joke in the presence of colleagues.

"Kidding," Beck said, then gave her a sidelong glance. "Or am I?"

Nelly couldn't help but laugh.

"So, Nelly," Beck said, sizing her up, "are you a runner?"

"Not lately," Nelly said.

Exercise had not been a priority in the last year. Nelly had been too busy getting divorced, leaving her job, and looking for a way to restart her life.

"Me neither." Beck clutched her nonexistent stomach. "All those drinks last night aren't helping either."

"You're young," Nelly said. "Wait till you're my age."

"Excuse me," Beck said. "I'm *twenty-five.* Old enough to have already suffered my quarter-life crisis."

Nelly was beginning to like this woman.

"So you've met everyone?" Beck asked.

"Everyone except...what's his name? The one running around?"

"Emmett." Beck rolled her eyes, but there was no spite in the gesture. "Mr. Wonderful himself."

Nelly enjoyed their banter. "Why is Emmett Mr. Wonderful?"

"He's a great guy," Beck said, meaning it. "He's the one who organizes this race every year. All the proceeds go to the women's shelter. He's very active in the community. And he coaches our basketball team, leads the youth group, and every summer he volunteers for Habitat for Humanity."

Nelly nodded, impressed. "Sounds too good to be true."

Beck lowered her voice. "Now that Patti might be gone, Emmett is probably our next assistant principal."

Nelly pulled a face. Patti Alston had taken an unexpected leave of absence due to some kind of medical emergency. Nelly had been hired to fill in for the woman, though Miguel had intimated that her employment would likely become permanent if things went well.

"And when Miguel retires," Beck went on, "that means Emmett will run the show."

"Is he married?" Nelly asked, joking.

Beck laughed.

"You just missed the boat." Beck shook her head. "Recently engaged."

Nelly snapped her fingers, feigning disappointment. Truth was, she had no desire to jump into a relationship. She was still recovering from the dissolution of her marriage. She'd been with John for a long time and couldn't imagine getting involved with anyone. She wanted to be alone for a while, get herself sorted.

"Good for him," Nelly said.

"Oh—that's him." Beck pointed. "The guy about to get on the microphone."

Nelly followed the aim of Beck's finger through the crowd, toward a knot of people standing about thirty feet away. A man wearing a gray St. Peter's Church T-shirt was passed a microphone. She couldn't make out Emmett's face from this angle. All she could see was his wavy, dirty blond hair.

Emmett brought the microphone up to his mouth. The people hovering near him raised their hands and signaled for quiet, but there were hundreds, if not thousands, here, making lots of noise, so few noticed. Emmett addressed the crowd over a staticky PA system.

"Thank you all for coming..."

His voice seemed familiar, though Nelly couldn't place it. Perhaps it reminded her of the baritone of some famous actor. Either way, she didn't know anyone named Emmett.

The PA system was of poor quality. Nelly picked out every third or fourth word he said. There were times when the crowd burst into laughter or cheered at something he'd said. He thanked everyone for their support, then asked one of the priests, who was also wearing a gray St. Peter's Church T-shirt, to offer a blessing. When that was done, Emmett reclaimed the microphone and whipped the crowd into a frenzy. He had the charisma of an energetic MC and seemed perfectly at ease addressing such a large gathering. And the whole time, that sense of his voice being familiar nagged at Nelly. The longer he spoke, the more she was certain she'd heard it *somewhere* before. But that was impossible.

Because she didn't know anyone named Emmett.

Finally, Emmett concluded by offering yet another heartfelt expression of gratitude, which was met with enthusiastic applause. Everyone adored this guy. Nelly couldn't help but be impressed and, surprisingly, a little envious. Not of Emmett specifically, but of the sense of community here. She couldn't help but feel like an outsider.

Emmett handed the microphone off to another man, who went on to explain the route and markers. He made a joke about having the most difficult job of all, the starter, which required him to fire a fake gun into the sky to signal the beginning of the race. The participants intending to run quickly moved toward the front of the starting line. Nelly's group, the Overland faculty, remained in the middle of the pack.

Beck waved her hand and raised her voice over the din. "Over here, Emmett!"

Nelly shifted from one leg to the other, staying on the balls of her feet. Though she'd run her fair share of 5Ks over the years, she was experiencing pre-race jitters now. She hadn't jogged more than a mile in quite a while, and she'd abandoned her admittedly modest exercise regimen when life had taken a turn. She was worried she wouldn't make it through the race and didn't want to embarrass herself in front of coworkers she hardly knew. She'd felt compelled to participate when Miguel had mentioned the event in passing, suggesting it was a great opportunity for her to meet her new colleagues before she got started.

But now she was regretting it.

"Emmett!" Beck called out. "Come meet Nelly!"

Despite her nerves, Nelly was excited to meet this man. If what Beck had said was true and Emmett was the next in line to succeed Miguel as principal in the near future, then it was very important to make a good impression with him also. Putting on a big smile, Nelly turned and came face-to-face with…

"Emmett," Beck said, touching the man's shoulder, "this is Nelly, our new history teacher. And Nelly, this is Emmett."

Nelly's smile slipped. Emmett looked an awful lot like someone she'd known, briefly, many years ago. He was a few inches taller than her, with gray, narrow-set eyes, and wavy, dirty blond hair. He looked to be about Nelly's age, around forty or so. This close, Nelly could see he was in fantastic shape, with a trim waistline and broad shoulders. As he flashed her a thousand-watt smile, she got a good look at his teeth, pearly white and perfectly ordered.

But there was something about Emmett that reminded Nelly of someone else. Of someone terrible. A boy named Marshall.

She felt all eyes on her. Nelly propped up that smile, hoping it looked genuine, though she was absolutely terrified. She wasn't certain she could move.

There was a change behind Emmett's eyes, a fleeting recognition, as he continued to flash his bright smile. Or was she imagining it? She couldn't be sure. All of the sudden, Nelly was in a sweat, and the race hadn't even started yet.

"Nelly, it's so nice to meet you." Emmett stuck out his hand. "I'm Emmett. I teach English language arts. I've heard so many good things about you."

His hand hovered between them. Nelly felt the scrutinizing gazes from Beck and others nearby. She knew she needed to shake this man's hand, but the very thought of pressing her palm against his, of allowing him to grip a part of her body in any way, made her light-headed. She was breathing heavily, as if she'd *already* run the race.

"Likewise," she forced herself to say, "it's nice to meet you too."

Somehow she managed to shake Emmett's hand. His palm was callused and cold. She hid an involuntary shudder. His grip was firm. A little too firm. She could feel how strong he was. The cords in his arm stood out. His pecs strained against his T-shirt.

He looked deeply into her eyes.

"I really look forward to working with you." One corner of his mouth turned up in a strange grin. "And getting to know you better."

BANG.

3

"Are you okay?" Beck asked.

"Fine," Nelly said. "Just out of shape."

Beck gave her what the kids called a side-eye. They were only a few minutes into the race, and even though the pace the faculty had set was comfortable, Nelly was struggling.

Emmett led the way, moving at what appeared to be a leisurely lope for him, while Beck ran alongside her.

"Don't worry," Beck said. "Only another two and a half miles to go."

Nelly faked a smile. Beck, for all her complaining and worry a moment ago, seemed perfectly fine.

But Nelly's eyes turned inevitably ahead. To the man calling himself Emmett.

He looked so much like Marshall. The resemblance was strongest in those gray, close-set eyes. And Nelly was certain she'd caught a look of recognition in those eyes, as if Emmett had met her before as well. Marshall had had curly blond hair, whereas this man had wavy dirty blond hair, but age could have dulled both features. Nelly thought about other people she'd known with blond or curly hair, and how they'd changed over time. Both men had the same pinched features as well, as if their nose were a magnet pulling their eyes and mouth toward it. The mouth was a little off-center too and possessed the same shape, higher on one side than the other.

There, however, the similarities ended. Emmett was a physical specimen, with broad shoulders and a tiny waist. He carried a lot of muscle and very little fat. Marshall, that sixteen-year-old boy she'd known so briefly, had been pudgy and oafish, his waist wider than his shoulders. She recalled that he'd tried out for the football team in high school but hadn't made the cut. Or had he been kicked off the team? It was difficult to remember. Emmett, on the other hand, glided along with little effort, looking very much like an athlete. She suspected he could run this race much more quickly if he desired.

But the differences went beyond the physical. Marshall had been awkward, leering, lurking. The kind of guy who hung out *around* everybody else, but not quite *with* them. He pretended not to be gawking at you from the corner of the room. He muttered things about your appearance just softly enough that you couldn't be sure he'd said them. When someone engaged him in conversation, he had trouble meeting their eye. His friends called him "funny," but she'd always thought they were being polite. Marshall's jokes were non sequiturs, punchlines to the strange ramblings of someone who'd been having a conversation with themselves in their own head.

"You sure you're okay?" Beck asked, sounding genuinely concerned.

Nelly clutched her side. A stitch was beginning to form.

"I don't know what's wrong with me," she said.

"Why don't we walk a minute?" Beck said.

They slowed. Beck told the other members of the faculty they'd catch up. Nelly didn't know about that. Her side was hurting. She was out of breath. And out of sorts. She'd be embarrassed by this poor showing if she weren't so preoccupied thinking about Emmett and Marshall.

Was it him? Was Emmett the man who...

With that emotional sixth sense most women seem to possess, Beck intuited there was something the matter with Nelly that went beyond the cramp in her side. The younger woman reached out and put a hand on Nelly's shoulder, giving her a meaningful look.

"Are you alright?"

"I'll be fine." Nelly forced a smile. "Just need a minute, then we can pick up the pace."

"Take your time," Beck said.

As dozens of people zipped by them and the faculty disappeared past the bend in the road ahead, her mind turned to the past, back to that horrible rainy day in September. It had been over twenty years ago, but to her it would always feel like yesterday.

4

"It's going to rain," I say. "Maybe we shouldn't go?"

Thunder rumbles in the distance, an ominous sign if ever there were any. But my best friend, Tina, ignores it and pedals on, picking up speed on her bike as we zoom down the hill.

"Don't be lame, Nelly," she says.

I pump my legs. It's difficult to catch up to Tina. I don't own a bike, so when we get together, I borrow the one she grew out of—it's too small for me, and only the lowest gear works, which is annoying. For every pedaling motion Tina performs, I have to do about four to match her.

But even if I had a nice new bike like Tina, it'd still be difficult to keep up with her. She's always moved a lot faster than me, in every possible way. Three years ago she announced we were done playing with dolls because she had French-kissed Alan Berowitz. And this summer, when I asked if we could play some board games, she laughed like I was making a joke and told me we were going to the pool because she wanted to flaunt her new bikini and planned on touching Sean Pepper's penis.

"I'm really not supposed to go here," I say, which I know is an even lamer excuse than the threat of bad weather. "My mother will kill me if she finds out."

Tina glances over at me. "You need to lighten up, Nelly. She won't find out."

"But if something happens—"

"Nothing horrible is going to happen."

We're biking to the old factory about a half mile up the road from Tina's place. It's been abandoned for so long, you can barely see it from the road anymore. The trees and other vegetation have crowded it; vines cover the face of the building. I've never been inside, but ever since we started eighth grade a month ago, Tina's done nothing but talk about it. It's where teenagers—usually high schoolers—go to have a good time.

The "bad" teenagers, that is.

If Mom knew I was coming here, I'd be in big trouble. She doesn't want me hanging around boys yet. According to her, the only honest man is the one who isn't talking, and even then you can't be sure about him. Two years ago, when I first got my period, we had the Talk, and that nipped what little growing interest I had in boys in the bud. Mom told me that most men just want to use women for sex and then leave them when they get pregnant. She told me they "couldn't help themselves." Though I had some friends with married parents who seemed happy, Mom was speaking from personal experience, so it was difficult to argue with her. That was the same day I found out she had gotten two abortions. One before and one after she had me. I didn't have the nerve to ask her why she decided to keep me but not the others. It makes me feel both incredibly lucky and undeserving, all at the same time. Maybe one day I'll ask Mom why things turned out this way.

In about forty years, maybe.

But even putting Mom's worries about horny boys aside, coming to the factory still isn't my idea of fun. I would have preferred to hang at Tina's house, where we watched R-rated movies in the basement and sometimes called boys and usually ordered pizza. Her parents were separated but not divorced, and Tina lived with her mother, who worked an important job as a lawyer and never seemed to have enough time to pay attention to what her mischievous daughter was up to.

So here I was, riding Tina's old bike to the factory, where we were supposed to meet some other people. She said something about beer and cigarettes. I don't plan on touching either and will have to keep my distance from anyone who indulges. Mom has the nose of a bloodhound, and if she gets a whiff of alcohol or smoke on me, I'll be in trouble.

"What did you tell your mom?" I ask.

"That we were going for a bike ride," Tina answers, like I'm being an idiot.

Thunder booms, this time much more loudly. "In a storm?"

"Nelly." Tina rolls her eyes. "You're overthinking this."

"If my mother calls her and asks what we're doing—"

"Nelly. For. The. Love. Of. God."

"I'm just saying—"

Tina brakes. As I slow to a stop beside her, a light drizzle starts.

"If you don't want to go, that's cool," Tina says, an edge to her voice. "I'm not forcing you to. Go home if you want."

I'm hurt by her attitude. She's my best friend, and we made plans today. We were supposed to watch a movie, and her mom had offered to order out. While that might not have been the most exciting afternoon ever, it beat whatever I had going on at home by a mile. Mom would have probably made me do all the chores around the house, then complained about how poorly I'd done them, then gotten angry when I didn't complete the ones she'd never asked me to do.

"Look, Nelly, hanging out in my basement to watch an old movie or whatever, it's lame. So is calling random boys and all that. I'm about to turn fourteen.*"*

Right. Fourteen. *Not twenty. We weren't in college. We weren't even in high school. Tina had always moved faster than me, but the differences of late were becoming more glaring. We were like these bikes: she kept changing to a faster gear, while I was stuck on the lowest one.*

I bite back tears. Tina's been my best friend since second grade. She's called me lame before, but I always took it as a joke. But now I'm starting to wonder if she means it.

Her expression softens when she registers my reaction. "Hey, come on. It's going to be cool. We don't have to stay long. And who knows? You might meet a cute guy."

I want to go home, but I don't want her thinking I'm lame either.

"Okay."

The rain picks up while we bike the rest of the way to the factory. Ducking under the rusty chain displaying a KEEP OUT sign, we walk our bikes up the overgrown entrance to the building. Behind the tree line is a parking lot filled with weeds taller than I am, crushed beer cans, broken glass, some needles, and a dumpster that looks like it was forgotten about. The building itself is missing some windows, and there are KEEP OUT signs posted in several places. One faded orange piece of paper nailed to the main entrance reads CONDEMNED.

"Are you sure it's safe?" I ask, not able to help myself.

Tina rubs my shoulder. "They just post those signs to scare people off."

With a growing sense of dread, I walk my bike around to the side of the building where a large roof juts out and there are big bays with sliding panels. This must be where the deliveries came in. The abandoned factory doesn't look any more stable or inviting back here, but at least we're out of the rain.

"How do we get inside?" I ask.

Tina smiles. "This way."

After leaning our bikes against the side of the building, I follow her to an old metal door. She turns the knob. The interior is dark, weak afternoon light streaming in through the few windows that haven't been boarded up or papered over. A strong metallic odor hits me.

I must make a face, because Tina says, "Don't worry about that. You won't smell it in a minute."

Stepping inside, I find myself in a large open room that's filled with junk, old machines, office equipment. I pretend I don't notice something small and furry scurry away from us, seeking refuge under a rotting desk.

"Great, isn't it?" Tina asks.

I can't bring myself to lie. My skin is crawling.

"Come on," she says. "I'll give you the tour."

We move carefully around dangerous-looking, rusting equipment through haphazard aisles of clear space into another area with a long hallway and a series of doors on both sides.

"This is the best place to hide," Tina says. "Not out there."

"Hide?" I ask.

"Yeah." She smirks. "For hide-and-seek."

I frown, puzzled at this. For all Tina's bluster about childish things being lame, I can't picture her enjoying a game of hide-and-seek anymore. Though, perhaps the ominous setting of an abandoned building makes it more thrilling.

Either way, I'm not much interested in playing hide-and-seek here of all places, with boys I hardly know. Mom has put the fear of God into me when it comes to the opposite sex.

"Come on," Tina says.

We move down the hallway. They could film a horror movie here. This place is creepy. There's all kinds of junk strewn everywhere, almost giving the impression that the people last here left in a hurry, like they were afraid of something terrible. Like they just found out a huge asteroid was on a collision course with Earth. Or like there was a group of sociopathic serial killers out hunting them. I don't know. My mind goes to dark places sometimes.

I step over what appears to be a used condom floating in a yucky puddle of standing water. A few short months ago, I would not have known what it was. But at the beginning of the school year, we had health education. The few pictures they showed us were funny. Half the class erupted in laughter at the sight of a penis.

I hear dripping somewhere. As we proceed down the dingy hallway, the soft murmur of voices in a distant room reaches my ears.

"Are you going to hold it together?" Tina asks. She's teasing me, trying for a laugh, but I'm not really in the mood. Every alarm bell inside my brain is going off. This is not my thing.

But I don't want her to think of me as her lame friend who only wants to play with dolls and make tie-dye T-shirts and talk about the Babysitters Club books.

"I'm fine," I lie.

At last we reach the end of this hallway, coming to a T-junction. Tina makes a right and leads me to a large office. I can hear a lot of voices now, loud and clear. I smell smoke and something else too—must be alcohol. At least I've gotten used to that godawful metallic smell. I don't notice it anymore.

"We're here," Tina says, stepping in front of the doorway.

I take a deep breath and follow her inside. There are about fifteen people here. She and I are the only middle schoolers. Everybody else is high school age. It's a small town, so I recognize them all, with the exception of one heavyset boy with long, curly blond hair. When our eyes meet, half his mouth curls upward in a gross smile. I know what's on his mind as his eyes slowly pan up and down my body.

"Everybody, this is Nelly," Tina says.

A few of them say hello. The rest don't bother. They can tell, just by looking at me, that I don't belong here. That I'm lame. The boy and girl standing closest to the door pass what I think is a joint back and forth, while that chubby kid on the other side of the office takes a swig from a bottle of malt liquor.

Tina strides right up to Sean Pepper, who offers her his can of beer. She runs her hand up and down his stomach first and then sips from his drink.

I put my back against the wall and try to activate my superpower: invisibility. I don't want to be here, and it's obvious from the muted reaction I got that nobody else really wants me here either. I'm not sure Tina even does, to be honest. Perhaps she just brought me along out of habit or a sense of obligation. Maybe to her I'm that annoying friend she can't bring herself to cut ties with. Another boy and girl sitting on a tarp-covered sofa go back to making out. The boy's hand disappears under her shirt. He's groping her boobs in plain sight of everyone else.

Tina and Sean are already deep in conversation. A trio of freshmen girls are shooting me scathing looks, and though I can't hear them, they're obviously talking about me. A couple of boys who I think are sophomores smoke cigarettes. Two more girls, with their skirts hiked way up on their thighs, dance provocatively even though there's no music playing.

I don't know why I'm here.

I'd rather be home, helping Mom with chores.

I'd rather be studying my least favorite subject: math.

I'd rather be anywhere else. Doing anything else.

Eventually, everyone loses interest in me, even the nasty girls in the corner. I melt into the wall, becoming part of the background. Tina begins teasing Sean, rubbing his stomach and thighs, drinking his beer, pushing up against him. It's clear what's on her mind. And even in the strange gloom of this office, it's impossible not to notice the bulge in Sean's shorts. It's almost like he wants her—and everybody else—to see what he's packing.

I want to go.

The chubby blond guy continues to leer at me. I pretend I don't notice him, but he must be able to tell how uncomfortable I am. Forcing myself to catch him staring in the hopes he'll be embarrassed and look away, I meet his eyes.

He doesn't avert his gaze. His mouth cracks open slightly, and again he offers me that same icky smile.

I have to leave.

The rain picks up. It hammers the roof, making a racket. Now is not the best time to ride a bike half a mile up this narrow, two-lane road missing a shoulder. Somebody driving through this deluge might not even see me. I could be killed if I tried to bike back to Tina's house right now.

And what exactly am I supposed to say to Ms. Hirshberg when I show up at her door without Tina? I can't tell my friend's mother where Tina is, certainly not what she's doing or who she's doing it with. I'd have to sneak around the back of the house, leave the bike, and then walk to the convenience store and call Mom for a ride from the payphone. Do I even have change?

Despite these practical impediments to my departure, the urge to run out of here does not go away.

"Alright, I think everybody's here," Sean announces suddenly. "You all wanna get started?"

"Let's do it!" one of the girls in the corner answers.

I have no idea what they're talking about, but I sincerely hope it's not playing this game of hide-and-seek Tina was talking about.

"Alright, cool!" Sean says. "Last time, the guys hid. So this time, it's the ladies' turn."

Someone hoots. The other girls congregate near the door, with the exception of Tina, who remains beside Sean.

"You all know the rules," Sean says. "You get caught, you have to kiss. At least."

What? How is that a rule?

Seeing the panic in my face, Tina detaches herself from Sean and comes over.

She rubs my shoulder. "You are going to love this, girl."

"I don't want to kiss anybody," I say, much too loudly. A few of the boys look offended.

"Don't worry." One laughs. "Nobody wants to kiss you either."

I could die right now.

Tina sighs, looking disappointed. "Like I said, you don't have to be here. You can go."

I can't contain my anger. Tina knew I didn't want to come to the factory at all but coaxed me into it. And she didn't say a thing about playing this kind of game with a bunch of older boys, one of whom keeps creepily staring at me.

"Do you hear the rain?" I ask. "And what am I supposed to say to your mother?"

"Nelly, for God's sake. Tell her whatever you want. I don't care. I'm going to have some fucking fun now. You do what you want."

Everyone has overheard our short, heated exchange. Practically dying of embarrassment, I lower my eyes.

"Everybody plays," Sean says. "If you don't, you have to take your top off for everybody to see."

There's more cheering. One of the other girls tugs her spaghetti-strap top up from the bottom, baring her bra. All the boys go wild.

"Yeah, girl, that's the spirit," Sean says. "Ladies, you have sixty seconds to hide. Starting now!"

Two more girls peel off their tops. One of them isn't even wearing a bra. Then they hurry out of the office. Tina struts back over to Sean and puts her forefinger on his lips.

"You'd better be the one to find me," she says.

As she leaves the room, I swallow what little pride I have left and shoot her one last pleading look. But Tina ignores my gaze and high-fives one of the other girls on her way out.

"Fifty seconds," Sean says, turning his eyes to me.

I'm the last girl in the room.

The blond boy puts his big bottle of malt liquor down and crosses the room, stopping in front of me. His breath reeks of alcohol, and he can't quite keep his eyes still. I've never had a drink in my life, but I can tell he's wasted.

"I'm going to find you," he says.

I could throw up. Not that I want to be forced to kiss anyone here, but if I had to choose, it would not be this guy.

"I'm Marshall," he says.

Moving away from him, I look at Sean.

"Yeah, so, I'm not going to play. I'm just waiting out the storm."

Sean checks his watch. "Forty seconds."

The other boys are laughing at me. Marshall eyes me greedily. I feel naked under his gaze.

"I said I'm not going to play."

"You don't have to hide," Sean says, "so long as you don't mind taking your top off for us."

"Ewww, gross."

The boys start chanting, "Take it off! Take it off! Take it off!"

I'm ready to cry. How could Tina do this to me? She obviously doesn't care about my feelings if she's willing to let her friends treat me like this. For the first time in my life, I experience the bitter taste of betrayal.

"Thirty seconds!" Sean calls out.

All of these people, the girls included, will pressure me to flash my bra. If I refuse, I'll be the laughingstock. For some reason, both those options seem worse than playing this stupid game. I'll hide, some boy will find me, and I'll kiss him. That's all. Maybe it won't even be this Marshall creep. That sounds much better than baring myself to all these people.

"I'm going to find you," Marshall says as I dart out of the room.

5

After the race, the faculty met near the navy blue canopy in the church parking lot. Many vendors had set up for the occasion, including several food trucks and a handful of microbreweries. Nelly was surprised at how quickly—and how much—her colleagues were grabbing drinks, but Miguel didn't seem to mind. Nearby, one vendor boasted the county's best pulled-pork sandwiches. The food smelled great to Nelly, but she didn't have much of an appetite.

A knot of young men—Nelly thought they were college-aged—were stuffing their faces and horsing around nearby. They must have finished the race quickly and gotten started drinking immediately. Judging by the volume of their voices and the barbecue sauce smearing their faces, they were already in their cups, as her mother would have said.

"This fucking pulled pork is amazing!" one of them declared, timing his profanity perfectly to coincide with the passing by of a mother and her two young daughters. One of his buddies swatted his shoulder, telling him to watch his language, but the kid was unabashed.

Nelly turned away from them. Her colleagues were all in good spirits, but she was going through the motions. She couldn't stop thinking about the past and wondering if this man, Emmett, and the boy she knew briefly, Marshall, were one and the same. At least Emmett had disappeared, attending to his post-race duties as the event organizer. It gave her some space and more time to think. Was she being paranoid? Seeing things that weren't there?

That was what John, her ex-husband, would probably say. Not that she cared anymore what he thought.

Beck appeared carrying two red plastic cups. "Sorry it took so long."

Nelly didn't normally drink beer, but she needed something to take the edge off. "Thanks."

Miguel was waving his hand to get everyone's attention. "Group picture!"

"Where's Emmett?" someone called out.

"I think I saw him with Vanessa," one of the other faculty members answered, "over by the volunteer tent."

At the mention of Emmett, Nelly felt sick. "Who's Vanessa?"

"Emmett's fiancée," Beck said.

"Did she run the race?" Nelly asked, hoping she hid her shock well. She couldn't believe this man was engaged.

"Vanessa?" Beck gave her an incredulous look. "She's afraid that if she lifts a finger, one of her fingernails will get dirty."

Nelly felt like there was more to the story behind Beck's dislike of this woman. But it was her first day here, and she didn't want to come across like she was prying.

"How did they meet?" Nelly asked.

"She teaches at the high school," Beck answered. "Foreign languages."

"What's she like?" Nelly asked. Though the woman had been standoffish at the race, Nelly felt an odd kinship toward her. They were both connected to Emmett.

Beck gave her a sidelong glance. "More stuck-up than a liquor store in a bad neighborhood."

Nelly stifled a laugh and followed Beck's gaze. Emmett approached the group with a striking blonde woman who was an inch or two taller than him. She wore a long skirt and an expensive-looking blouse under a shawl. Vanessa was put-together, and judging by her dress and manner, Nelly assumed she came from money. Emmett was in the middle of scarfing down a pulled-pork sandwich. Nearby, a group of high school boys began playfully shoving each other.

"I don't want to hear the word no," Miguel said, stepping in front of Emmett. "You're joining us for a group photo."

Emmett's smile slipped. "You know I hate having my picture taken."

"Come on," Miguel said. "It'll look good on the school's social media accounts."

An alarm sounded in Nelly's head. Why would someone as attractive as Emmett, who seemed to suffer from no shortage of vanity, be camera-shy? It made her even more suspicious. If you were pretending to be someone you were not, you wouldn't want your picture all over the internet.

"Oh, don't make him, Miguel," Vanessa said, putting her hand on her fiancé's chest. "You know how Emmett feels about social media."

"It's going to be the death of us," Emmett said.

But the rest of the faculty applied peer pressure, and

eventually Emmett capitulated, demanding he stand in the back row. While they positioned themselves in front of the canopy, one of the nearby rowdy college boys accidentally bumped into Emmett. Barbecue sauce ended up all over Emmett's wicking shirt. He took it in his stride, but Vanessa laid into the drunk college kids, who apologized and made themselves scarce.

"You can't take your picture looking like that," Vanessa said, looking her fiancé over. "You'd better take your shirt off."

"No," Emmett said. "I don't want to be *that* guy."

She rubbed his chest, her hand avoiding the stains. "You're allowed to show off that body. You've earned it."

"Take it off!" one of the other faculty members shouted, teasing Emmett. And then everybody else took up the chant.

Nelly's nausea worsened. Hearing everyone shout *take it off* struck too close to home, with the memory of that horrible afternoon fresh in her mind. She remembered what it had felt like to have those boys pressure her into playing that awful game of hide-and-seek, as they all chanted the same thing at her.

Take it off.

Emmett finally peeled his shirt off to reveal an impressive torso. Not an ounce of flab anywhere on that body of his. He blushed when several members of the faculty hooted appreciatively at him. A long scar ran diagonally from his shoulder nearly to the other side of his stomach. It looked like an old wound, but it hadn't been there when Nelly knew him.

Nelly felt a bit odd posing for a group picture with these people when she hadn't technically started working with them yet. But she would have felt even more awkward standing off to the side and waiting to be asked to join the shot, so in the end she wedged herself between Steve and Beck.

Miguel arranged for a passerby to take their picture. While that person had them tighten up their arrangement and moved a few people around and made sure nobody was blocked, Nelly thought about math. She would be the first to admit to its utility, but it had always been her least favorite subject in school. More specifically, she thought about odds, and what the odds must have been for her to move across the country to live in a new state so that she could work in a small town in a small school district, and wind up being colleagues with a man who had assaulted her twenty-some years ago, who was now posing as someone else.

Of course, she couldn't put an exact number on those odds. But it didn't take somebody with a PhD to know they were *long*.

Maybe they were too long.

Sure, Emmett bore a passing resemblance to Marshall. But there were just as many differences between the two men, most notably in their personalities. Nelly knew a thing or two about that, having worked with so many children and keeping in touch with, or hearing about, them over the years. She hadn't been shocked when she heard Joey DeVito was accepted into Harvard, or when Melanie Rodgers became a decorated soldier, or when Patrick Newman was arrested for receiving stolen goods.

Personality was largely set in childhood. People changed gradually over time, by degrees, but for the most part, they were who they were. The gauche, creepy, and criminal

Marshall transforming into the gregarious, charming, respected teacher and beloved community member Emmett was the stuff of fairy tales. Not reality.

Maybe it wasn't him.

The truth was, Nelly had been through a traumatic childhood experience that had left her scarred for life. She was intellectually honest enough to admit that that damage affected the way she saw things. Perhaps this was just her overactive brain generating a false positive.

"Young lady, I need you to smile."

Nelly realized the man taking the picture was talking to her. He couldn't have been much older than her, but she had always appeared young for her age with her smallish stature and youthful features. It was only a few years ago, at the age of thirty-three, that she'd been carded at a liquor store, a story her then-husband had loved sharing with his buddies, giving him an opportunity to brag about how youthful his wife looked.

Perking up immediately, she plastered a smile on her face and hoped it was convincing. She was embarrassed to have been caught not paying attention and holding everyone up. While they posed, Nelly told herself she should take this slow, not jump to any conclusions. Though, at the same time, she couldn't ignore that terrible feeling of certainty. Part of her was *convinced* Emmett was Marshall. The rational and intuitive sides of her mind were in disagreement, and she didn't know how to reconcile that.

Nelly lingered after the photo was taken, not wanting to be the first to leave and be seen as antisocial by her new colleagues. She chatted up a few people she hadn't gotten the chance to talk to, all the while keeping one eye on Emmett. Not once did the man glance in her direction, though she got the feeling he was acutely aware of her presence.

By the time several faculty members had left, Nelly's half-finished beer was warm. The skies had turned gray, and the air was cold. She was looking forward to getting back to her apartment so she could spend some time looking both Emmett and Marshall up online. She didn't know what she expected to find, but she had to do *something.* She said goodbye to Miguel and Steve, who were deep in conversation. Beck noticed she was leaving and hurried over.

"Nells," she said. Apparently, they were already on a nickname basis. Nelly liked it. "Do you want to go out for drinks?"

It took Nelly a moment to realize Beck meant *tonight.*

"I'd love to, but I'm still getting settled," Nelly said. "Maybe later this week?"

Beck mock-pouted. "Alright, but I'm going to hold you to it."

They exchanged numbers. While she had her phone out, Beck held it up for Nelly to see the screen.

"By the way," Beck said, "you look great in this picture."

It was one of the group photos from earlier. Miguel had forwarded them around. Nelly didn't think she looked *great* in it. The sun was in her eyes, forcing her to squint a bit, but she appreciated the compliment. While she examined the photo, she couldn't help but scrutinize Emmett for a moment. In this photo, with his shirt off and that ugly scar prominent, he didn't resemble Marshall as much.

"What?" Beck asked.

"Nothing," Nelly said, catching herself. "I can't get over how old I'm starting to look."

Beck shook her head. "You look great. Are you on social media? You should post this."

"My Facebook is on life support," Nelly said.

"You should post this," she repeated. "You'll have about fifty guys asking for your number."

Nelly laughed. She'd always been plain-looking, cute on her best days, forgettable on the others. Now that she thought about it, she wasn't sure fifty guys had shown an interest in her entire life.

She didn't plan on posting the group photo, but now that Beck had mentioned it, she realized she should update her profile. At the very least, she should friend request, or whatever the appropriate term was, the Overland Middle School page. Beck gave her a hug, then went off looking for food. Nelly was about to leave when she heard a voice.

"Nelly."

She turned to find Emmett's fiancée standing behind her. The woman had at least half a foot on her, with icy blue eyes and long, straight blonde hair that fell to her shoulders.

"I'm Vanessa," she said, holding her hand out. "It's so nice to meet you."

"Hi."

They shook hands. Emmett, conversing with the PE teacher whose name Nelly couldn't remember at the moment, looked over at them with a blank expression.

"I teach French and Spanish," Vanessa said. "From what I hear, we're lucky to have you. Tell me, what brings you all the way from sunny California to our quiet little town?"

Nelly was distracted by Emmett's gaze and a bit intimidated by this striking woman with a rather patrician manner.

"I was looking for a change," she said, keeping her

answer intentionally vague. "And this seemed like a good fit."

"Really?" Vanessa frowned. "I heard you were coming from a very large school district. It must have been incredibly well funded, too, being situated in California. Not too many teachers I know would want to leave that. You must have been looking for quite a big change."

The woman had put Nelly on her heels. She felt the need to explain herself, but thought better of it.

"Yes, I was."

Vanessa arched an eyebrow as if she didn't believe Nelly. "Well, like I said, we're lucky to have you. Though you have some big shoes to fill. Patti is a wonderful teacher."

Nelly smiled. "That's what I hear."

"I do hope she comes back soon," Vanessa said. "The children *love* her."

Nelly didn't say anything. Miguel hadn't shared the details of Patti's abrupt leave of absence, but Nelly had gotten the sense that Miguel had been taken by surprise by the request.

It was also a strange thing for Vanessa to say. If Patti suddenly returned from her leave of absence, as unexpectedly as she had taken it, then Nelly would likely be out of a job. Miguel had made assurances that he would "try" to place her in the event that happened, but she had known that was as soft a guarantee as he could make.

"Oh," Vanessa said, as if realizing her gaffe, "I'm sure Miguel would figure something out if that happened. Don't worry."

Nelly didn't say anything. Everyone else had been so welcoming of her, but this woman was frosty.

"We're a tight-knit faculty," Vanessa said. "More family

than co-workers. When you prove yourself, you'll be welcomed in with open arms."

Nelly gaped. She'd been teaching for fifteen years. While she wanted to do a good job and gain Miguel's approval, she also felt like she didn't have to *prove* herself to anyone, least of all this woman. Her experience should have spoken for itself. Her references were glowing. And despite whatever problems she'd had at her last school, her reputation had remained intact.

"Vanessa, dear, are you giving our newest colleague a hard time?"

Emmett approached them with a big smile and a beer in hand. He had an easy, almost carefree manner, which surprised her. Nelly had wanted to skip out without engaging with the man again, but no such luck.

He put his arm around his fiancée's shoulders, giving her a little squeeze.

"I was not," Vanessa said, giving him a peck on the cheek. "I only wanted to introduce myself."

Emmett gave Nelly a knowing look, like they were in on some joke together at Vanessa's expense. It made her uncomfortable.

"You'll have to forgive my fiancée," Emmett said. "She's lived in Overland her entire life and has been teaching here for eighteen years. She can be a bit territorial."

Nelly smiled, keeping her eyes on Emmett. Now that they were face-to-face again, the resemblances between him and Marshall were stark, much more prominent than the differences.

Vanessa playfully batted Emmett's stomach. At some point between the photo opportunity and now, he'd donned another St. Peter's T-shirt. This one was a bit too small for him, though, taut against his pecs and tight around his bulging arms.

"Nelly," Emmett said, leaning in, "I'm afraid I owe you an apology."

6

Emmett's words froze Nelly.

Why did he owe her an apology?

He hadn't been rude before the race. To anyone watching, as a matter of fact, he would have appeared warm and kind.

Welcoming.

Nelly was at a loss, her eyes drifting to the man's fiancée.

But Vanessa's expression didn't give anything away either. She didn't look surprised or embarrassed or nervous about her fiancé admitting to owing Nelly an apology.

There was only one thing Emmett—Marshall—could have apologized to Nelly for. But surely he didn't mean that?

"I really am sorry," he said.

Nelly had no idea how to respond. They seemed to be talking about something specific, but also not. Was he owning up to his crime?

While nothing had come of his allegations before, the cultural landscape around sexual crimes had improved much. Back then, people said things like—

He said, she said.

Can't blame a guy for trying.

Did you see what she was wearing?

But these days, it was different. These days, men were playing with five fouls.

As impossible as it seemed, Nelly wondered if her presence had jarred him. If seeing her had stirred up remorse.

People changed. It often took them years, but it happened.

Was he sorry? Was he finally ready to account for his sins? Or had he even regretted his actions for some time, been too ashamed to face her and admit to them?

Nelly didn't know. But her thumb, the one he'd dislocated while holding her down, began to ache. Her body's way, perhaps, of reminding her of the pain from that day.

It would have been foolish of him to apologize. While the statute of limitations had run out, a public apology for such terrible behavior would have been professional suicide.

But the man did look genuinely sorry. Nelly had never expected this moment to come, had no idea what she'd say, and couldn't stomach the thought of him begging her forgiveness. While Nelly considered sympathy one of her strong suits, she had her limits.

"I did something that really put you off," Emmett said. "And I'm sorry."

Put her off? That was one way of putting it.

"When we were introduced," Emmett said, frowning at her confusion. "I can explain, if you'll let me."

Nelly didn't follow. She hated how weak her knees were. How terrified she felt. How this man had destabilized her.

"How many times have I warned you, Emmett?" Vanessa said, rubbing his belly.

"You're right, hon," Emmett said before turning back to her. "I was painfully shy growing up. I'd freeze up if I was in the middle of a big group. Wouldn't be able to get a word out. But I knew that I had to get over it if I ever wanted to teach."

Nelly was utterly confused.

"One day, I met a man. I didn't know it then, but he was going to change my life. He was always perfectly at ease around others, no matter the context. Eventually, I worked up the nerve to ask him how he did it. Back then, we didn't use the term 'hack' like we do today, but that's what he taught me. For a month straight, he forced me to introduce myself to twenty people every day. Everything changed for me after that. I grew comfortable around strangers, around large groups of them. I learned how to command a room, feel at ease, and make others feel at ease. It was life-changing."

"I don't understand."

"Sorry. I'm coming to it." He offered another ingratiating smile. "He taught me this hack. When you're meeting someone for the first time, you *pretend* they're an old friend. It's a way to trick your own brain. It changes the way you smile and look at this other person. You act like you *recognize* them."

Nelly understood.

He wasn't really apologizing. He was attempting to explain away that flash of recognition in his eyes when they'd been introduced.

"It's habit now," Emmett said, looking embarrassed. "I do it without thinking whenever I meet somebody new. It's supposed to make the other person feel comfortable and create this instant connection."

It sounded made-up to Nelly. And she felt like he was

using this as an opportunity to flaunt himself. While other faculty members heard him say how sorry he was, he was secretly communicating something else to her: that he wasn't sorry at all.

"He does it to everyone," Beck said, coming up beside her. "And it works. I've, uh, *borrowed* the hack and used it myself. It's helped me a lot in those awkward meet-and-greet social situations."

Nelly's head was spinning.

"The thing is," Emmett said, holding out his palms, "the trick works with nearly everybody. But when it *doesn't* work, when you try it on that one person in a thousand, it's *very* off-putting."

Nelly didn't trust herself to speak.

"That's all a long-winded way of saying sorry." Emmett stuck out his hand. "I wanted to make a good first impression with you, but I blew it. Can we start over? I'm Emmett."

She looked down at his hand. Touching him once had almost brought on a panic attack. Now here he was, using an insincere apology and the social context to all but force her to shake once more.

"I..."

Nelly didn't want to shake his hand again. But she was also the new teacher at Overland. She was starting her new job tomorrow, and she needed it to go well to help get her life back on track. She wasn't in a position to accuse this man of being a fraud. No one would take her seriously.

Besides, what if she was wrong about Emmett? Sure, there was a resemblance between him and Marshall. But Nelly hadn't seen that boy in twenty-four years.

Emmett smiled apologetically. "I'm terribly sorry about this."

He began to retract his hand. Nelly felt shamed into shaking.

"I'm Ellen *Peak*," she said. "But everybody calls me Nelly."

Marshall knew her as Nelly *Gordon*. But she realized after the fact how silly it was to emphasize her married name. If he'd recognized her, and she was almost certain he had, then what difference did a name make?

"Again, I'm really sorry, Nelly. It's nice to meet you."

It took all her strength to say, "It's nice to meet you too."

7

Eventually the rain that had threatened all day came, ending the post-race festivities early. Before it turned into a downpour, Nelly hustled back to her car. As soon as she started her engine, the windows fogged, and she was forced to sit there a moment while the defogger did its slow work.

While she waited, she watched the vehicles going by. A new BMW slowed next to her. The driver waved excitedly.

It was Emmett.

He smiled and continued to wave, as if waiting for an acknowledgment. Her skin crawling, Nelly forced herself to wave back so as not to offend or arouse his suspicion, but her movements were mechanical, unnatural.

She'd been able, at least temporarily, to not think about Emmett. But now as she watched his BMW disappear ahead, her intrusive thoughts returned. Her knuckles whitened as she gripped the steering wheel.

Now he knows what car you drive.

The thought made her start to hyperventilate. A line of

cars passed while she got her breathing under control, including several police cruisers.

While Emmett knowing her car wasn't ideal, she realized she couldn't have prevented that from happening. Overland Middle was a small school with a tiny faculty. He would have been able to pick her car out anyway quickly enough.

But all the same, it made her nervous.

What should I do?

Nelly mulled it over on her drive home. For longer than she cared to admit, Nelly considered inventing a story about a suddenly sick family member who needed her help, offering Miguel her sincerest apologies before leaving town in a hurry.

As tempting as the idea was, Nelly couldn't go through with it. She wasn't a liar, and she also didn't want to leave Miguel in the lurch. Having taught for so many years now, Nelly understood how challenging it was to be down one staff member, especially in a small school like this.

And perhaps most importantly, she didn't want to feel like a coward. If she ran away, would she ever be able to look at herself in the mirror again?

Besides...was she *certain* Emmett was Marshall?

She wanted to talk this over with someone she trusted, but she and her ex didn't really speak anymore, and Nelly didn't know anyone in town. She was tempted to contact her new boss, Miguel, but she had no idea how he'd react to what was admittedly an outrageous accusation. Her few close friends back in California had distanced themselves following the divorce and the other nasty business, clearly not wanting to get involved in the mess that had become Nelly's life. She didn't even consider calling her mother.

She felt all alone.

On her way home, she passed her new place of employment, Overland Middle School. Instead of continuing past, she pulled into the lot and parked illegally in front of the building.

With it being Sunday night, the school was dark, and nobody else was in the lot. She'd already visited the school's website prior to formally accepting the job offer, but online pictures never did a physical location justice. Overland looked both smaller and older than how it appeared on the internet.

Not for the first time, Nelly wondered if she'd made a mistake taking the job.

She'd had trouble finding work the last year. Money had been a concern of course, but she had her savings, and John was good about alimony. The truth was, she'd started to worry she'd never teach again. She feared she'd be forced into some office job she'd never wanted, the last fifteen years of teaching good for nothing.

When Miguel had offered her the job, she'd accepted on the spot. The principal had chuckled at her overeagerness, telling her to give it some thought and get back to him. Afterward, she'd been embarrassed by how desperate she must have seemed. When she had a moment to reflect, Nelly acknowledged that being out of work had made her jump at the offer even though it meant moving all the way back to the East Coast and starting over in a small town where she knew no one. She agonized for two days over the decision. But in the end, she didn't think she could wait any longer in the hopes a position more local, or in a larger school district, or both, would materialize. Keeping her misgivings to herself, she formally accepted the offer.

Not only did she have reservations, but now she also had Emmett to contend with.

NELLY PULLED into the long driveway, driving past the big old house where seventy-two-year-old Orville Lange resided, and parked in front of the barn, where her second-floor apartment was. Her legs ached as she climbed the wooden stairs. Once upon a time, running a 5K would have been a breeze. But she could tell she'd be sore tomorrow. Her lower back was also tight from being in the car for so long. She had no appetite and spent twenty minutes moving around the small apartment, having no outlet for all her nervous energy. Eventually she managed to get herself under control. With a deep, calming breath, she opened her laptop and started searching.

Marshall Dawes had no online presence.

No social media.

No LinkedIn.

He had graduated from Lenape High School twenty-two years ago. Nelly found his name on a list of graduates. But that was it.

She tried MySpace but discovered it was a very different website than the one she'd used, briefly, decades ago. Either way, she couldn't find a profile for Marshall Dawes.

Emmett Moore was a bit more active online, but that wasn't saying much. Like Marshall, he was not on social media. He did have a LinkedIn profile, but there was no photo. According to his page, he'd worked at Overland

Middle School for three years. He had graduated from Marist College in New York and worked at two other schools before winding up at Overland.

Nothing about his résumé suggested anything sinister. Instead, his history painted a picture of a dedicated teacher who spent several years at each place of employment before moving on.

He did appear on Overland Middle's faculty page, though Nelly almost didn't recognize him. In the professional photograph, Emmett wore large, black-rimmed glasses and had a close-cropped beard. His face slightly angled away from the camera, he wore a serious expression, no hint of a smile. He appeared to be both younger and heavier-set in the image too.

She recalled Emmett being actively involved in his church, so Nelly spent a few minutes scrolling through St. Peter's publicly available photos on Facebook. Emmett appeared in only a few and never quite in the foreground.

Nelly had only performed about twenty minutes of online snooping, but already she felt like she was approaching a dead end. Nothing on the internet proved Emmett was an impostor. The lack of photographs could simply be put down to his being a private person, perhaps camera-shy. As for Marshall, it was like the man had ceased to exist after he graduated from high school. Though this was merely a preliminary search, Nelly had to admit there was also nothing tying the two men together. They hadn't attended the same schools, and there was nothing to indicate they would have otherwise crossed paths.

As she had been driving back to her apartment earlier, Nelly realized she needed help. Contacting a private detective seemed like overkill, and if word got back to Emmett or her new boss that she'd hired someone to look into one of the most respected members of the Overland community, she could kiss this job and her reputation goodbye. Hiring a PI would be a last resort, the proverbial nuclear option.

But at the same time, simply continuing to probe online didn't seem like it would get her anywhere. Approaching local law enforcement with her gut feeling that Emmett was actually Marshall wouldn't go over well either.

There was one person Nelly thought about contacting. Her childhood friend Tina. They were Facebook friends, but beyond Nelly sending a friend request and Tina accepting, they hadn't interacted at all. When Nelly occasionally popped onto social media, she'd sometimes check out Tina's page, looking at pictures of the other woman's children. But if Tina ever did the same with her, Nelly had no idea. When nothing had come of their online connection, for lack of a better word, Nelly feared Tina had accepted the friend request out of a sense of obligation rather than desire, and eventually she gave up on the idea of ever talking to the woman again.

Nelly sighed. Contacting Tina didn't seem like a viable option. If the woman still harbored a grudge—rightly or wrongly—then she'd be loath to help Nelly at all.

There was a knock at her door.

8

Nelly checked the peephole before opening up.

The owner of the property, Orville, stood on the wooden stoop outside her apartment. He wore a plaid shirt, jeans, and an old baseball cap and gave her a toothy grin.

"Heya, Nelly," he said. "How's it going?"

"Oh, fine. Just getting ready for class tomorrow."

"I see." He turned toward his house. "I installed some floodlights near where I keep my trash. Raccoons have been bad this year. I'm hoping the lights will scare the critters off. They're on motion sensors. I wanted you to know in case they came on in the middle of the night. Didn't want you worried."

"Thank you for telling me," Nelly said.

Orville lingered. "I don't suppose you'd want to keep an old man company over dinner?"

Nelly smiled. Being around another human being sounded wonderful right now.

Orville's home hadn't been redone in a long time. The walls were covered with pictures of family. In the photographs, Nelly was treated to a time-lapsed montage of his children, from very early ages to adulthood, to becoming parents themselves. The carpet bore the stains of long use, of children and grandchildren too, worn down in many places, bunched up in others. A deer head hung on the lintel above the den. But for as old and outdated as it was, Nelly adored the place. She could picture Orville's children running through the living room, jumping on the couch, throwing pillows around, building makeshift forts out of the space's raw materials. In the entryway to the kitchen, names and ages and lines were penciled on the white paint to signify the children's increasing height over time. Some newer markings appeared lower in pen. Nelly guessed they belonged to Orville's grandchildren.

"You have a lovely home," Nelly said.

"Thank you," Orville said. "But I can't take credit for any of it. Lauren did the decorating. I haven't changed a thing."

Lauren had passed unexpectedly almost ten years ago. Nelly offered the man a sympathetic smile.

"Have a seat," Orville said, pulling a chair out at the kitchen table. "Nothing fancy, I'm afraid. Just steak and potatoes."

Nelly asked if she could help with dinner, but the old man was having none of it, insisting she was his guest and all but forcing her to sit. While Orville heated the leftovers and got the dishes and silverware out, Nelly reached into her pocket for her phone out of habit.

"Ah," she said, remembering.

Orville retrieved some Italian bread from the oven. "Something the matter?"

"My phone," Nelly said. "I'm trying to break my bad habit of constantly checking it, so when I'm just sitting around, I keep it away from myself."

"That's a good idea," Orville said. "I should do the same. I'm always on mine too."

"Problem is," Nelly said, "now I leave it places. Two weeks ago, I left it on the windowsill of a coffee shop. I had to retrace my steps that day to find it."

Orville smiled. "Can't win for trying, sometimes."

The Italian bread smelled delicious, and the steak and potatoes didn't look like leftovers to Nelly. She wondered if he'd pretended they were when he'd asked her to dinner so she didn't feel compelled to accept his invitation. Now she was beginning to suspect the old man had gone to quite a bit of trouble to prepare this meal.

"Thank you so much for having me over," Nelly said. "I really appreciate it."

"It's no bother. I get lonely these days, what with Lauren gone and the boys moved out. You're doing me a favor by being here." Orville brought some napkins over. "I know you're working tomorrow, but would you like some wine?"

"Sure would," Nelly said.

He poured her a glass of red. The microwave dinged. Orville brought the food out.

Nelly spooned some food onto her plate; it smelled delicious. They made small talk while it cooled. Orville asked her about California, politely steering clear of the subject of her ex-husband.

"Nervous about tomorrow?" he asked.

"I got the chance to meet my colleagues yesterday,"

Nelly said. "Everyone seemed nice, but yes, I'm nervous. Before this, I was at the same school for fourteen years. I'd planned on working there forever. This is a big change for me."

He nodded along. "First day at a new job. That's normal. But don't worry. You're in good hands here. All my children attended Overland Middle. Miguel taught my youngest English composition, if you can believe it."

"He's a nice man," Nelly said.

Orville nodded. "He must be getting ready to retire soon."

Nelly saw an opening. "There's talk that Emmett might succeed him?"

Orville's face brightened at the mention of Emmett Moore.

"Like I said, you're in good hands. I couldn't think of anybody better to succeed Miguel. Emmett is a great guy. *Great* guy."

Nelly kept her eyes on her food. "That's what everybody tells me."

"I saw him at church today. Mentioned you were staying here."

Nelly froze. "You did?"

The old man sat up, looking apologetic. "Oh, I'm sorry. I didn't think anything of it."

Nelly forced a smile, but her insides were churning. Emmett knew where she lived. That thought was terrifying.

"It's okay," she managed to say.

"I really am sorry," Orville said, sounding pained. "I didn't think anything of it. Small town, everybody talks. It's not like a big city. But I guess I shouldn't have told him that."

"It's just..." Nelly searched for the right words to say.

Some half-truth. "I've had problems with men before, and I don't want strangers knowing where I live."

"My gosh." Orville put his fork down. "Nelly, I'm so sorry. Won't happen again."

He'd apologized several times now, but Nelly said nothing. She kept her eyes on her food and forced some potatoes into her mouth, even though her appetite had vanished.

An uncomfortable silence developed. Orville fidgeted in his seat.

"You don't have to worry about Emmett," he said. "He's a good man. Really. That one wouldn't hurt a fly. He leads the middle school youth group at St. Pete's. He's wonderful with the children."

Nelly kept her expression neutral, but she wanted to scream. The thought of Emmett being a teacher, working with children...

"He runs the youth group?"

Orville's expression brightened. "Oh yeah. The best. The youth group had a lock-in event Friday night."

"A lock-in?"

"That's what they call a sleepover." Orville put his wine down. "Emmett usually coordinates one every season. The kids love them. They play games and watch a movie. The parents love it too. Their children get to socialize, and they know their kids won't get into too much trouble at church."

"He seems to have his hand in a lot of things."

Orville gave her a strange look.

Nelly forced a smile, feeling her cheeks turn red under Orville's gaze. "I'm impressed, is all. He's up all night with the kids; then he's managing the charity run. It's a lot."

Orville grinned, as if he took pride in the other man's good deeds. "That's Emmett. Always up to something."

Always up to something.

9

FIVE DAYS AGO – MONDAY

I run while Sean calls out how much time is left. Every time I think I've found a good spot to hide, I discover one of the other girls has already taken the spot, and they shoo me away. With only ten seconds left, I duck into a small room at the far end of the factory and hunker down behind a filing cabinet. I do my best to ignore the tiny black insect that scurried away when I disturbed some trash in the room.

"Ready or not, here we come!" Sean calls out, his voice barely reaching me in this room.

I hear snickers from the factory floor. The other girls are actually excited to be chased. They're enjoying this moment, savoring the idea of what's to come next when so-and-so finds them and they're "forced" to make out. But I'm not like them. Sure, I've thought about kissing certain boys in our grade, but not just any *boy. I really don't want any of these characters to find me, especially that mouth breather Marshall.*

It's only when I'm sitting here, worrying about being found, that I realize I don't know what the rules of the game are. Do the boys only have a certain amount of time to find us? They can't be allowed to take all afternoon—that wouldn't be fair. And what if they do find us? Do I really have to kiss them? Could I get away with kissing on the cheek? Or does it have to be lip to lip?

What happens if I refuse? I mean, I know I'll be the laughing-stock and will have to run out of here embarrassed, but they're not going to demand I show off my bra to everyone if I refuse.

Right?

Am I allowed to go outside? Nobody said I couldn't. But it's pouring with rain now, and I realize this white T-shirt isn't the best outfit when you're stuck outside in a squall. Just the thought of any of them getting a glimpse of my bra makes my stomach flip. Being the youngest and, uh, least matured girl here, I would die of embarrassment.

I stay in my crouch beside the filing cabinet, hoping no one comes back here. There are a few windows to my right. If worse comes to worst, I can sneak out through those. I mean, assuming those things even open. They're probably rusted shut.

If I do go outside, then I'm getting on that bike and taking my chances in the storm. If I go fast, I can make it back to Tina's house in a few minutes. If Mrs. Hirshberg asks, I'll tell her Tina met up with some friends, and they're playing hide-and-go-seek up the road in the rain, but that I wanted to get out of the storm. It's not a lie, and given how permissive Tina's mother is, I doubt she'd get into trouble for it. On her best mothering days, Mrs. Hirshberg can't be bothered to go out and find her daughter. I doubt she'd jump in her car in a downpour and drive around.

But even if Tina does *get into trouble, do I really care at this point? She says she's my friend, but she obviously doesn't treat me like one. She brought me here knowing I'd be uncomfortable and that I would feel out of place. Hiding from horny high schoolers in this eerie factory is not my idea of fun.*

I don't have time to grow angry with Tina again because I

hear someone rooting around nearby. My insides turn to liquid. I don't want to kiss anybody, but now I'm bargaining with fate, telling God or the universe or whoever's listening that I'll kiss one of them. Just please, please, please don't let it be Marshall. Anybody but him. Maybe it'll be one of the guys who doesn't want to kiss me—then I'll get out of having to do it altogether.

I hear them getting closer. I don't dare poke my head out to look for fear of being spotted, but they sound like they're just outside the door. A sneaker squelches as the person moves. It sounds like they're in the room with me...

"One minute!" Sean announces.

I feel a sliver of hope. It turns out there is a time limit to the search. I just have to hang in there for a little while longer.

The sneaker squelches again, and I cover my mouth to muffle the sounds of my breathing. It feels like there's someone in the room with me now—the air has shifted and is different.

"Thirty seconds!" Sean calls.

I close my eyes, willing whoever it is to go away. Though I can't say why, I have a bad feeling it's Marshall. I picture him lurking on the other side of the room in his untied basketball sneakers, mesh shorts, his hairy belly poking out from the bottom of his practice jersey. I shudder at the thought of him pushing all that mass against me, one of his hands on the back of my head, his lips seeking mine...

I hear a door open farther down the hallway. Did Marshall leave the room?

"Fifteen seconds!" Sean yells.

I dare to hope.

NELLY BARELY SLEPT SUNDAY NIGHT.

She would have been nervous and preoccupied anyway, starting a new job, but she also had to contend with the prospect of seeing Emmett. What would she say? How should she act? It was probably best to pretend everything was normal. Be polite but not overly friendly. Make him think there was nothing wrong, while also establishing the parameters of their relationship: colleagues but not friends. Nelly didn't want him to know she suspected anything. Or, if she knew, that she was intent on doing anything about it.

That was all easier said than done, however. The mere thought of interacting with the man put her in a cold sweat. While she peered into the bathroom mirror and fussed with her makeup, a wave of nausea hit her. Gripping the rim of the sink, Nelly put her head down and drew deep breaths.

She took antacids to combat the nausea and got dressed. She checked her bag multiple times to ensure the lesson plans and her lunch—leftovers from last night—were there, but she almost walked out of the apartment without her phone. This time, she'd left it on the kitchen counter next to the stove.

The drive to Overland Middle School was only fifteen minutes from her apartment. She drove through beautiful country, passing long green pastures and fields of cornstalks. Some of the leaves had changed color too, the landscape beginning to take on its autumnal hues. Nelly loved this time of year. As much as she enjoyed summer break, returning to school in the fall was always exciting. She loved what she did for a living.

But she wasn't excited this morning, and the beautiful view did nothing to calm her nerves. The antacids had helped a little bit, but the nausea returned as she neared school. She arrived nearly forty-five minutes early, wanting to make sure she had enough time to get settled. There were a handful of cars in the small parking lot, one of them being Emmett's BMW.

Nelly parked as far from his vehicle as possible without making her choice comically obvious. She checked her makeup again in the rearview mirror and tried not to think about Emmett. She needed to focus on her job this morning. Outside of accusing the man of being an impostor without any proof whatsoever, there was nothing Nelly could do about him right now.

She hated how powerless that made her feel.

Checking her makeup for the umpteenth time was just a stalling tactic, so Nelly forced herself out of the car. The autumn air was crisp and damp and smelled of earth. Her breath came out in tiny white puffs as she crossed the parking lot.

"Hey, Nelly."

She froze at the sound of Emmett's voice. Trying to recover quickly, she put a smile on her face and turned to greet the man. She'd given his car a wide berth, not realizing he'd been sitting in it.

"Good morning, Emmett."

As he approached, she took him in. Emmett wore an expensive black overcoat, a white shirt that looked freshly pressed and starched, and an orange and navy striped tie that matched the school colors.

He was well put together, albeit a little overdressed, Nelly thought. Maybe he liked wearing nice things, but Nelly suspected his garb was a subtle power play. John, her ex, had constantly worried about such things, being a salesman and working in a highly competitive environment where your colleagues could be friends one minute and bitter rivals the next. He'd always told her that you didn't want to dress better than your boss, but you did want to outclass your coworkers. It was a sly way of establishing a higher place in the pecking order than your peers.

If Emmett was gunning for the open assistant principal position, then John's theory applied here.

"Ready for your first day?" he asked, blowing the steam off his hot cup of coffee.

While Nelly had tossed and turned all night, Emmett looked well rested. He looked like he'd slept like a baby.

"I'm ready."

"Great," he said, giving her a thousand-watt smile. "I'm so glad you're here."

She wondered if her smile looked as fake as it felt. They fell in step as they headed for the school entrance. Another car pulled in, hip hop blasting so loudly from the speakers that Nelly thought the windows must be open. But they weren't. Emmett waved enthusiastically at Beck as she whipped through the parking lot, driving way too fast.

"Remember when you used to listen to music that loudly?" Emmett asked, shaking his head. "I can't do that anymore."

"Right," Nelly said, hating how timid she sounded.

Emmett used a badge to unlock the door, then held it open for her. "After you."

Things had happened so quickly with the job offer. Nelly would have liked to take a day to get acclimated to the building and set up her classroom. But there'd been no time. Miguel had begged her to start immediately, and the cross-country drive had taken its toll. She'd arrived later than expected Saturday afternoon and had spent Sunday getting her apartment together, then participating in the charity run.

As a result, this was the first time she'd set foot in the building.

A thirtyish-woman with big curves and long brown hair looked up from the front desk as they entered. Nelly had met her on Sunday but was glad the woman's name plate was visible; otherwise she would not have remembered.

"Good morning, Megan," Nelly said. "Nice to see you again."

"Welcome!" Megan said, rising at her desk. "I'm glad you got in early. I can give you the tour."

Nelly was about to thank her, but Emmett jumped in.

"I'm happy to show Nelly around," he said.

Megan looked tentatively toward the closed door behind her desk. Miguel's office. Her smile slipped. "Miguel asked me to."

Emmett smiled easily. "You've got a lot to manage this morning, especially with the changing bus routes. That phone of yours will be ringing off the hook. Let me take care of it."

Nelly couldn't think of a tactful way to ask if Megan could show her around instead.

"Thanks." Megan looked relieved. "You're the best."

Emmett oozed charm. "You get pulled in a lot of directions, Megan. It's the least I can do."

"Well," she said, glancing back at Nelly, "I'm so happy you're here. Good luck! And, oh, I almost forgot: your name plate hasn't come in. I hope to have that for you later in the week. Here's your security badge."

The woman's words barely registered. Nelly took the badge and smiled. "Thanks."

"This way, Nelly," Emmett said, extending an arm.

HE SPOKE. She listened. But Nelly hardly heard him.

He showed her the gymnasium first. Coming from a well-to-do school district in California, with a campus to rival that of a small college, Nelly was struck by how tiny the gym was. The basketball court was not full sized. It was so narrow, the three-point line was cut off on the wings, not extending to the baseline. There was also no room along the sidelines to stand, and no space on the far side of the court to sit. Spectators must have watched the game from the stage behind one of the baskets.

"Nelly?" Emmett said, like she hadn't responded to something he'd said. "Let's head this way."

She nodded mutely. Emmett held the door for her but positioned himself awkwardly in the doorway, leaving little room. He gave her a wink and a smile as she approached.

"It's cozy," Emmett said. "But it's home."

Nelly waited a moment for Emmett to move out of the doorway. But when the man didn't take the hint, Nelly was forced to squeeze past him. His aftershave was strong and smelled like cedarwood. Only inches from the man, Nelly averted her eyes but still felt uncomfortable. Emmett wasn't unusually tall, but he had an undeniable physical presence about him. Whatever space he occupied, he filled it.

She followed him as he droned on about the upcoming soccer game, the middle school dance in a month's time, and back-to-school night, which was only a few days away. Nelly groaned at the thought of having to meet the parents of her brand-new students so quickly—she wouldn't have much substantive feedback for anyone unless their child was poorly behaved.

"My eighth-grade class is focused on essay writing right now," Emmett said, beaming a proud smile. "They really are a gifted bunch. I'm fortunate to have such great kids."

Nelly smiled politely and nodded at opportune moments. She felt like Emmett was dragging the tour out. Not wanting to come across as rude, she kept her thoughts to herself, but the whole time she was just hoping he'd lead her to her room so she could prepare for the day. That was why she'd come in early. If this went on any longer, she'd have to say something.

"Our next topic is the MeToo movement," Emmett said, giving her a meaningful look. "Miguel thought that might be too sensitive a subject for eighth graders, but I pushed back because I feel very strongly."

Nelly's breath got stuck in her throat.

Emmett kept his eyes on her. "I expect some of the parents won't be too happy, but it's an important moment in history. Men must learn to respect boundaries. Women should be made to feel *safe*."

Nelly felt her pulse in her temple. She dared to meet Emmett's eyes, but the man gave nothing away in his expression. He simply gazed down at her with that same warm smile.

"Don't you agree, Nelly?" he asked.

She was in a nervous sweat now.

"Ye-yes. Of course."

His smile relaxed, as if he'd been worried she'd disagree.

"I've divided the class in half," Emmett said. "One group

will write from the perspective that MeToo hasn't gone far enough, while the other half will take the opposite position."

Nelly nodded, not trusting herself to say anything.

"Not to get all personal or, God forbid, political, but I'd like to hear your thoughts on the matter," Emmett said. "It's our goal to build a safe space here for everyone."

Nelly had strong opinions on the subject, but she was too unnerved to think of anything meaningful to say.

"It's difficult, right?" she said, chuckling nervously and hating herself for it. "I mean, on the one hand, women should be safe, but on the other, it's important not to jump to conclusions..."

She wanted to scream. That was not how she felt, but she was not at all ready to have this conversation with Emmett, all the while having to pretend like the feeling of utter dread in her stomach wasn't real.

"Fair point," Emmett said. "It's important to protect women, but it's also important to assume a person is innocent until proven guilty. Right, here is the art room."

"Coming through!"

Beck barreled out of the art room, already in her paint-spattered smock.

"Morning, Nelly!" she said as she raced by. "Forgot my coffee in the car!"

Emmett chuckled and shook his head. "I love that young woman's energy. Wish I still had it. By the way, do you drink coffee?"

Nelly forced a smile. "Can't function without it."

He nodded knowingly. "We'll grab a cup in the lounge. Up here is my beautiful bride-to-be. Vanessa, darling, are you in there?"

Vanessa popped out of the next classroom. She was dressed smartly, in gray straight pants and a white blouse that looked like it had just come out of the store this morning. The woman was truly striking.

"Good morning, Nelly." Vanessa gave her fiancé a quick peck on the cheek before offering Nelly a cold look. "What are you two doing?"

"Emmett is giving me the tour." Nelly had almost said *Marshall*.

Vanessa nodded silently. She didn't seem too happy about that. The woman wasn't offering a very warm welcome, but Nelly had more important things to worry about.

"Well, he's the man for the job," Vanessa said flatly. "He's only been here for a few years, but he knows everything."

Nelly wondered if there was more to what the woman had said. Was Vanessa implying that Emmett knew about Nelly and her suspicions?

No, that wouldn't make any sense. That would mean Vanessa knew Emmett was actually Marshall and, at the very least, that Nelly had accused him of attempted rape. Nelly couldn't imagine Vanessa intending to marry the man while knowing that.

"She's being modest," Emmett said, putting his arm around Vanessa for a moment. She stiffened at the display of public affection. "Vanessa has lived in town her whole life and taught here longer than me."

She awkwardly squirmed out of Emmett's grasp. "Nelly, would you like to see my room?"

Nelly got the impression Vanessa was only being polite —and barely at that. She couldn't help but notice how

Vanessa had reacted to Emmett's putting his arm around her. Perhaps the woman was uncomfortable with PDAs while at work, though Nelly wondered if there was more to it.

Had Emmett come clean last night and told her about his previous experience with Nelly?

"Would you like to see my room?" Vanessa asked again.

Nelly realized she hadn't answered. "I'd love to, but now isn't the best time. I'd really like to get to my classroom so I can prepare for the day."

"Of course." Emmett looked at his watch. "Wow, look at the time. Students will be arriving in twenty minutes. We'd better keep moving."

Vanessa extended a long arm. "Glad you're here, Nelly. Good luck today."

The woman's hand was icy to the touch, her grip a little too strong.

"I do hope you're a good fit," Vanessa said, holding on for a moment too long. "We had to bring someone in for third quarter last school year, and she was—"

"Now, honey," Emmett said. "I'm sure Nelly won't be a troublemaker. She has a good reputation and strong references."

"I'm sure she won't be either," Vanessa said, her voice growing haughty. "I was only remarking about the last time Miguel was forced to hire someone quickly under special circumstances. It did not work out, unfortunately."

Nelly couldn't help but feel the sting of the woman's words.

Forced to hire someone.

Under special circumstances.

Though she couldn't be sure, she wondered if the woman was slyly suggesting that Nelly might not have gotten the job if Miguel had had more time to make his decision.

She felt Emmett's eyes on her again.

"Nelly doesn't seem like a troublemaker to me," he said.

He was smiling brightly, but the gesture didn't quite reach his eyes.

10

"I know you want to get to your class," Emmett said, "but I want to show you the teachers' lounge first. Don't worry. It's on the way."

Despite his promise to get her situated quickly, Emmett had stopped off at the bathroom, where they ran into another teacher coming out. Not wanting to be rude, Nelly made small talk with the man in the hallway. Before they could get moving, an older woman who taught sixth- and seventh-grade math came around the corner. She hadn't participated in the charity run yesterday, so Nelly felt compelled to introduce herself.

By the time they reached the teachers' lounge, home room was starting in fifteen minutes. Nelly was growing antsy.

"It's a new Keurig." Emmett tapped the coffeemaker proudly. "What can I make for you?"

Nelly picked out a dark roast and went to make it herself, but Emmett stood in front of the machine.

"I'll show you how it works," he said.

"I've used a Keurig before," Nelly answered, an edge to her voice.

Emmett shook his head. "It's the latest model, not as intuitive as it used to be. Here."

He held out his hand for her coffee mug. Nelly reluctantly handed it over. Emmett placed it under the machine's funnel and punched a few buttons. The procedure didn't seem any more complicated to Nelly. The Keurig immediately whirred to life.

"You're free fourth period, right?" Emmett said.

Did he have her schedule memorized? "Yes."

He smiled. "I know because you've got the same schedule as Patti. I'm also free that period, if you'd like some company for lunch."

Nelly was at a loss. "Don't you want to eat with Vanessa?"

"She's not always free fourth period." Emmett looked offended that she hadn't immediately said yes. "But I understand if you'd prefer to eat alone. Some days I like to do that, close the door to my classroom and sit in peace."

"First day and everything." Nelly managed a sweet smile. "I'll see how I'm feeling."

When her coffee was done, Emmett handed her the mug. "Oh, I wanted to show you what's in our supply clo—"

"Sorry," she cut in, "do you mind if we keep going?"

"No problem," Emmett said.

They passed another teacher, and Megan hustled in the opposite direction. They were almost to the end of the hallway now.

"And here we are," Emmett said, spreading his arms wide. "You and I are neighbors."

"What?" Nelly blurted out, regretting her tone immediately. "Oh really? That's funny."

Emmett was still smiling, but his eyes narrowed. "I hope that's...*alright*?"

"Of course it is," Nelly said quickly. "Why wouldn't it be?"

"Because your reaction..." Emmett's voice trailed off. "Sorry, what an idiot I've been. You are probably itching to get settled, and I've been going on and on. How rude of me."

"It's okay," Nelly said, peering past him toward her room.

Emmett smiled again. "I'd better let you get to it."

He opened the door for her once more. This time she waited until he moved out of the doorway. Nelly had no intention of ever getting that close to him again.

"Before I let you go," Emmett said, leaning toward her and lowering his voice, "I wanted you to know that the faculty at Overland Middle is one big, happy family. We're happy you're here, and everyone wants to see you succeed."

Nelly heard a but coming.

"We might be working in a small town with a modest budget, but we hold ourselves to the strictest academic, not to mention highest moral, standards. If you're interested in this becoming a permanent position, I'd recommend bringing your A game and working incredibly hard. The woman Vanessa referred to had also come from a large school district and thought this job would be a walk in the park, but she was wrong. She had *twenty* years of experience but couldn't hack it."

Nelly was shocked at this man's nerve. He was her peer, not her boss. And Nelly's experience should have spoken for itself.

She wondered, too, if he was trying to intimidate her for other reasons.

"I doubt this is the case with you, but in a school with a larger faculty, it's easier for a weaker teacher to hide,"

Emmett said. "Similar to bystander syndrome, when you've got a sizable group, people can avoid responsibility."

Nelly couldn't take any more of this. "I'm an excellent teacher, and I plan to work hard."

He smiled. "I'm sure you will, Nelly. Good luck today. And if you want some company during fourth period, I'm just across the hall here."

He started to leave but remembered something.

"I almost forgot. Miguel plans to audit one of your classes tomorrow. He wanted me to give you the heads-up this morning. He would have told you himself, but he's tied up with a school board meeting right now."

Her boss intended to sit in her class on her *second* day? While she'd expected to be audited, she didn't think it would happen so quickly. Maybe there was something to what Vanessa had said: Miguel had hired her out of necessity, not entirely out of desire. The thought was disheartening. She would have to wow the man.

"Don't worry," Emmett said. "As long as you have the right attitude, keep your nose down, and—most importantly—avoid drama, I'm sure you'll fit in here. If it's one thing we don't abide at Overland Middle, it's someone who doesn't know how to play nicely in the sandbox."

He gave her a pointed look.

"But I'm sure you'll fit in perfectly here. You want this to work out as much as we do, right?"

What Nelly wanted was to open the floodgates and let everything she was thinking come spilling out with the force of a tidal wave. Accuse him of being a fraud. Threaten to tell Miguel and the community about what he'd done. Yell and scream at him for having the gall to bully her. Expose his hypocrisy.

But she couldn't.

Emmett had the power.

He was not only known around here, he was respected, even admired. His reputation, as unearned and fraudulent as it might have been, was spotless. With many years of teaching behind him, including three here, and with his free time spent dedicated to community service, the man seemed bulletproof.

Nelly, on the other hand, had been in town for three days. No one knew her. She hadn't had time to build up any credit. She was the stranger here, the unknown. If anyone in Overland looked into her background, they'd know her as the woman who'd left her last job under a cloud and couldn't find work for nearly a year.

"Yes," she said. "I want this to work out."

"Great." He flashed her one of those charming smiles. "I'm glad to hear it."

She watched Emmett slip into the classroom opposite hers. Nelly couldn't believe her bad luck. This man would be teaching English a mere ten yards from her.

Short on time, Nelly forced herself to get over her shell shock. There was nothing to be done about Emmett right now. And besides, he was right: as unfair as it might have felt, she *did* have to prove herself to her new boss.

Her classroom was rather small to accommodate the twenty-five or so children who would fill it. Patti had decorated the walls with cutouts of famous historical figures, white dialog bubbles appearing near many with memorable quotes. There were maps and artists' renderings of the ancient wonders of the world too. In one corner, a faux-marble bust of Herodotus looked out over the classroom.

Nelly was just sitting down at her new desk, removing

the lesson plans from her folder, when she heard the murmur of the first students arriving. She thought she'd had time to get herself situated, but Emmett's protracted tour had robbed her of that opportunity. And she was certain he'd done it on purpose.

11

"So, Nelly, how did your first day go?"

Nelly found herself in Miguel's office. It had a lived-in feel, no doubt a result of Miguel having held his position as principal for so long. The walls were decorated with student art, term papers, and school memorabilia. There were many pictures of Miguel with students. In some of them his hair was even jet black, and he looked about forty pounds lighter. She noticed a few awards as well, though these weren't prominently displayed, and she appreciated that. Though the man sitting across from her at the mahogany desk was in charge, Miguel seemed the humble sort, not one to draw attention to his achievements or boast about his accomplishments.

Although Nelly hadn't had as much time to get settled as she would have liked, she thought the day had gone well. In the afternoon, she'd had to deal with a rather disruptive student, but otherwise it was smooth sailing. She did need to get a better handle on this material, but she'd take care of that this evening.

"I'm glad to hear that," Miguel answered after she gave him a brief recap of her first day. "By the way, did Emmett tell you about the audit tomorrow?"

"Yes." She kept her smile in place to hide her nerves. "I'm looking forward to it, actually."

"Nothing to be worried about. I do it with every member of the faculty, once a term, regardless of tenure. I won't be there to trip you up, just to observe. We'll sit down after school lets out tomorrow to discuss any constructive feedback I might have."

Nelly nodded. "I want you to know I welcome that."

"I've got a good feeling about you," Miguel said. "I don't know if anyone's mentioned, but we have a home soccer game tomorrow. No pressure to attend, obviously, but I wanted to let you know that most members of the faculty make an appearance. It's part of our culture. We want to fully support the student body both inside and outside the classroom."

No pressure, Nelly thought. Already demands were being made of her that hadn't been discussed during the interview. While Nelly enjoyed attending sporting events, and was apt to wildly cheer her students on, she did not like what her ex-husband, John, would have referred to as scope-creep: the tendency for supervisors to give you more and more responsibilities over time, usually through implication and without additional compensation.

"I'll be there," Nelly said.

"Wonderful." Miguel beamed a smile at her. "Now then, get out of here. Go home and relax. I don't want you thinking about this place or anyone here for a few hours. Okay?"

Nelly knew that was impossible.

She stepped out of Miguel's office. His assistant, Megan, was gone for the day.

"You survived," Beck said.

Nelly hadn't noticed the other woman filling her bottle at the water cooler on the other side of Megan's desk. Beck was petite and was barely visible behind the filing cabinet.

Nelly chuckled. "It was a good first day."

Beck motioned toward the office behind her. "I meant with Miguel."

"We had a nice conversation."

Beck finished at the water cooler and approached Nelly. "Wanna grab dinner? Bellamy's does a wing special tonight."

Nelly wanted to spend time going over the material for class in anticipation of Miguel's audit tomorrow. But it wasn't even four o'clock yet. She had plenty of time, and it would be fun to get out, see the town, socialize with someone who might turn into a friend.

"Come on," Beck said, mistaking her thoughtfulness for reluctance. "I'll even give you the grand tour."

"The tour?" Nelly said.

"Yeah. I'll show you Main Street...then more of Main Street...and the rest of Main Street."

Nelly had a good laugh at that. "Sounds thrilling."

"Pick you up at seven?"

BECK WAS TWENTY MINUTES LATE.

She powered down the passenger window as Nelly approached her two-door sedan. "Whoa, nice place, Nelly. How'd you afford this on a teacher's salary?"

Beck was gawking at the farmhouse.

Nelly got in the car. "I'm only renting a room on the second story of the barn, aka the guesthouse."

"Damn," Beck said, her face falling. "I was hoping you were loaded. I was gonna ask you to pick up the tab tonight."

They had a good laugh at that, and the laughter continued as Beck had trouble backing out of the gravel driveway. After several near collisions with trees or jutting branches, Beck let out a sigh of relief.

"You'd think, being an artist, I'd be good with spatial dimensions," Beck said.

"You're fine. The driveway is crooked."

She gave Nelly a grateful look. "You're too nice."

Beck's car was a mess. There were empty bags of potato chips and pretzels and half-finished bottles of diet soda on the floor and in the backseat. There were also a bunch of drawing pads and student art and a pile of clothes back there too.

"It's a rental," Beck says. "This is how the car came."

She whipped around a bend and turned in the opposite direction Nelly was expecting. They passed a handful of newer developments on their right, while on their left farmland stretched far and wide.

"I'm not living out of my car," Beck joked. "I swear."

Nelly chuckled. "Remind me where we're headed?"

"Bellamy's," Beck answered. "They've got great wings, which means there will be plenty of guys who like to eat wings."

It was hard to argue with her logic, but Nelly hadn't planned on hunting for men tonight, or being Beck's wing girl. Did the kids still call it that these days? She had no idea.

"Isn't Bellamy's back the other w—"

"Yeah. But I promised to give you the tour." Beck winked.

"You'll thank me for this. Nobody showed me around when I got here."

Nelly smiled politely. She liked the idea of someone being quirky more than the reality of it. Or maybe she was just getting old and fussy. More than ten years separated her and Beck, and it was beginning to show.

Nelly had thought they were grabbing a bite to eat, but Beck was on the prowl. Nelly had also assumed Beck's offer of a tour was figurative, not literal. But Beck apparently intended to show her around Overland, population seven thousand. It wasn't exactly the night Nelly had in mind, and she wished she could ask Beck to skip the tour so they could get to dinner. But she didn't want to come off as rude. For all her quirks, Beck seemed like a good person, and Nelly had no friends here. She decided to make the best of the evening. If she was out later than expected, it would be fine. She'd still have time to go over the material for class tomorrow again before bed. Besides, she'd already put in an hour's work.

"So why'd you take this job?" Beck asked bluntly.

Nelly smiled nervously and hoped Beck didn't notice. "I needed a change."

"I hear you." Beck took her eyes off the road to glance at her. "I wasn't dying to work in Overland either."

"I didn't say I didn't want—"

Beck talked right over her. "My last principal was a real asshole. I was there for about three days when I realized it was never going to work."

"Where was that?"

Nelly was genuinely interested in hearing Beck's story, but she was just as determined to keep the spotlight off herself. She wasn't ready to talk about her past. It wasn't old enough yet.

For the next ten minutes, Beck proceeded to detail the many ups and downs of her nascent teaching career, digressing several times to share juicy tidbits about her incredibly active love life, which, unwisely for her, too often intertwined with her professional life.

Nelly got to hear all about a former partner's favorite sexual position and the size of another ex's genitalia. When she managed to guide Beck back to her career, the other woman explained how she'd changed schools twice in those four years and ended by stating she didn't plan on making Overland her permanent home.

"I'll stay another two years, maybe three," she said. "I know principals don't like to hire teachers who have moved around a lot, so I have to stick it out here for a stretch. But this place is a little too Make America Great Again for me."

She laughed, shaking her head.

"It's not *bad*. But in a school this small, the non-instructional duties can be a bit much."

"Oh really?" Nelly frowned. "Miguel hasn't asked me to do anything extra yet."

Beck rolled her eyes. "That'll change. He did the same thing to me. I was new, he didn't want to put too much on my plate during the transition, but by winter term I was managing the car line and monitoring recess. He even asked if I could help assist the coach of the girls' softball team. I've never played a sport in my life, but that didn't bother him. I finally had to say no."

Nelly didn't like the sound of that. "How did he take it?"

"Pretty well," Beck said, as if the thought had just occurred to her. "You know, for a principal, he's alright."

"He seems nice."

"He is," Beck agreed. "But he's also talking about a lower budget next school year. We don't have a music program to cut, which means the art department is next. Needless to say, I'm keeping my eyes open."

"That's a shame," Nelly said. "We do a disservice to our children when we slash art and music programs."

"I know, right?" Beck slowed and pointed out Nelly's window. "See that big place over there?"

They hadn't passed any other homes for a bit, so this sprawling house stood alone, sitting back away from the road. A high stone fence surrounded the property, though from what little Nelly could see, the grounds appeared immaculate. Whoever lived here, their grandchildren wouldn't have to worry about money.

"Guess who owns it."

"I don't know. Who?"

"You'll never guess."

"Emmett?"

"Try again."

"Miguel?"

"Nope."

"You."

"Ha. Ha. Very funny."

They passed the house. A detached garage, big enough to be a small home itself, came into view. And beyond that, there was another structure off to the side. It looked like a pool house.

"I don't know, Beck. Who lives there?"

"Her Royal Highness, the Lady Vanessa herself."

Nelly laughed at Beck's tone. "She's not that bad."

"You're right. She's worse."

Nelly hadn't much cared for the woman, but she also didn't want to speak out of turn. Thinking of Vanessa, however, called Emmett to mind.

Beck rolled her eyes. "If you saw the inside, you'd agree with me. Family portraits hang on every wall. It's a bit creepy, what with those old, dead guys staring down at you in every room."

Nelly was shocked. "You were *inside* her house?"

"It's this big, three-hundred-year-old place. Even though it's been updated and some additions have been put on, I could still feel its age. Its *history*. The original owners were part of the Underground Railroad. The basement is enormous, and it's filled with all these secret passages and places to hide."

Nelly couldn't help but wonder how Vanessa could afford such a property on a public school teacher's salary.

Beck smiled, somehow reading her mind. "You're too polite to ask, so I'll just tell you. Vanessa's grandfather owned the local lumber mill and made a fortune. Her father took over the business and eventually bought the property. When Daddy retired and her parents moved away, Vanessa got the house. She's sitting on a fortune."

"Wow."

"But could you imagine living in that place *by yourself*? Everywhere you go, it's empty. How creepy is that? It's like something out of one of those awful Gothic novels."

Nelly pictured the strange, haughty woman moving about the enormous, quiet place by herself. It was an odd image.

"Anyway, I accepted her invitation. Big mistake."

"What happened?"

Beck braked at the intersection controlled by stop signs,

then hung a left. They passed a farm advertising corn mazes and haunted tractor rides for the upcoming Halloween season.

"She's a no-soul," Beck said.

"What do you mean?"

"Have you looked into her eyes?" Beck said. "There's nothing going on behind them."

Nelly laughed. She was beginning to see how Beck was a bit dramatic. But this time Beck did not laugh along with her. She was deadly serious.

"Sounds like you had a great time," Nelly said.

"Best night ever." Beck snorted. "The moment I got there, Vanessa asked me these insanely personal questions."

"Like what?"

"She asked if I'd graduated with honors, what my parents were like, if I'd ever been in trouble with the law. Then she asked me what I thought of Emmett."

"What about Emmett?"

Beck shot her a quick look. "It was really strange. They'd just started dating when I was over, and I got the sense that Vanessa wasn't so sure about him. I felt like that was why she'd invited me over—to get another woman's opinion of him."

"But you two hardly knew each other, right? And *you* hardly knew Emmett yourself."

Beck nodded. "It was the weirdest convo of my life, and that's saying something."

"What made her ask you about Emmett, if you had to guess?"

Beck thought it over. "I got out of there so quickly, she didn't have a chance..."

Nelly knew she was prying a bit too much, but she couldn't miss out on this opportunity.

"But?"

"It was like she didn't trust him," Beck said. "Or trust her own judgment of him, if that makes sense."

Nelly tried to hide what she was thinking.

Beck laughed. "Anyway, I didn't even finish my vodka tonic. And believe me, that is out of character."

Nelly wanted to keep Beck talking about Emmett. She had to find out everything she could about the man.

"Vanessa and Emmett make an odd pairing," Nelly said.

"Right?" Beck slapped Nelly's thigh excitedly. "I said the same thing. Neither of them have been married before."

"Vanessa's never been married?" Nelly asked. "You'd think guys would be beating down her door."

"She's stunning, I'll give her that," Beck said. "And she's loaded. But like I said: no soul."

Nelly chuckled. "What do you think of Emmett?"

"I hate to admit this, but Emmett's a good guy," Beck said.

"Why do you hate to admit it?" Nelly asked.

Beck rolled her head side to side. "You know how some people seem too good to be true, and you just want to find something—*anything*—wrong with them? Only you can't? Like Mr. Rogers. He really is that good. If he weren't forty years old, I would have thrown myself at him."

"He's also engaged," Nelly pointed out.

"Details," Beck said, waving a hand.

Nelly couldn't tell if Beck was joking.

"Let's be a hundred percent with each other," Beck said suddenly. "Why don't you like Emmett?"

There was no judgment in Beck's tone, only curiosity. But still Nelly had to be careful.

"What makes you think I don't?"

"*Nells.*" Beck gave her a sidelong glance. "We are cool. What happens in the sedan stays in the sedan. Most of the time, anyway."

Nelly was stricken. She tried some humor to avoid answering Beck's question. "I don't want to think too hard about what's happening in this car."

"Oh." She gently whacked Nelly's shoulder. "You're right: you probably don't."

Nelly laughed along as Beck related yet another lewd story, while hiding her disappointment. She'd been hoping Beck would have some dirt on Emmett. But like everyone else in this town, the other woman had fallen under Emmett's spell.

12

Bellamy's was a local sports bar, and Beck's prediction turned out to be correct: the chicken wing special the place was running tonight had attracted a load of men. For every woman in the place, there appeared to be four or five guys. Most of the men looked to be in their thirties, but there was a pocket of guys playing pool in the far corner of the place closer to Beck's age.

A lot of heads turned when they entered the place. Most eyes glommed on to Beck, who was a curiosity in a small, fairly conservative place like this. She was dressed provocatively tonight, wearing a skirt that might not pass the dress code at a strip club and a white top that left little to the imagination.

Nelly did, however, catch a few men checking her out as well. She couldn't remember the last time *that* happened, and it was a welcome distraction from her troubled thoughts. While they waited for a table, Beck spent most of her time banging out text after text on her phone.

"My ex," she said, rolling her eyes. "Check out his junk."

Without warning, Beck stuck the phone in Nelly's face. She was treated to a view of a man's privates. Red-faced, she turned away.

"He's what they call underemployed and lacks ambition." Beck shrugged. "But can you blame me for dating him?"

The man was inarguably well-endowed. Through a fit of shocked laughter, Nelly managed to mumble an incoherent acknowledgment of Beck's reasoning. Her new friend sensed Nelly's embarrassment and turned a devilish grin her way.

"What?" Beck asked, acting like what she'd just done was perfectly normal. "It's not weird that I showed you a dick pic, is it?"

Nelly couldn't control her laughter. She was in near hysterics when the host waved at them to follow.

IT WAS LATER than Nelly would have liked when Beck dropped her off. As Nelly was about to ask their server for the check, two guys who had been playing pool in the corner approached and offered to buy them drinks. Beck had already had two and didn't need another, and Nelly wasn't interested in more alcohol. But Beck eagerly accepted their offer.

As a result, Nelly had spent the next forty-five minutes listening to this twenty-three-year-old guy tell her all about his last six months working out at the local CrossFit gym, doing her best to keep her eyes from glazing over, while Beck chatted the other young man up. Nelly had held out as long as she could, not wanting to spoil Beck's fun, but in the end she told Beck she had to review her lesson plans.

Back in her apartment, as the night grew long, Nelly tried to focus on schoolwork but found the task almost impossible. While she was nervous about Miguel's audit tomorrow, Emmett kept invading her thoughts. She would only get through a sentence or two of her worksheet before he would appear in her mind, or the things he said would echo in her ears. She was almost certain about who he really was.

But she had no proof.

Eventually she gave up trying to do more work. It was approaching ten o'clock, time for her to go to bed, but Nelly knew that wasn't happening. She was too amped up.

She boiled water on the small stove for chamomile tea and sat at the kitchen table while it brewed, unable to rein in her racing mind. When the kettle whistled several minutes later, she realized just how lost in thought she'd been. After pouring herself a cup, Nelly moved to the couch. Her laptop sat on the coffee table in front of her.

Think, Nelly. Think. Then take action.

She wanted to approach the sheriff. But all she had was a story and her word that Emmett was Marshall. She needed *more.*

Nelly went online. She decided to probe social media again. Perhaps there was some mention of Marshall Dawes elsewhere, a distant relative or perhaps an old friend discussing him. Anything to get her started.

She spent the better part of an hour searching but not coming up with anything new. Once more, doubt wormed its way into her mind. Was she just imagining the whole thing? What was more likely—that Marshall Dawes had assumed someone else's identity and now worked as a middle school teacher of all things? Or that this man, Emmett Moore, merely resembled someone from her past? Nelly had to admit the latter was more probable.

The more she thought about it, the wilder the idea seemed. In this day and age, it must have been nearly impossible to live your life as an impostor. People left too many footprints, both in-person and online, for that.

More importantly, if you were going to pretend to be someone else, why would you settle down to become a middle school teacher of all things? The job was public-facing and required multiple and periodic background checks. Nelly herself had recently updated her clearances, as a matter of fact. And as a teacher, you interacted with dozens if not hundreds of new people each year, every new contact serving as a potential problem.

Nelly had to admit, there were better ways to keep a low profile. Marshall would have been better served working for a small company, where he could keep his contacts to a minimum. Even better, he could have found a job working from home, where he could get away with very little human interaction, where other people wouldn't be staring him in the face every day.

What was she thinking?

Emmett was probably Emmett. The idea that Marshall could have transformed himself into this charming man was absurd.

But no matter how rational those lines of thought were, Nelly could not ignore what her gut was telling her.

Eventually she gave up on her search and drifted over to social media. Other than posting that picture yesterday, she hadn't been on Facebook in ages. Perhaps she could find something here.

As she was about to enter the name Marshall Dawes in

the search bar, however, she realized there were private messages waiting for her. After opening a new page, Nelly was in for a shock.

She had a message from Tina.

The subject line was:

MARSHALL?!

Nelly opened the message.

Hey, Nelly. Long time no talk, but I had to reach out when I saw that picture of you with Marshall.

Nelly gasped.

She wasn't imagining things.

Tina had gone on to write that she missed Nelly and would love to catch up, providing her phone number. Though it was getting late, Nelly noticed that Tina had only sent the message about twenty minutes ago. She decided to throw caution to the wind.

Nelly grew incredibly nervous as she dialed Tina's number.

The two women hadn't spoken since high school. And the last *pleasant* conversation they'd ever had went all the way back to eighth grade. Their falling-out had been terrible. It had left Nelly, who at the time was already in a dark place, reeling. She had needed support after Marshall assaulted her, but instead Tina had shunned her. Nelly's reporting of the crime had resulted in Tina getting into some serious trouble at home, and Tina had never forgiven her for it.

When Nelly had turned to her mother for support, her

mother had told her to get over the loss of her friend, dismissively telling Nelly that this was typical teenage behavior. It was only years later, when Nelly arrived at college, did she see Tina's poor behavior for what it truly was.

"Nelly Gordon?" Tina answered. "Is that you?"

If Nelly hadn't known whom she was speaking with, she might not have been able to place the surprisingly hoarse voice. Hearing it now, Nelly was reminded that Tina had started sneaking cigarettes when they were twelve. From the sound of it, she'd been chain-smoking ever since.

"It's me."

"As I live and breathe."

For a moment, neither woman said anything. Nelly thought enough time had passed that their history should have been water under the bridge. But she didn't know if Tina felt the same way.

"It's still Nelly Peak," Nelly said, filling the awkward silence. "I haven't gotten around to changing my name back."

"Right. I've been saying the same thing for five years."

Nelly had taken note of Tina's last name on Facebook. "Walker...so you're divorced?"

"It's complicated."

Nelly wasn't surprised. With Tina, things were always complicated. "I'm sorry to hear that."

"It is what it is."

There was wailing in the background.

"Oh wow, is that a baby I hear?"

"Yes," Tina said. "Long story, but then again, what isn't?"

"Right." Nelly chuckled nervously. "How have you been?"

Tina didn't answer for a moment. Nelly wondered if she'd hung up, but then she heard Tina putting the phone down. Nelly listened while Tina cooed at the baby, getting the child to stop fussing.

"Sorry," Tina said, coming back on. "Colic."

"Ah," Nelly said. "That's too bad."

Again the awkward silence bloomed. Nelly was beginning to think this was a bad idea. Tina no longer seemed angry with her, but she also wasn't in a very expansive mood, despite her message on Facebook. Perhaps she was now regretting having made contact with Nelly at all.

"Listen, Tina—"

"Nelly, would you mind if I got some things off my chest?" Tina asked.

Nelly went very still.

"Are you still there?" Tina asked.

"Yes." Nelly didn't know what to expect. "Please go ahead."

"I've thought about contacting you for years," Tina admitted. "But every time, I chickened out."

Nelly just listened.

"It was all so long ago, everything that happened, but... Nelly, I'm so, so sorry."

Nelly was dumbfounded.

"I'm sorry," Tina repeated. "I've wanted to say that to you for a long time now. But I was so ashamed. Do you ever look back on your childhood and wonder what the hell you were thinking?"

Nelly chuckled. "All the time."

Tina went on as if she hadn't heard Nelly. "Not you, I'll bet. You were always kind."

"Tina, I—"

"Please let me finish. This is really difficult for me, but it needs to be said." Tina's voice grew heavy. "Nelly, I've screwed up so many things in my life that I've lost track of all the apologies I owe. You've always been at the top of my list, but I didn't think you'd ever want to hear from me again."

"Of course I would," Nelly said, not sure that had been true. But it felt true *now*.

"I treated you badly. But it wasn't until I heard about Marshall a few years later that I really felt terrible."

Nelly was at a loss. "Heard what about Marshall?"

"You didn't hear?"

"No."

"Oh, Jesus." Tina drew a breath. "I thought you knew."

Nelly waited for it. She was glad she was already sitting down.

"Another woman came forward."

13

Nelly hadn't known what Tina was going to say.

But it certainly wasn't this.

"When did this happen?" Nelly asked.

"He was in his twenties," Tina answered.

"What happened?" Nelly asked.

"Are you sure you want to hear this?" Tina asked.

Nelly appreciated Tina asking the question. "Yes."

"It's a bit of a story," Tina said. "I'll start at the beginning."

TINA WAS twenty years old and just beginning to show with her second child. Being the single mother of a toddler and pregnant with another, she didn't get out much, so when her mother unexpectedly offered to babysit for a long weekend, she jumped at the offer.

With a full weekend at her disposal, Tina reached out to someone she'd met at work. The other woman had temped at Tina's office during her winter break from college, and the two had struck up an unlikely friendship: the sorority girl undergraduate and the twenty-something single mother.

The last thing Tina wanted to do was spend her Friday and Saturday nights at the local pubs, seeing all the same brain-dead guys she'd partied with in high school. She also did not want to risk bumping into either of the two men who had gotten her pregnant and who now wanted nothing to do with her or their children.

She wanted to be somewhere else. With her decent grades in high school, and a mother willing to pay for her education, at one point Tina had been destined for college. But then the baby came, and whatever vague plans she'd had to go away for school evaporated.

Her unlikely friend, Alice, had invited her to the on-campus apartment. Tina was overjoyed. Though she'd only be there for the weekend, she would be getting a taste of the college experience at least.

Tina packed a bag, kissed her young child goodbye, and hit the road. She was so looking forward to this weekend, but almost as soon as she arrived, Tina wondered if she'd made a mistake. She sat around while Alice and her friends talked about class and the boys they knew, while pregaming at the apartment, throwing back just enough drinks to get themselves buzzed but not drunk, so they were in that perfect frame of mind, riding a blissful wave of booze, when the party started. She felt like an outsider. She didn't go to college and didn't know any of these other people around whom these young women's lives revolved.

Tina had been so looking forward to a college party. Every guy was handsome, put together, intelligent, and fit. They were all *going somewhere.* But after the introductions were made and the polite small talk quickly died out, none of the young men paid her any mind. Her baby bump was the ultimate deterrent. The only guy remotely interested was a wasted scuzzball who drunkenly quipped he wouldn't have to wear a condom if they screwed because he couldn't make her more pregnant.

While Alice had the time of her life, chatting up the hottest guy at the party, Tina found herself alone in the corner. Being pregnant, she couldn't drink. And she didn't know anybody else. Within an hour, Tina wished she had stayed home and gone to the local pubs. It would have been better than this.

She wanted to leave, but her friend was having a great time, so Tina stayed in her corner and drank her soda. The other girls ignored her, and the guys acted like she was invisible.

She was about to fake nausea and ask her friend for the key to her sorority house when another group of guys walked into the party. She recognized one.

Marshall.

"YOU HAVE TO UNDERSTAND," Tina was saying. "I was really feeling sorry for myself. Under different circumstances, I wouldn't have even talked to him. But my friend disappeared with this guy, and I didn't know anybody else there. So Marshall and I started talking."

Nelly was afraid she knew where this was going.

"He was different," Tina said. "He'd come out of his shell and had turned into an actual human being. He was funny. And, uh, kind of charming."

Nelly said nothing.

"He'd lost all his baby fat. He'd gotten himself in amazing shape. I thought he was hot." Tina made a gagging noise at the memory. "Anyway, there were other girls at the party, and Marshall could have talked to any of them. But he spent the whole night with me."

Nelly closed her eyes.

Tina was getting choked up. "I slept with him."

Nelly had to put the phone down. She walked away from the table.

Without the phone to her ear, she could barely hear Tina's voice.

"Nelly? Are you still there?"

Nelly folded her arms and stared down at the phone. This was too much.

"Like I said," Tina added, her voice small, "I was in a really bad place. I didn't know if I was going to keep the baby or if I was going to have it taken care of. But more than that, I didn't know if I could keep being a mother to the child I had. I was thinking about adoption, or asking my mother to raise Marnie. I was twenty years old, and it felt like my life was over."

Nelly picked the phone up. "How could you sleep with him?"

"I'm sorry," Tina said.

"After what he did to me."

"At that point," Tina admitted in a pained voice, "I still didn't believe you. He was so kind to me. Gentle, even. I was never scared. He was almost *too* polite when we were hooking up, stopping to ask if this was okay, if that was okay."

Nelly wanted to scream, but she choked down her rage. "But now you believe me?"

"I should have then."

"What changed your mind?" Nelly asked, her voice icy.

"A month or so later, my friend from college called with the story. A friend-of-a-friend situation. This poor girl accused Marshall of rape."

Nelly closed her eyes. She felt vindicated. Then she felt terrible for feeling vindicated, because Marshall had terrorized another woman.

"I hope the university kicked his ass out of school at least."

"He wasn't a student," Tina said. "He lived near campus and knew some of the guys enrolled. It was a long time ago. I don't remember all the details. But I never saw him again."

Nelly pushed her anger at Tina aside.

"Tina," she said, "I was actually calling to talk about Marshall."

"Nelly, before you go on, let me just say how sorry I am again."

The woman sounded pained and sincere. Nelly knew she should have accepted Tina's heartfelt apology. She'd done plenty of things she wasn't proud of when she was young and dumb and hurting. But the shock of this was still too much.

Tina filled the awkward silence. "Anyway, I have to admit I was completely shocked. I never thought I'd see you anywhere near Marshall again, never mind posing in a group photo together."

"This is going to sound crazy," Nelly said, not addressing Tina's apology. "But the man you saw in that picture—"

"You mean Marshall?"

"Are you sure it's him?"

"Yeah...why are you asking? I'm confused."

"Because I need to know. You're sure it's him?"

"Yes."

Nelly closed her eyes and took a deep breath and held it. All her wild emotions threatened to burst out of her, but she kept them inside.

"I don't understand why you're asking me these questions," Tina said. "You saw him with your own eyes, didn't you?"

"He's on the faculty where I took a job," Nelly said.

"Are you *serious*?" Tina asked. "That guy shouldn't be anywhere near children."

"Right." Nelly's heart was racing. "Do you know where he went after he left campus?"

The baby started to wail.

"Hang on," Tina said.

Nelly heard Tina put the phone down again. She called out to someone that the baby needed to be fed. When she came back to the phone, Nelly regretted not accepting Tina's apology. The moment for it seemed to have passed.

"How old is your baby?" Nelly asked.

"She's not my baby," Tina said. "She's my granddaughter."

Nelly's jaw dropped. Tina was only half a year older than her. She'd turn thirty-eight next July, on the twenty-third. It was amazing how they hadn't spoken since graduation, yet Nelly still remembered Tina's birthday. It reminded her of the times she'd been invited back to Tina's house after the party, watching her friend open presents, that one time they ate an entire ice cream cake together, the crippling stomach aches that ensued.

"You're a grandmother?" Nelly asked, incredulous. "That's wonderful. Congratulations."

"Marnie was younger than me when she got pregnant. I warned her, but nobody listens to their mother when they're seventeen."

Tina had been pregnant with Marnie during senior year of high school. By then, she and Nelly weren't on speaking terms. But Nelly would never forget seeing Tina at the graduation ceremony. Her former friend had always been whip-thin, but on that hot June day, Tina was as big as a house. She gave birth to Marnie not long after.

"Where were we?" Tina asked.

"I asked where Marshall went after he nearly got arrested."

"No idea," Tina said.

Nelly mulled it over. "Did your college friend, Alice, know him?"

"Yes," Tina said. "He was in with those guys at the party, and they hung around with the girls a lot."

"Are you in touch with any of those guys? Remember their names?"

"They didn't give me the time of day, Nelly."

"How about your friend?" Nelly asked. "Alice might know them. Or she might know someone who—"

"Alice is dead."

"I'm so sorry." Nelly was taken aback. "What happened?"

"It was a house fire," Tina said. "She and two of her roommates died. Only one of them survived, and barely at that. Third-degree burns all over her body."

"That's terrible."

"It happened a couple of months after I went to see

Alice," Tina said. "But I only knew her. I wasn't close at all with the others."

Nelly's head was spinning. "The man in the picture...he says his name is Emmett. Emmett Moore."

Tina read between the lines. "Wait a minute—are you saying Marshall has a new identity?"

"That's exactly what I'm saying."

Tina was quiet for a moment. "Let me look again."

Nelly held her breath. Part of her wanted Tina to admit she'd made a mistake. That it wasn't Marshall. That the man named Emmett might have resembled Marshall in some small way, but they were clearly two different people.

Life would be so much easier that way.

"No," Tina said. "I'm positive. It's him."

14

Nelly could feel her entire world begin to crumble.

She wasn't crazy.

This wasn't her past trauma making her see things that weren't there.

This was real.

Emmett was Marshall.

And all those things he'd said today, all those off-putting warnings, they were veiled threats. Emmett was absolutely trying to intimidate her.

Tina said, "I recognize the scar."

"You do?" Nelly asked.

"I've seen it before," Tina said. "He got it in a knife fight."

Nelly's knees felt weak. It was a good thing she was sitting down.

"I don't believe this," Nelly said.

"I don't either," Tina said. "And you're telling me he's a *teacher*?"

"Yes," Nelly answered. "He's going by Emmett Moore. He's worked here for three years."

"This is insane," Tina said. "Where's *here*, by the way?"

Nelly brought Tina up to speed.

"This is unbelievable," Tina said. "What are the odds?"

"Not long enough, apparently."

"How has he acted toward you?" Tina said.

Nelly shared the details of her meeting Emmett and of her interactions with him today. When she was done, Tina was still incredulous.

"What are you going to do?" she asked.

"I'm going to the police tomorrow."

15

FOUR DAYS AGO – TUESDAY

"Time!"

I've never been so happy in my life to hear that word, except when we were last forced to run wind sprints in gym class. The terrible game of hide-and-seek is over. I can come out now from behind the filing cabinet. My legs are tingling from having held the deep squat position uncomfortably for so long. When I stand up, I'm a little light-headed too and have to steady myself against the filing cabinet. The world slowly stops spinning, and only then do I notice that Marshall is standing in the doorway.

"I knew you were in here," he mutters.

His eyes are angry.

I force a smile. "Better luck next time, I guess."

There will never be a next time.

Marshall doesn't budge. He stands there, in his crimson football practice jersey, number 16, simmering.

I can't leave the room.

"You're a cock tease," he says.

I know what that means, but nobody has ever accused me of

the behavior before. I fake a laugh, pretending I think he's joking when I know he's not.

"Ha-ha. Very funny."

"I'm serious," he says, practically growling. "You know what I'm talking about. You kept looking at me before the game. You made me think you wanted it."

I involuntarily shudder at the thought of what he's suggesting.

"Uh, no...you were making me uncomfortable."

He shakes his head, huffs angrily. "Liar."

My throat has gone dry. I want to scream, but my body seems incapable of producing a loud sound at this moment.

"Could you please move?" I ask.

He doesn't. "You know you want it."

He locks eyes with me, and I freeze. I can't move, can't scream, can't even think. A wicked smile plays on his face. Marshall enjoys seeing me frightened. He steps into the room, and the murky light of this rainy afternoon grows even dimmer, and the world seems to grow smaller and close in on me as he approaches.

"There you are!"

It's Tina. She pokes her head in the doorway.

Marshall turns angrily to look over his shoulder.

"Maybe I should give you two some privacy...?" Tina asks.

I'm furious at Tina, but seeing her there and hearing her voice has snapped me out of my terrifying paralysis.

"No!" I blurt out.

I hurry past Marshall, past his chubby hulking body that smells like old sweat and alcohol and cigarettes, and rush out of the room.

I run toward light, a strange illumination that did not fill the factory before...

Nelly was aware of light hitting the curtain in her bedroom window. But that was confusing, because her body was telling her it was still the middle of the night. Groggy, she checked her phone. It was three o'clock in the morning.

She sat up in bed. Her curtain was lit up like it was daytime. As her mind began to work, she recalled Orville mentioning the floodlights he'd installed to deter the raccoons from getting into his trash. The nocturnal critters must have been up to their mischief, their movements tripping the motion sensors.

Nelly shifted the curtain and squinted against the glare. She didn't see any animals moving about near Orville's house. As she was about to let go of the curtain, a dark shape moved, disappearing around the corner of the home.

Now she was fully awake.

The shape had been large. That was no raccoon. Nelly got on her knees for a better look out the window. Orville's garbage cans hadn't been disturbed.

As she peered into the darkness beyond the floodlights, Nelly's eyes began playing tricks on her. Shadows seemed to move. One moment she was certain *something* was there, but the next her brain made better sense of what she was seeing: a tree, a clump of firewood, Orville's old riding mower.

She stared out the window for a long time, even after the floodlights went dead and darkness settled on the house once more.

The shape had been large enough to be a man.

And Emmett knew where she lived.

HER ALARM JARRED her awake in the morning. Nelly had had trouble falling asleep after speaking to Tina, both excited and nervous at the prospect of approaching the police with her suspicions now that it wasn't just her who thought Emmett was an impostor. And then the floodlights had activated in the dead of night. It had been difficult dropping off after that. Every few minutes she'd heard a noise, or *thought* she'd heard a noise, and had to work up the nerve each time to look out the window. Thoroughly spooked, she had tossed and turned for another hour or two.

She yawned her way out of bed and through her shower and during her breakfast. The last thing she needed on the day Miguel was scheduled to audit her class was to be tired and yawning. And she hadn't gotten the opportunity to spend as much time on the material as she would have liked, with dinner running long and being constantly distracted by intrusive thoughts. She was very nervous now thinking about Miguel observing her, but as long as she had her lesson plans, she knew she'd manage.

No outrageous amount of makeup could cover up the bags under her eyes. Tea wasn't going to cut it this morning. She needed a strong cup of coffee to get her going. After dressing quickly, Nelly collected her things, making sure her lesson plans were in her bag, then headed out. As she walked down the wooden staircase, however, something about her car struck her as odd. When she reached the ground, Nelly realized what it was: the car was tilted at a funny angle.

Rounding her vehicle, Nelly groaned. Her rear passenger tire was flat.

Great.

It wasn't even seven o'clock in the morning yet. She

doubted there was a local tow service open for business at this hour. Even if Nelly knew how to fix a tire, she didn't think she'd be able to do it quickly enough to arrive at school on time. What a horrible way to start her second day.

She felt like she couldn't catch a break.

Her tire being flat made no sense, however. During her cross-country trek, she'd made sure halfway through her journey to check her tire pressures. Everything had been fine. If this were a slow leak, she would have noticed. That meant—

She opened the passenger door to put her things down, then stooped to examine the tire. It wasn't a little flat—it was completely airless. She reached for her phone to use her flashlight app, but it wasn't in her pocket again. Cursing, Nelly searched her bags and found it crammed between some textbooks. She was going to have to be more careful about keeping it in certain places.

Switching on the flashlight app, Nelly did a double take. Now that she could see much better, the puncture wound in the tire was obvious. She could fit her pinky in the hole.

Had someone slashed her tire?

Nelly stood, immediately spooked. Who would have done this? And why?

There was only one person she could think of.

Emmett.

But when would he have done this? It would have been too risky at the school parking lot. Another teacher might have seen him messing with Nelly's car.

Then it struck her.

The floodlights.

The dark shape.

He'd been *here*. In the middle of the night.

Nelly trembled at the idea of Emmett creeping around in the darkness like some deranged psychopath.

"Nelly, everything okay?"

She jumped at the sound of Orville's voice. She hadn't heard the man come out of his house. He stood on the porch in a robe, a steaming cup of coffee in one hand.

"Sorry," he said. "Didn't mean to frighten you. But I'm an old man, so I barely sleep anymore. I was sitting down to read my paper when I looked out the window and saw you here crouched by your car."

Nelly took a deep breath. "Somebody...I've got a flat."

"Mind if I take a look?" he asked.

"THANK you so much for the ride," Nelly said, opening the passenger door of Orville's old truck out front of the school. "I appreciate it."

"It's no problem," he said. "I'm sorry I couldn't change it quickly enough so you could drive yourself. Want me to pick you up?"

"That's not necessary," Nelly said. She didn't want to put him out.

"But how are you going to get home? Call an Uber-thingy?"

She smiled. "Yes, that's what I'll do. Or maybe Beck can give me a ride."

He nodded. "Okay, then. Like I said, I'll get that spare on for you."

"Thank you so much," Nelly said. "You'll let me know how much your time is worth to—"

He stuck out a palm. "I won't have that. I needed something to do anyway today. You're doing me a favor."

Nelly didn't put up much of a fight. She'd pick up a bottle of wine or perhaps bake some cookies as a way of repaying Orville for his troubles.

She slid out of the truck, thanking the man again, and headed for the entrance. Emmett just so happened to be coming up the sidewalk. He flashed her a smile, but Nelly wasn't in the mood. She turned away from him and headed for the entrance.

"Hey, Nelly, hold up a second."

She stopped in her tracks, feeling terrified and angry and outraged and panicked, all at the same time.

"Morning, Emmett," she said, an edge creeping into her voice.

He hustled up to Orville's truck and waved at the old man. "Hey there, Orville. How are you?"

Orville rolled his window down. "This poor young woman had a flat."

Emmett's face fell as he turned to Nelly. "Gosh, I'm sorry that happened."

Nelly fought to keep her voice even. "I think someone slashed it."

Emmett frowned. "Huh. The same thing happened to Patti a few weeks back. We're pretty sure it was one of the kids."

"Kids getting into mischief," Orville said. "It's annoying, but they could be doing worse things, I suppose."

Emmett nodded. "Thanks for driving Nelly this morning. I'm glad she got in alright."

"No problem," Orville said. "I'll see you both later."

As the old man drove off, Nelly forced herself to lock

eyes with Emmett. As panicked as she was, she searched his face for some tic, in the hopes she could spot his duplicity.

"I'm sorry that happened," Emmett said before smiling. "But you got here on time. No harm, no foul, I guess."

"Not really," Nelly muttered. "I need to buy a new tire."

"Oh." Emmett pulled a face. "If money is an issue, I'm sure we could—"

He was goading her. Nelly tried to remain calm, but it was getting more and more difficult.

"Money's not the problem," she said.

He smiled sympathetically. "I understand. It's the time and the hassle, right?"

"It's knowing that someone did this to my car intentionally."

Emmett shrugged. "You know how kids are."

"I haven't been here long enough for any of them to bear me a grudge, Emmett," Nelly muttered.

He considered her point. "Didn't you mention you had to discipline someone yesterday? Tom Stovitch, I thought?"

"You think Tom Stovitch slashed my tire because I told him to keep quiet?"

He shrugged again. "Kids act out for less compelling reasons. And I don't have to tell you this, I'm sure, with all your teaching experience, but you know that sometimes kids do things for *no reason.*"

"He wouldn't even know which car is mine," Nelly pointed out.

"You never know, Nelly. It's a small staff here, and you know how deceptively observant children are. If he saw a new car in the parking lot, he'd rightly assume it was yours."

Nelly was having trouble keeping her emotions in check and feared she'd say something that would get her in trouble. Emmett, on the other hand, was perfectly at ease. With the corner of his mouth turned up in what could have been a mocking smile, Nelly got the sense he was *enjoying* this conversation.

"To be clear, I'm not accusing the boy of anything. And who knows?" he said. "Maybe it was just some kid doing it on a dare. Whose car it was didn't even matter. Or it could have happened somewhere else. Where did you go after you left school yesterday?"

She didn't want him knowing about her comings and goings. "I'd better get to it. I'm off to a later start than I'd hoped this morning."

"That's a shame," Emmett said.

He played the perfect gentleman, holding the door and then telling Megan how unfortunate Nelly was to wake up to a flat tire this morning. Megan was terribly sorry, and Emmett went on and on about how unlucky Nelly was. Megan matched Emmett's mood, expressing sympathy for Nelly's inconvenience, but the whole time Nelly watched Emmett.

He was a good actor.

But he wasn't *that* good.

He was giving a performance, not expressing genuine emotion. He said all the right things, but the emotion wasn't quite right. He emphasized the wrong words, and his expressions were ill-timed, coming a beat too early or late.

Even worse, Emmett seemed to know that she saw through him. But rather than be worried about it, that same small, mocking grin appeared at the corner of his mouth.

He was eating this up.

"Can I call a garage for you?" Megan said. "I know a really good one—"

"Thank you," Nelly said. "But someone is taking care of it for me. Now I really have to get to my classroom."

Before Nelly could turn to leave, Miguel's door opened. The principal appeared and smiled at her.

"You decided to give us another try?" he said, drawing laughs from Megan and Emmett.

"Morning, Miguel," she said. "And I look forward to seeing you later."

"I'm sure you'll do great," he said.

She'd been hoping he'd tell her which period he'd be auditing, but Miguel did not offer any information. As she turned to leave, Emmett spoke again.

"Say, Miguel, what do you think about Nelly taking a look at our policies?"

Frowning, she turned around.

Miguel thought about it.

Emmett added, "It'd be nice to have a different perspective on them." Emmett turned to her. "We're updating our bullying and safe-space practices."

Nelly ground her teeth. Was this asshole for real?

"I think that's a great idea," Miguel said. "It'd be nice to have a fresh set of eyes on the policies, especially with Nelly coming from a much larger district. But it's only her second day. I don't want to put too much on her plate already."

Nelly felt trapped. Emmett should have had this conversation with Miguel behind closed doors, outside of her presence, so no one felt obligated. And it didn't help that Megan was present either. Nelly felt like she couldn't say no.

"I wouldn't ask her to do any of the heavy lifting," Emmett said, as if she were fragile or not up to the task. "Perhaps we could read them over during fourth period when we're free. If she has any feedback, I'll incorporate it myself."

"I know you're probably not used to this," Miguel said, turning to her. "But in a small school like this, I'm afraid we're all forced to wear many hats. What do you think?"

Nelly felt the weight of their stares.

"Sure, Miguel. I think I can spare a few minutes during fourth period. But I still have a lot to do in my classroom, and I'd like to use some of the time lesson planning as well."

"That's generous of you, Nelly," Miguel said.

"Don't worry," Emmett said. "I won't take up too much of your time."

16

Miguel did not audit her first three periods. Nelly had been hoping to get that over with early so she wouldn't be nervous the rest of the day.

At the end of the third period, Nelly stood and erased the board behind her, then gathered her lesson plans and notes.

"Heya, Nelly," Emmett said.

He filled her doorway.

"Are you ready?" he asked.

"Yes, just let me grab my phone," she said. Nelly had been leaving it in her desk drawer.

"If you don't mind, we have a policy here," Emmett said. "No phones in small meetings."

Nelly thought he was joking at first, but his serious expression disabused her of the notion.

"I suggested the idea to Miguel last year, and it's worked out incredibly well," Emmett explained. "Meetings are not only more productive these days, they're also much shorter because everyone is laser-focused."

"I didn't realize this was a meeting," Nelly said.

"Kind of, sort of." He moved his head back and forth. "But don't worry. I promise it will only take a few minutes."

Nelly closed the drawer and left her lesson plans on the desk under her laptop, then she followed Emmett down the hallway. The lounge was empty when they arrived. The bell signaling the start of fourth period sounded as Emmett took a seat at the table by the window overlooking the athletic fields.

He opened a ring binder. "There are three policies we're updating. They're the ones with the yellow tabs. Don't worry about the work instructions right now. I want to respect your time."

"Okay."

Nelly took the binder from him.

"I don't want to be standing over you while you read," Emmett said. "I'm going to step out for a minute. When I come back, I'll stay out of your hair, alright?"

"Okay," she said.

"Thanks. You're the best."

Emmett disappeared.

Nelly sighed and flipped through the binder. The three policies were all several pages, with the last one being the longest. So much for this only taking a few minutes. Nelly was still nervous and edgy around Emmett, but now her anger was rising. She was certain Emmett didn't need, or even want, her feedback. He was doing this to steal her time. This was yet another subtle and petty exertion of authority over her. He knew she had more important things to do, yet here she was reviewing documents needlessly.

Bastard.

There was no way to prove that, of course. Just like there

was no way, short of eyewitness testimony or forensic evidence, that Emmett had slashed her tire last night.

She was practically frothing at the mouth when she realized several minutes had passed, and she'd been reading the same sentence over and over. Forcing herself to concentrate, Nelly decided to quickly scan these documents and provide him with vague, minimal feedback. If he wasn't happy about that, then too bad.

When Emmett returned, he was humming happily. Giving her a bright smile, he removed several Tupperware containers from the fridge. Nelly wanted to shut the binder, tell him the documents were fine, but not enough time had passed for her to have plausibly read everything. And the last thing she needed was for Emmett to paint her as uncooperative to Miguel. So she bit back her anger and continued to read.

"Don't mind me," Emmett said, interrupting her. "I have to count every calorie, or I blow up as big as a house."

He opened one of the cabinets above the sink and produced an opaque bottle and an oversized container of vegan protein. He made himself a protein shake, carefully measuring out each grain before filling the bottle with just the right amount of water. Then he got to work on the food in his Tupperware containers, which looked like chicken, brown rice, and broccoli. Nelly realized she was staring at him.

"Everything okay?" he asked.

"Fine," she muttered, moving to the second policy.

Like its predecessor, it was several pages' worth of boring, mechanical prose. She thought about how each second of her time was being wasted.

Emmett continued to hum to himself while the

microwave zapped his food. Nelly worked through the second policy quickly.

Steve entered the lounge. He greeted them both and went to the fridge, removing a brown paper bag. Emmett sat at the same table as Nelly but gave her a little space. She heard Steve rummaging through the drawers by the sink. Distracted by the sound, she looked up to see what he was doing.

"Hey, Emmett," Steve said. "Any chance you've seen that knife I brought in?"

Nelly was about to return to her reading, but the thought struck her.

A knife is missing from the kitchen.

Nelly couldn't help but draw a connection between the misplaced utensil and her slashed tire, especially since Emmett was sitting only a few feet away.

"Sorry, buddy," Emmett said. "You know how things disappear around here."

Nelly looked over at the man. He spooned some brown rice and chicken into his mouth.

"Yeah, I know," Steve said.

"Care to join us?" Emmett asked.

Steve shook his head apologetically, his expression becoming distracted. "Sorry, but I've got some work to do."

He left the lounge, and Nelly went back to reading. She flipped to the third policy about creating safe spaces at school.

"I think that one's really important." Emmett pointed with his fork. "The students and faculty need to feel like this is a place where they can be free from bullying, aggression, and intimidation."

The irony was not lost upon her. In what horrific

universe did she find herself being forced to read an anti-bullying policy written by the man who'd attempted to sexually assault her years ago?

Nelly blazed through the text. The policy said all the right things, but the words rang hollow to her because this vile man was sitting only a few feet away, slyly doing all the things he had just railed against.

After a quick scan, she sped her way through the document, acutely aware of the passing time and wanting to get back to her classroom.

Though Orville had been kind enough to stop for coffee on the way to school, one cup wasn't enough. She stifled a yawn.

"I hope these things aren't boring you," Emmett said in a disapproving tone. "These policies are important. Ideas matter. The goal here is to craft a message that will positively shape the landscape of this learning environment."

Nelly wanted to gag at his overblown, self-important corporate-speak.

"Sorry," she said, "I haven't been sleeping well."

"Must be the time difference and the big transition."

"Yep." She kept her eyes on the document. "That's it."

"Nelly," Emmett said, leaning forward, "you didn't have to agree to look these over. If you felt like you had too much on your plate and couldn't take on anything else, you were allowed to say no."

Nelly looked up and met his eyes.

"I was allowed to say no?"

Emmett stiffened at her question. "Of course you were."

I was allowed to say no?

She knew she shouldn't have said that. But the words had

just come out, all on their own. There was no mistaking their double meaning.

Emmett looked almost offended. "We care about work-life balance here. At Overland, we want to put our teachers in the best possible position to succeed. Don't ever feel like you have to agree to something out of pressure."

Nelly closed the binder. "These look good to me."

He arched his eyebrows. "Oh, you're done?"

"I read quickly," she said, rising.

Emmett held out a palm. "Hold on, there was one more thing I wanted you to take a look at."

"What?"

Emmett took the binder from her. "It's the...oh, where is it?"

Nelly forced herself not to roll her eyes. She'd already lost fifteen minutes to this pointless busywork, and now Emmett was asking for more. He flipped through the binder.

"Emmett, if it's alright with you, I can take a look after sch—"

He snapped his fingers. "Here it is. This won't take but a minute."

Without waiting for her response, he spun the binder back around. Nelly reluctantly sat, choking down her anger. Only a moment after telling her she could have politely declined this task, Emmett was asking her for more. This was getting to be absurd.

At this rate, she'd have to scarf her lunch down if she wanted to take any time reviewing her materials.

She glanced at the one-page document. "What do you have for me?"

"This is the certification I crafted," Emmett said. "The faculty will sign this, or something like it, to acknowledge they've read and understood these policies. We're also considering—"

"It looks fine to me," she said, her anger rising.

He seemed offended by how little thought she'd given it. "I value your feedback, Nelly, and want to know what you think. Don't worry about offending me. I've got thick skin."

"It's a one-page document that basically says *I've read and understand*," she pointed out. "I don't have much to add."

He nodded. "Fair enough. But how about the policies themselves?"

"I think you've done a good job," she said, rising. "Now if you'll excuse me, I really do have to prepare for the rest of the day."

He checked his watch. "Look at the time. I'm sorry to have kept you. I honestly didn't think it would take so long. If I'd known, I would have asked you to do this after school."

NELLY DIDN'T HAVE another break until seventh period. She rushed to the bathroom, fixing her makeup and hair, then filled her water bottle at the cooler by Miguel's office. The principal's door was closed, and Megan was away from her desk.

Nelly strode back to her classroom. Someone had snuck a soda into her last class, apparently, and she found an empty snack-sized bag of potato chips in the corner. She tidied up quickly, then returned to her desk to go over the lesson plans. She'd been holding out hope Miguel would pop in during second or third period, when she taught the much more familiar material about colonial America. For fifth period, she was switching back to early South American history.

Moving her laptop aside, however, she discovered her lesson plans were not on her desk. That was odd. She swore she'd left them here.

Growing worried, Nelly searched her desk and then riffled through her drawers. Her phone was where she'd left it, but the lesson plans were gone.

"What the hell?" she muttered, her panic rising.

Nelly expanded her search. She checked her bags, the trash can by her desk, the trash can near the back of the room. She looked inside desks and under them. She stuck her head out of the room and peered up and down the hallway. Now frantic, she returned to her desk. What had she done with them?

Mentally, she retraced her steps. She was almost one hundred percent certain she'd left them under her laptop for the coming period. But had she taken them with her to the lounge? It was worth checking.

Hurrying down the hallway, Nelly re-entered the teachers' lounge. Emmett was still at the same table, enjoying his lunch. He gave her a concerned frown.

"Everything okay, Nelly?"

"Oh, yes." She didn't want him to know she was panicked. "I thought I left something in here."

Emmett went through the motions of looking around, even getting out of his chair and searching under the table.

"I don't see anything," he said. "What did you lose?"

She wanted to tell him that she didn't *lose* anything, but her time was short. She thanked him for looking, then hurried back to her classroom. Though she'd already turned the room inside-out, Nelly went through the same routine. The lesson plans were *not* here.

"What the hell is happening?"

Nelly knew she hadn't misplaced them. But that meant someone had snuck into her classroom and taken them. She couldn't imagine a student doing it. Couldn't imagine anyone except Emmett. But that wasn't even possible. She'd just spent the last twenty minutes with him. He'd never had the opportunity.

Then she realized that wasn't true. Emmett had stepped out of the lounge, claiming he'd forgotten something. Had that been enough time for him to get to her class?

Either way, there wasn't much she could do about it now. Fifth period was fast approaching. Nelly had always preferred to create her lesson plans by hand. Taking the time to write her thoughts down made them easier to recall later, she'd found. But from now on, she'd do this digitally.

Flipping to a fresh page in her notebook, then opening the text, Nelly attempted to recreate her lesson plan from memory. She hadn't gotten very far by the time the bell sounded. Her notes were a jumbled mess, reflecting her haphazard recall. The students filed in a moment later. Nelly asked a girl sitting in the front row to take roll, giving herself another minute to conjure up the important details for today's lecture.

Then Emmett walked into her classroom.

"Apologies for the last-minute change of plans," Emmett said. "But Miguel was called into something important."

It took Nelly a moment to grasp what he was saying.

"*You're* going to sit in my class?" she asked.

"Megan is proctoring my test for me," Emmett said by way of explanation, then realized he'd answered a question that Nelly hadn't really asked. "Is something the matter?"

Nelly scrambled to come up with a good reason why the audit should be cancelled. But she couldn't and feared she would come across as worried and desperate, afraid of being reviewed.

"No," Nelly said. "But, unfortunately, my lesson plans have disappeared."

Emmett arched an eyebrow. "I'm sorry?"

Anger ripped through her. He'd heard her perfectly well. And, she suspected, he'd had a hand in their going missing. But he was going to play the innocent and feign surprise. He was going to make her explain herself.

Force her to grovel if he could.

"I left them here before you and I met," she said. "You probably remember that? I put them right under my laptop."

Emmett looked lost. He slowly shook his head. "I'm sorry, Nelly, but I wasn't paying attention to what you were doing with your lesson plans when I came by."

"But you must have noticed," Nelly said, as the bell signaling the start of fifth period sounded. By now, her conversation with Emmett had drawn everyone's full attention. The children knew something was up. "When you came in, I was holding them in my hands. Remember? And I slid them under my laptop when I mentioned grabbing my phone?"

Emmett shrugged. "I'm sorry, Nelly, but like I said, I wasn't paying attention to whatever you were doing."

The children had gone quiet. She heard snickers in the back of the room. They could sense she and Emmett were having a disagreement—and that she might be in trouble. Nelly's face turned red.

"Either way," Nelly said, "they're gone. Someone must have moved them."

Emmett frowned, looking back over his shoulder at the children. "We'd better discuss this in the hallway."

The children were eating this up. Red-faced, Nelly followed Emmett into the hallway like she was a student herself, about to be reprimanded. Emmett, at least, closed the door so the students wouldn't be able to overhear their conversation.

"Someone must have taken my lesson plans," Nelly said, wanting to take charge of the conversation. "When I realized they were missing, I managed to recreate what I could from memory. Under the circumstances, I don't think it's fair that I be audited when—"

Emmett's expression grew stern as he thrust out a palm.

"Nelly, I don't know what happened to your lesson plans, but I can assure you *no one* moved them. As you know, we take roll every period. If I check around, I'm certain all students will have been accounted for during fourth period."

"Someone could have asked to use the bathroom," Nelly said, wishing she didn't have to play this game of make-believe. She wanted to say what she was thinking, but without proof, she couldn't accuse a colleague of such outrageous behavior. "Or it might not have been a student."

He gave her an exasperated look. "Really, Nelly. This is getting ridiculous. Now you're accusing a member of the *faculty* of stealing your lesson plans. Who would do such a thing?"

Under other circumstances, such an accusation would be

ludicrous. But she was staring into the eyes of a fraud, a dangerous man she was certain was trying to sabotage her.

"I don't know," Nelly said. "But the point is, it's hardly fair for—"

"Nelly." He folded his arms and gave her a patronizing look. "Part of being a good teacher is being able to solve unexpected problems on the fly." He looked down at his watch. "Class started two minutes ago, and you've got a roomful of idle seventh-graders in there. What are you going to do about it?"

Nelly couldn't believe this was happening. He'd set her up. She didn't know how he'd managed this, and had no proof that he did, but all the same she was certain. Now he was going to force her to teach without a full lesson plan and perform the audit himself.

He was setting her up to fail.

Nelly swallowed hard. He wanted to break her, but she would not go down without a fight.

17

The audit hadn't been a total disaster.

Only a minor one.

She had managed, eventually, to foster a productive conversation toward the end of the period after explaining that the explorers had slyly played off different groups of indigenous peoples against each other, effectively driving a wedge between tribes that could have allied against the Europeans.

But that had been the sole highlight of an otherwise disjointed class interrupted many times by a few students who'd just been looking for any reason to be disruptive. Nelly had done a good job under the circumstances, but she assumed Emmett was providing Miguel with only criticisms of her performance.

"Knock, knock."

Beck was at her door. Nelly motioned for her to come in.

"You made it through another day," Beck said.

"Close the door, would you?" Nelly asked.

Beck did and sat in the chair beside Nelly's desk. Her

smock was covered in what appeared to be fresh paint, but Nelly didn't have the energy to worry about her chair getting messy.

Beck had picked up on her mood. "Is something wrong?"

"My lesson plans disappeared," Nelly said. She was still livid about it, as well as Emmett's insistence on auditing her, but she had to be careful about what she said. "I didn't have them for fifth period, when Emmett showed up to audit me. But he went through with it anyway."

"Uh-oh." Beck pulled a face. "So you winged it?"

"Half-winged it," Nelly said.

Beck looked pained. "How did it go?"

"I've taught better classes."

Beck winced. "I'm sorry."

Nelly shook her head. Her anger was getting the better of her. "Though it wasn't half as bad as Emmett is going to make it out to be."

Beck's expression changed to one of confusion. "I don't think you have anything to worry about. Emmett has always been fair. I'm sure he'll take that into account when giving Miguel his feedback."

Nelly pushed away from her desk and stood. She was dangerously close to saying things she shouldn't. Beck was startled by her sudden, dramatic motion.

Nelly walked over to the window so Beck could not read her expression. She could just make out the edge of the athletic fields. Several students wearing soccer uniforms ambled toward the pitch, reminding her of the home game scheduled to start in the next half hour. Now she was regretting the promise she'd made to attend.

"I left them right on my desk," Nelly said, hating how her voice betrayed her emotions. "I remember it specifically."

"You think someone moved them?" Beck asked.

Nelly nodded.

"Maybe it was the same jackass who slashed your tire," Beck said.

Nelly turned. "No student did that to my tire."

Beck frowned. "Where else did you go yesterday?"

"Nowhere else but home," Nelly said.

Beck slowly put it together. "Are you saying that a *teacher* slashed your tire? *And* moved your plans?"

Nelly faced the window again. She hadn't said yes, but Beck must have known what she was thinking.

"When did this happen, again?" Beck asked.

"Fourth period."

"Well, let's see...who's free fourth period...Steve, Jen, and Emmett...sometimes Vanessa and Lee. I think that's it. So it'd have to be one of them. But you said you were with Emmett, so he's out."

"Not the whole time," Nelly answered, a bit too quickly. "We walked to the lounge together; then he left for a few minutes."

Beck palmed her forehead. "Right, he came to see me."

Nelly narrowed her eyes. "He did? Are you sure?"

Beck nodded. "He asked me about the signage for the upcoming Halloween dance. I'm doing the artwork for it."

Beck's classroom was on the other side of the building. Emmett wouldn't have passed by Nelly's room to visit Beck.

"How long did you two speak?" Nelly asked.

Beck gave her a look like she was being paranoid. "A few minutes. We talked about the signage, and then he asked me if I was coming to the soccer game."

Nelly shook her head. She hadn't timed Emmett's absence, but the man had only been gone shortly. Was there enough time for him to have gone to Nelly's room, catch up with Beck, and return to the lounge? She couldn't be sure.

Either way, what could she do about it? If she accused Emmett of something, he had an alibi in Beck.

"Come to think of it," Beck said, "I noticed him stopping by Megan's desk on his way back to the lounge after we talked too. Something about the dance."

Nelly pinched the bridge of her nose. It was only her second day, but already it felt like things were getting out of control. Emmett had all the power here, and she had been made to look a fool.

There was a knock. Nelly peered through the window in her classroom door to find Megan standing in the hallway. After Nelly motioned for her to enter, Megan stuck her head into the classroom.

"Miguel would like to see you."

"HOW'D YOU FARE TODAY?" Megan asked.

Nelly got the sense that the woman already knew how she'd done. Having all these fake conversations was beginning to wear her down.

"Good," Nelly said, hoping she sounded confident. "I'm looking forward to the soccer game."

Megan smiled as they headed toward Miguel's office. "We should win this one. Red Lion isn't as good as us."

They walked the rest of the way in silence. Megan went back to her desk. Nelly heard people talking in Miguel's office, but she couldn't make out any of the words. She knocked gently on the door.

"Come in."

Miguel was sitting behind his desk, his hands folded on his belly. He did not smile at Nelly.

There was only one other person in the room. Emmett sat in one of the two chairs facing Miguel's desk. He gave Nelly a perfunctory nod.

"Please have a seat," Miguel said, pointing to the empty chair.

Nelly knew they had been talking about her. Inwardly groaning, she sat in the chair next to Emmett. She steeled herself for what she knew would be a difficult conversation. She'd have to defend herself without getting defensive, which was always difficult.

To her surprise, Emmett opened the conversation. "Nelly, we asked you in here—"

"Emmett," Miguel interrupted him, "why don't you give us the room? I'd like to speak to Nelly one-on-one."

Emmett's mouth hung open. Nelly suppressed a smile. She knew she was in for some trouble, but she would at least enjoy this moment of watching Emmett at a loss.

"Of course," Emmett said, rising. "Nelly, I do hope you're still coming to the soccer game?"

She gave him a steely-eyed look. "I wouldn't miss it."

Emmett closed the door behind him after he left. Nelly's joy was short-lived as Miguel cut right to the chase.

"Nelly, I took a chance on you," he said. "And I want to believe in you. But what happened today is simply unacceptable."

After his curt dismissal of Emmett, Nelly was hoping Miguel would go easy on her. Instead, the man had been blunt, and now she was worried about her job.

Nelly opened her mouth to protest, but Miguel raised a hand.

"You are responsible for your classroom," Miguel said. "You are responsible for your lesson plans. From what I hear, the lecture went poorly. You didn't know the material well enough to teach without the plans, and you lost your place several times. This is not good, Nelly."

This time she did not wait to speak.

"I left the lesson plans on my desk, right under my laptop. I know I did."

"What are you saying?" Miguel asked.

"Someone must have moved them."

Miguel tipped his head back in disbelief. "Who would have done such a thing, Nelly?"

"I don't know," she said, wanting to shout Emmett's name. "But I am certain I left them on my desk."

"Though you haven't named anyone, you are making a very serious accusation." Miguel narrowed his eyes. "Do you have any proof of this?"

She swallowed hard. "No. But I swear I left them on my desk."

Miguel was unmoved. "Put yourself in my position, Nelly. What's more likely here? That a teacher accidentally misplaced her notes? Or that one of her colleagues purposely moved them? I mean, really, who would do such a thing? This is your second day here. Which member of my faculty wants to see you fail?"

Nelly hated to admit that he was right. From his perspective, the idea was preposterous. He took her silence to be an acknowledgment of his point.

"And either way, you did not prepare well enough to teach that class," he said.

Nelly thought that was unfair. "I haven't taught early South American history in *years.* No teacher is an expert on everything. Fifth period was literally the second time in over a decade that I've lectured on that subject."

She felt herself tear up.

"All the same, you lost control of your students." Miguel's lips grew thin. "Classroom management is an important aspect of teaching."

Nelly was outraged. "Emmett told you that?"

Miguel nodded. "I understand what it feels like to be flustered. Lord knows I was in that position plenty of times myself as a young teacher."

Nelly bristled. She wasn't a *young* teacher anymore. She had fifteen years of experience and knew what she was doing. Emmett had fed this man outright lies about her performance.

"But you have to keep your composure, especially when the situation goes left," Miguel added.

Nelly shook her head. "I did *not* lose control of my classroom."

"I wasn't there," Miguel said. "But I trust Emmett. I've known him for a long time. He's always been fair."

Nelly realized she was shaking.

Seeing her getting worked up, Miguel's face softened.

"I appreciate how difficult this must be for you," Miguel said. "You went from being out of work for quite a bit while going through a divorce, to moving across the country, and starting a new job immediately, one month into the new school year, no less. I know this has been a major transition, and I want to be sympathetic to that, Nelly."

Nelly managed not to cry.

"It's only your second day, and you're still getting acclimated obviously." Miguel smiled. "And I'd be a hypocrite if I acted like I never made mistakes."

Nelly's messy feelings were threatening to come out. She resented the fact he thought she'd made a mistake.

Miguel said, "I'd like you to come up with a plan of action for your lessons moving forward. Please have that ready for me tomorrow morning. And also, please let me know how I can support you. I want to see you succeed here, Nelly."

A plan of action...Nelly knew what that meant. It was the beginning of a paper trail in her personnel file. She didn't get the sense Miguel was planning to fire her, but this document would serve as a starting point in the event he decided to let her go.

Two days in, and she felt like her job was already in jeopardy.

"Yes, of course. This won't happen again," Nelly said. "I promise you."

Her phone buzzed in her pocket. Nelly had forgotten to leave it in her desk in keeping with the school's policy on meetings. Miguel's smile vanished.

"We don't like for people to bring phones to small meetings," Miguel said. "Emmett should have mentioned this already. If you must absolutely have it on your person, then make sure it's muted."

Nelly's face was on fire. "Sorry."

Miguel was not happy about the interruption. The good humor and compassion he showed a moment ago were short-lived.

Even though Nelly hadn't done anything wrong, she still felt compelled to make up for what Miguel viewed as her poor showing today.

"I've noticed that everybody around here wears many

hats," she said. "I wanted to ask if there's anything I can help with. I'd like to do my fair share."

Miguel gave her a pointed look. "Are you sure you can handle it?"

That was unfair, but she forced herself not to get defensive. "Yes."

Miguel thought it over. "Come to think of it, Megan has to leave early tomorrow. Could you handle the car line at dismissal?"

Nelly groaned inwardly. Car line and recess were the most demanding and also most thankless jobs.

"I'd be happy to."

BACK IN HER CLASSROOM, Nelly closed the door and slumped in her chair. The soccer game was about to start, but she needed a moment to herself and figured it wouldn't be the end of the world if she showed up a few minutes late.

What a day.

It had started off lousy and only gotten worse. And perhaps the worst part was yet to come. She still had to speak to the police. As necessary as that conversation was, she dreaded baring her soul to a perfect stranger while accusing a beloved member of the community of being a fraud. Maybe she was just feeling low after a terrible school day, but right now Nelly was certain the police wouldn't take her seriously.

Outside, a whistle sounded. The soccer game must be starting.

Nelly quickly tidied up the room and gathered her things. She put her notes for tomorrow in her bag and made sure she'd left nothing valuable or essential behind before closing up. On her way down the hall, she remembered her phone buzzing in Miguel's office.

Taking her phone out of her pocket, she tapped the icon for her text messages. Her screen went black. A few moments later, her screen flickered back to life and partially froze.

"Really?" Nelly said, wondering what else could go wrong today.

Sighing, Nelly was about to try turning the device off and back on, but then her text messages opened. Nelly breathed a sigh of relief. She wasn't tech-savvy. Her ex-husband had handled the selection and purchase of their electronic devices. This phone was almost three years old, she realized. It was probably time to get a new one.

"When it rains, it pours," she muttered.

Tina had texted to ask how her day went. It was only a short message, but all the same Nelly was touched. She thanked Tina for thinking of her and mentioned she was nervous about going to the police station later. Then she headed outside for the game.

18

Outside, the air was chill. Nelly zipped her jacket and hunched against the cold. As she made her way to the soccer field below, she was surprised to see a police vehicle parked on the blacktop beside the building. There was a badge and official insignia painted on the door. Above the emblem was the word SHERIFF.

She made her way down the gentle but long hill to stand near the middle of the field behind the home team's bench.

The game was in full swing. Beck sported a pair of old pom-poms and performed a discombobulated cheer routine loudly and unabashedly, drawing laughs from the parents and the remainder of the faculty. Despite her poor mood, Nelly found herself smiling at Beck's goofy enthusiasm while the students raced across the field, haphazardly sending the ball in one direction or the other.

But the sight of Emmett approaching wiped the smile off her face. She turned slightly, laser-focusing her eyes on the field to deter any conversation. But all the same, the man came up beside her anyway. He stopped only two feet away and settled his narrow-set eyes on her.

"Hey, Nelly," he said.

She decided not to look at him. Nelly cheered when one of her students made a good play.

"Emmett."

He drew a deep breath, as if stung by her short reply.

"Look, I wanted to connect with you about what happened in fifth period," Emmett said. "We didn't really get a chance to speak because I had to run to my next class."

Nelly folded her arms against the surprising cold.

"I've already spoken to Miguel," she said. "I'd rather not go over it again."

He was silent, and for a moment she thought he'd respect her wishes.

But he didn't.

"I feel it's important for us to be honest with each other," Emmett said. "I'm not one to sneak around and do things behind other people's backs."

She shook her head. The absolute nerve of this son of a bitch galled her. His duplicity. His utter two-facedness.

"So I wanted to share what I told Miguel," Emmett went on. "Because I feel like I owe you that."

She tore her eyes off the field and whirled on him.

"Like I said, Emmett, I've already spoken to Miguel and don't really need to hear it all again." She narrowed her eyes. His proximity made her nervous, but her anger trumped her fear. "But I do agree with you, I think it's important that we be completely honest with each other."

Emmett's eyes flashed in surprise. For the briefest of moments, she had caught him unawares in an unguarded moment. But he quickly composed himself. The man's presence of mind, she hated to admit, was impressive. And intimidating.

"You have something you'd like to share?" Emmett asked innocently.

"First of all, I will find out who moved my lesson plans, and that person will have to account for themselves."

"*Nelly*—"

She talked over his condescending voice. "Second, you and I both know that your auditing me under those circumstances was hardly a fair test of my capabilities."

His grin was mocking.

"And most importantly, I did a good job in fifth period teaching material I was unfamiliar with under those circumstances. And never *once* did I lose control of that classroom. I don't appreciate your mischaracterizing my performance. We both know that if Miguel had been there, he wouldn't have seen it that way."

Emmett was taken aback. "Nelly, I'm many things. But a liar is not one of them."

She couldn't stop herself from scoffing.

"I offered Miguel my honest opinion of your performance," he went on. "I understand why you're getting defensive, though. People identify with their jobs and draw much of their self-worth from their performance. It's very difficult for some to take constructive feedback. I get that."

She had half a mind to walk right over to the sheriff, point at Emmett, and loudly proclaim his identity so that everyone standing on the sidelines could hear.

"I'm not getting defensive," she muttered. "I'm standing up for myself. You—"

"But if you want to work here," Emmett said, "then you

must learn to accept feedback, Nelly. It's the only way you'll improve. I understand why you're upset. The experience is still fresh in your mind, you've just had a difficult conversation with Miguel, and you're naturally worried about your job. But don't turn this around on me. I didn't touch your lesson plans, and let's be honest, the most likely explanation isn't that someone stole them. It's that you misplaced them. You need to take responsibility for that, as well as for your performance."

Nelly was so angry, she could cry.

"But I do apologize," Emmett said, offering a repentant grin that almost looked genuine. "I wanted to talk to you about what happened in fifth period, but I should have realized you'd need time to process everything. You're still a little raw, obviously, and I should have been more sensitive to that."

Screw you.

She wanted to say it. To scream it. She wanted to rake his face with her nails. Gouge his eyes. Kick him in the groin. Get him on the ground. Rain blows down on his head until it required the strength of three, no, four grown adults to pull her off him.

Nelly had never wanted to hurt anyone before.

Actually, that wasn't true.

She *had* fantasized about beating Marshall Dawes up. That was why she'd taken all those self-defense classes over the years, because she'd dreamed up this scenario where one day she would run into the man somewhere, and it would just be the two of them, and she'd beat the ever-loving shit out of the scumbag.

What childish thoughts, though. Even if she'd run into

Marshall in a dark alley, she couldn't attack him without facing serious repercussions. Showing that kind of aggression and turning violent would end her career.

Not to mention the fact that, even with her training, the man standing before her was a physical specimen. Emmett was in marvelous shape. He was bigger, stronger, faster than her. He could probably break her in half if he wanted. Sure, she might get a lucky shot or two, but once he got hold of her, the fight would be over. This man could have his way with her.

"I'm really sorry, Nelly," Emmett said. "How about we regroup later this week and talk? I feel like we haven't gotten off to a great start, but I want you to know I'm on your side. I want to see you succeed here. We all do."

Nelly bit back tears and choked down rage. She took comfort in the fact that she'd speak to the sheriff tonight. Then this monster would be in trouble. The thought made her smile. She couldn't wait to see this bastard's face when the sheriff hauled him down to the station for questioning, maybe even during an arrest. She hoped she could be there for it.

"Yes, Emmett," she said, an edge to her voice. "Let's talk later this week."

He smiled pleasantly, like they'd had a moment of reconciliation. Then he looked past her and moved along.

Nelly seethed while the game played out. She watched Emmett make his way through the crowd, chatting up parents, getting to be the "cool" teacher whom all the students liked, enjoying the naked adoration of his peers. He had everything going for him.

Everything.

At halftime, the sheriff approached Nelly.

She wasn't expecting him to stop and talk to her. He was a tall man with long arms and a beach-ball stomach, one of those guys who, if she'd looked at him from the back, she would have had no idea he was overweight.

"Bill Van Dyke," he said with a smile.

His catcher's mitt of a paw swallowed her hand. He must have been six seven or six eight. Nelly had to crane her neck to look up at him.

"Nelly Peak," she said.

"Nice to meet you," he said. "And welcome to Overland. How are you getting on?"

By degrees, Nelly became aware of Emmett watching her converse with the sheriff. She didn't want the man knowing she planned on speaking to Bill Van Dyke about sensitive matters, but at the same time she enjoyed making Emmett sweat a little. There was no harm in chatting the sheriff up. After all, they were only introducing themselves, and in a small community like this, it was perfectly normal for teachers to be acquainted with the sheriff.

"It's been an adjustment," Nelly said, thinking of how hard her day was. But she pushed that aside and smiled brightly at the sheriff, acting like nothing was wrong at all. "Everyone I've met has been so nice. Overland seems like a great community. I'm still getting settled, of course, but I don't think it's going to take me long."

"It's a great town, and we aim to keep it that way," he said, his voice growing serious. "When did you get in?"

She told him her story, bringing him quickly up to speed.

The sheriff listened politely, showing a genuine interest. When she was done, he smiled and nodded, explaining that his nephew attended the school and played for the team.

"Well, it was nice meeting you, Nelly," the sheriff said, offering his hand.

"Likewise."

"If you ever need anything, you give me a call," he said.

Little did the man know she'd be stopping by later.

They shook hands again. She took some satisfaction in knowing that Emmett was watching her converse with the sheriff, hoping the conversation he couldn't hear was making him uneasy. Then Bill was moving past her, working his way through the small crowd. He greeted each of the other faculty members by name, coming at last to Emmett. The sheriff greeted the other man with noticeable enthusiasm, patting Emmett on the shoulder as they pumped hands. Emmett's eyes drifted briefly to Nelly, and he flashed her a quick, mocking smile as if to say, *The sheriff likes me more than you.*

Nelly frowned. Was there anyone in this town not under Emmett's spell?

Beck shoved one of the ratty old pom-poms in Nelly's face.

"I need a co-cheerleader," Beck said.

Nelly laughed until she realized Beck was serious. "Uh, no, thank you."

Though she was used to standing in front of a classroom of middle schoolers, Nelly did not like calling attention to herself.

"Come on," Beck said. "It'll cheer you up."

"Yeah, come on, Nelly," Emmett said, putting his hands together. "Let's see your stuff."

Before she knew it, the rest of the faculty was egging her on. She really didn't want to stand on the sidelines and make a fool of herself in front of people she hardly knew. But Miguel was watching, and she wanted to come across as a good sport, so Nelly snatched the pom-pom from Beck and moved to the edge of the field.

Beck winked at Nelly. "Just follow my lead."

Nelly plastered a smile on her face. "I'm going to kill you."

Beck laughed. "This won't hurt a bit."

"You owe me," Nelly said, still smiling. "How about a ride home?"

"How about a ride to the bar instead?"

BECK DROPPED Nelly at home after the game. She pushed for a quick drink, just one, but Nelly politely declined enough times that Beck gave up. Before Nelly climbed out of Beck's tiny car, Orville popped out of his house and approached. He waved at Beck while she backed out of the gravel driveway.

"Heya, Nelly," he said. "How'd it go today?"

A lot of people asked that question out of habit. But Nelly got the feeling Orville was actually interested in her answer. She smiled at him, not wanting to relive today's experiences.

"Oh, fine." She pointed at her vehicle. "Thank you so much for...wait a minute, where's the spare tire?"

Nelly's spare tire was supposed to be smaller than her regular ones, just something to put on the car in an emergency so you could get somewhere else safely. But the new tire on her car was regular sized.

Orville shrugged. "I know a guy. He came out and put the tire on for me."

Nelly was happily surprised. "You did?"

"He owed me a favor," Orville answered.

"How much was—"

Orville waved the question away. "Don't worry about that."

"Oh, no, you have to let me pay."

"It's fine. Like I said, the guy owed me a favor."

Nelly couldn't believe it. She was so touched by the gesture after her lousy day that she teared up.

"Thank you so much."

"No problem." Orville grinned ear to ear. "He did say your other tires were a little bald and could at least use a rotation, if not changing altogether."

Yet another thing that her ex-husband used to take care of. Nelly pushed thoughts of John aside and thanked Orville again and went inside to change out of the clothes she'd worn to school. She needed to get to the sheriff's office, but at the last moment she decided to take a hot shower and wash the day off her. Emerging fifteen minutes later, she checked herself in the mirror. The bags under her eyes hadn't gotten any better, and now she seemed to be carrying the entire day with her. Nelly tried some different makeup, not wanting to show up at the sheriff's office looking like a vagabond, then pulled her hair into a ponytail. She donned her nicest pair of jeans and a sweater. She had to look presentable. If she went in there looking spotty, the sheriff would be even less inclined to believe her outrageous claims.

She popped a few more antacid tablets on her way out, grabbing her favorite shawl off the back of the door.

The sheriff's office was on the other side of town. It took Nelly nearly twenty minutes to get there, spending the last half of the trip on Main Street. She passed an ice-cream parlor boasting the world's best apple cider. Someone was burning leaves in the park—were people still allowed to do that? She watched a cute younger couple walk hand in hand through town, stopping to peer in the windows of an antique shop. There was a used-book store and a greeting card shop. It seemed like such a nice place to live.

But it was hell to Nelly.

The police station was old and looked more like a post office than what it was. As Nelly pulled into the tiny municipal lot, the concrete bulging upward in places as tree roots pressed against it, she realized that the building *also* housed the post office. Several men wearing mail carrier uniforms were conversing out front, both smoking cigarettes. She kept her head down as she hurried inside, not wanting to draw attention to herself.

A woman wearing the same-colored khaki uniform that Bill Van Dyke wore earlier looked up at Nelly from a big desk in the front of the office.

"Afternoon, ma'am," she said. "I'm Val Sullivan, sheriff's deputy. Can I help you?"

Nelly smiled nervously. She'd only been in a police station once before on a school field trip years ago and felt entirely out of place here. Looking past the woman, she counted only a handful of desks, two offices, and in the corner, what appeared to be bars. She recoiled at the thought of someone being held in there.

"Uh, hi. I was looking for the sheriff."

"Was he expecting you?"

"No."

"I'm sorry, but the sheriff's not here right now. What's your name?"

"I'm not trying to be rude," she said. "But I don't want to make my presence here, uh, official. Is that alright?"

"I understand," Sullivan said. "Do you mind if I ask what this is about?"

Nelly smiled apologetically. "It's a private matter."

"I see." The woman nodded sympathetically. "Well, he's due back in about twenty minutes. You can wait in here or come back, up to you."

Nelly thought it over. She didn't want word getting to Emmett that she was nosing around the sheriff's office, so she didn't relish the idea of hanging out here for all the world to see. But at the same time, if she left, she'd simply have to come right back.

"I'll wait."

"Can I get you something to drink? Our coffee is terrible, but at least it's free. You get what you pay for, I guess."

Nelly wasn't in a humorous mood, but she managed a smile. "I'm fine."

"Water?" Sullivan asked.

"Water would be great."

"Okay, great. Grab a seat, and I'll bring you one."

WHILE NELLY WAITED, she grew antsy. She wasn't thirsty but sipped the water to give herself something to do. The seconds ticked by. Despite the antacids she'd gobbled, she was still feeling queasy. In her head, she went over what she'd already gone over, again and again. Growing increasingly nervous, she stood and paced the small waiting area. On a normal day, she'd be preparing dinner right now. Six o'clock was the time she and John usually ate. Why was she thinking about John?

"Is there anything else I can get you?" Sullivan asked.

"No, thank you."

The deputy got on the horn, trying to reach the sheriff through a walkie-talkie unit clipped to her shoulder. But Bill Van Dyke did not answer. Nelly noticed her punching out a text and figured she was trying to reach her boss in that manner also.

"Ma'am," Sullivan said when she finished typing, "is there something the matter?"

Nelly was about to say no, but that would have obviously been untrue.

"I guess I wouldn't be here otherwise."

Sullivan nodded appreciatively. "What can I do for you?"

Nelly eyed the door. She was thinking about leaving. Putting off this conversation for another day or two. Did she really need more drama in her life today?

But she knew that was fear and rationalization talking. She knew that if she ran out of here today, she'd be less likely to come back tomorrow and even less likely to return the following day. She knew that if she left the sheriff's office right now, she might as well just keep on driving, right out of town. Might as well go find somewhere else to live and work.

That was how precarious her situation was.

"Nothing, thank you," Nelly said.

"Would you like to sit with me over here?" Sullivan asked, leaning back in her chair. "I could use somebody to talk to."

"Sure."

Nelly passed into the main area of the station. It smelled like coffee back here. Old filing cabinets were pushed up against one wall behind Sullivan with decaying paper tags denoting their purported contents. Nelly sat in the chair beside the deputy's desk and crossed her legs at the knee.

"My name's Val, by the way. Did I already tell you that?" Sullivan stuck out her hand, and they shook. "But most people just call me Sullivan. Even my mother."

The two women shared a laugh. Nelly was glad to have someone to talk to. It took her mind off the upcoming conversation.

"Nelly," she said. She didn't know why, but she felt like she could trust this woman.

Sullivan nodded knowingly. "I thought that might be you. The new teacher, right?"

"Yes."

"Welcome to town, then," Sullivan said. "What do you think so far?"

Nelly got to talking and was grateful for it. Before she realized it, the sheriff was coming into the station. Another twenty minutes had passed. He removed his hat and shrugged off his brown jacket, smiling at Nelly.

"Ms. Peak, it's your lucky day, getting to see me twice." He looked at Sullivan. "Anything doing?"

"Ten men tried to rob the liquor store across the street, but I managed to shoot and kill them all. No bystanders were injured either. I'll get to the report tomorrow."

Van Dyke smiled, but did not laugh, at the joke. He asked Nelly to follow him. His office was at the other end of the small station. The walk afforded Nelly a better vantage point into the holding cell. Nobody was in there, which made her feel unreasonably better. The sheriff asked her to sit and pulled the door closed. He sat behind his mess of a desk. Paperwork threatened to landslide off both ends.

"Ms. Peak." He sat forward. "What brings you in?"

Nelly took a deep breath. It was the moment of truth.

"This is going to sound crazy..."

19

The sheriff waited, his expression blank.

"But please hear me out," Nelly said.

Bill Van Dyke nodded at her. "Nelly, I've heard plenty of crazy things in my day. I doubt anything you have to say will surprise me."

She wasn't so sure. Her eyes drifted to the window behind him, which commanded a view of the street and municipal lot where her car was parked. She wanted to leave.

But Nelly decided to plunge in.

"I grew up in a small town, much like this one, in New Jersey," Nelly began. "From the time I was a baby all the way through high school. After graduation, I went away to college in California, and I haven't been back home since. I met my ex-husband not long after I started working and..."

Why was she telling him this? Nelly had already gone off-script. It felt like the walls were closing in around her.

"Just take your time," Bill said.

His voice was gentle, but it did not soothe her.

She laughed nervously. Her back was slimy with sweat. She peeled off her shawl but still felt overheated. Nelly just had to say it.

"When I was thirteen years old, I met a boy named Marshall Dawes at a party. He was three years older than me, so sixteen at the time. He..."

Her head felt light. If it weren't attached to the rest of her body, she felt like it would have floated away like a balloon.

Over the years, she had only shared her story with a handful of people. Telling it had never gotten any easier.

Bill came around to her side of the desk, pulling up a chair beside her.

"It's okay," he said. "You're safe here, Nelly."

She blinked away tears. "He tried to rape me. He *almost* raped me. He pinned me to this desk, and...anyway, the details aren't important."

"Okay."

She felt his eyes on her, but she could not look at him. Even after all these years, even after all the therapy, even though this had never been her fault, Nelly still felt ashamed. Like she had done something wrong.

"I reported him to the police. But this was a long time ago. Back then, people didn't believe women. Not even other women." She was thinking about Tina, and how awful her friend had been to her afterward. "It was always a misunderstanding. The girl sent mixed signals. Guys will be guys. Can't blame a guy for trying."

She took a deep breath.

"That's how it was until a few years ago when MeToo happened."

The sheriff didn't say a word. He just waited for her to go

on. But she felt him sitting next to her. His presence in the small office was like a tangible thing.

"Nothing came of it. He said, she said. Imagine the worst thing you can think of happening to you, then imagine nobody believing it happened. Not even your moth—it was a nightmare."

She thought of her mother, with whom she hadn't spoken now in almost two years. She'd cut Mom out of her life several times. But she always ended up feeling guilty, regretting her decision, and reaching out.

Only to regret *that.*

She recalled Mom's words. *You show up in a wet T-shirt with those shorts on and expected what to happen exactly?*

And Mom's other words, years later. *Nelly, you just need to get over it. Life moves on.*

She didn't know it then as a child. But she knew it now. Mom was damaged goods. She should never have been a mother. She wasn't equipped. Dad had run off when Nelly was young. She didn't even remember him and wouldn't know him by sight. Mom had destroyed what few pictures there were.

"Marshall left town not long after it happened. He came from a broken home, apparently. The story was that his mother couldn't support him and sent him to live with his father or uncle or a cousin. I don't know. There were a lot of stories. I never knew which to believe. Either way, as quickly as he came into my life, he was gone. I never saw him again."

There was a lump in her throat.

"Until Sunday."

She swallowed hard. Her vision was a hot blur of tears. Nelly reached blindly into her purse for tissues and dabbed at her eyes. The sheriff remained where he was, not moving, not speaking.

"He's *here*," she said. "In Overland."

"You said his name was Marshall?" the sheriff asked, finally breaking his silence.

"Was. Yes." Nelly managed to clear her vision. "Marshall Dawes. D-A-W-E- S."

The sheriff was jotting notes down on a tiny pad he'd pulled from his shirt pocket. "Where did you see him?"

Nelly couldn't bring herself to say it. Not yet. She wasn't trying to be dramatic. She simply wasn't capable of telling the sheriff exactly what she'd come here to say.

"At the charity run."

"Marshall Dawes," the sheriff said. "That name is unfamiliar to me."

He said it like he knew the name of everyone living in Overland. Perhaps he did. Nelly fought to get her breathing under control. She realized now she should have opened with the next sentence. She'd been pulling the proverbial Band-Aid off slowly as if that would lessen the pain of what was to come.

It was only making things worse.

"He's not going by Marshall anymore," she said, forcing herself to look the sheriff in the eye. "His name is Emmett Moore."

The sheriff went unnaturally still.

Nelly wanted to take it back. Wanted to get in her car and drive away. But now it was too late. She had crossed a personal Rubicon.

Life returned to Bill Van Dyke's body. Without perhaps even realizing it, his mouth took on a skeptical expression, a puckering of the lips. He adjusted himself in the chair, which was much too small for his height.

"I want to make sure I understand what you're saying. You're telling me you think Emmett Moore is the same person as this Marshall Dawes, who attempted to assault you...how long ago was this?"

Nelly knew then this had been a mistake. She noted his careful choice of words. *"You're telling me you think..."* And there was no misinterpreting his tone when he'd asked how long ago the assault had occurred, as if the number of years made her story less plausible.

"Twenty-four years ago," she said in a tiny voice.

He nodded, wrote something down in his notebook. For a moment, he would not look at her. Nelly felt the need to fill the silence. She had to plead her case, though she knew sounding desperate would only work against her.

"Like I said, I know how this sounds. But I'm certain it's him. I'd recognize that man anywhere. But you don't have to take my word for it. I contacted an old friend. Her name is Tina Hirshberg—*Walker*—her last name is Walker now. Anyway, we got in touch and she saw a picture of Mar— Emmett from the race. She's certain it's him too."

The sheriff nodded, as if he'd finally received a piece of information that made sense.

"As you can imagine," Nelly said, "I'm going out of my mind. I've had to interact with this man at school. Pretending like nothing is wrong while he..."

"While he what?" the sheriff asked, scooting forward on his seat.

"While he plays games," Nelly said. "Mind games."

Bill frowned. "Has he made you feel uncomfortable?"

"Well, yes. I mean, I don't like being around him."

"But has he done something specific to make you feel that way?"

Nelly had to think about it. They had interacted several times, but could she point to anything objective to support her assertion?

"He talked about having his students write an essay on the MeToo movement," she said. "You know that story about the actress who just came forward?"

The sheriff nodded. "I'm familiar."

"Well, there was that."

He looked up from his notepad. "Is that it?"

He asked like that wasn't enough. "You don't understand, it was the *way* he said it. He brought that uncomfortable subject up on purpose. He had to know it would upset me. It was his way of sticking the needle in. His way of demonstrating his power and how protected he is. He can literally reference the fact he tried to put his penis inside me without getting into trouble."

The sheriff winced at her choice of words, but Nelly didn't care.

"He has a great reputation in this community, and apparently he thinks that makes him untouchable."

"What else has he said or done?" the sheriff asked. "Has he explicitly threatened you?"

"No...but..."

"But what?"

This was not going well. "My tire was slashed."

"Your tire?"

Why was he acting like she was speaking a foreign language?

"Yes, my goddamned tire," she said, regretting her

outburst. "Sorry. I woke up this morning to a flat. You can ask Orville about it. He dropped me at school today."

"I see. And you think Emmett did this to your car?"

"I don't see who else would. I've been here all of three days," she said. "Nobody else knows me that well."

"Did you see him near your car?"

"No, I didn't catch him in the act, but..." She squeezed her eyes shut and pinched the bridge of her nose. "Like I said, who else would do this?"

The sheriff didn't answer, once more returning to his notes.

"I think someone was outside my apartment last night also," she explained. "Orville installed floodlights on a motion sensor to scare away raccoons. They came on about three, three thirty and woke me from a dead sleep."

"And you saw someone outside?" he asked.

The truth was, she thought she had seen a large shadow moving along the unlit side of the house.

"Not exactly," she said. "There was movement. It could have been a man."

His look said: *It also could have been an animal.*

But the sheriff kept his opinion to himself.

"Has he done anything else to threaten or intimidate you?" the sheriff asked.

She took a deep breath. While planning for this conversation, she hadn't decided on whether to bring this up or not. But she felt like she was sinking. Nelly needed him to take her seriously.

"Look, I don't bring this up lightly, but I have to say something because..." She didn't know if she should go on. If what she planned on saying next would make the sheriff more or less skeptical. "But the man is a teacher. If he's...he shouldn't be around *children*."

"I understand your concern." The sheriff scratched more notes. "How did you hear about Marshall's brush with the law?"

Nelly repeated her conversation with Tina, leaving out the parts where Tina had apologized for her poor treatment of Nelly in the past.

"And your friend—Tina—agrees with you? She thinks Emmett Moore is actually Marshall Dawes."

"Yes," Nelly said.

He asked for Tina's phone number. Nelly said she'd ask her friend first before providing it to the sheriff. She assumed Tina wouldn't mind, but better to ask permission prior to dragging her friend into a police investigation.

"Nelly," Bill said, putting his notebook down for a moment, "I want you to know that we take charges like this very seriously. I am going to use all my resources to look into this. You have my word."

He spoke solemnly, meaning it. Nelly wanted to cry grateful tears of joy. But she had to take things slowly. This was only the first step. A lot needed to happen between now and the arrest. She wondered how Emmett would react once the sheriff confronted him. He wasn't sixteen years old anymore, able to run off and hide away with another family member in a different town to avoid responsibility. He had built a career and life here. He had a reputation to maintain.

"I appreciate how difficult it must be to work with a man you believe assaulted you," the sheriff went on. "But unfortunately that will have to continue for the time being. I don't want Emmett knowing I'm looking into his past. So you'll have to keep showing up for work and, I'm afraid to say, acting like nothing is wrong."

Nelly couldn't help but feel disappointed. "Is that really the only way to go about this?"

"It's a tricky situation," the sheriff said. "He hasn't come out and threatened you explicitly. I don't think the court would grant a temporary restraining order under the circumstances. But let's say the judge was willing to entertain the idea. They can only issue a TRO against Emmett Moore, but all we've got is your word that Emmett is Marshall Dawes. The judge won't write out a TRO unless you can prove Emmett is Marshall, and again that's assuming you get over the hurdle of proving he's threatened you. Lot of hoops to jump through. I'm sorry to say your case isn't helped by the fact that nothing came of your previous allegations."

"It was the '90s," Nelly said. "If he'd tried to rape me yesterday, you can bet he'd already be locked up."

"I agree," the sheriff said. "Different times."

She wanted to press him on this. Surely there was another approach, one that didn't involve her constantly interacting with this creep. But Nelly realized the sheriff wasn't in a position to arrest Emmett Moore based merely on her accusations.

Besides...what if the man had legally changed his name? There was no law against that, she realized. And since nothing had come of her allegations before, even if Emmett was Marshall, Nelly had no evidence of a crime having been committed.

All the same, Nelly was crestfallen. It was totally unfair that she had to show up for work, act like there was nothing wrong, and be anywhere near that man.

But what else could she do? The investigation had to run its course if she wanted justice.

"I understand."

"I'm sorry about that," the sheriff said. "Truly, I am. But there's nothing to be done. Your only other option would be avoiding him."

"That's not possible," Nelly said, her frustration leaking out. "His classroom is fifteen feet away from mine. And I can't call out of work. It's literally my third day of school tomorrow."

The sheriff nodded glumly. "It's an unfortunate situation. But I promise you I am taking this very seriously. In the meanwhile, I'll work behind the scenes. I can call in a favor from a friend who works for the FBI. He and I go way back. But I'm going to need a few days to run this down. Do you think you can manage?"

What other choice did she have?

"Yes."

He nodded respectfully.

"If he does anything threatening, you call me immediately." The sheriff provided his personal number. "Doesn't matter what time."

"That was a lot of fun," Tina says with a devilish grin.

"Are you kidding?" I ask. "That was the worst. Marshall almost—"

I bite my tongue when Marshall Dawes emerges from the other end of the factory, where he nearly caught me in time, and joins the larger group in the middle of the open space. Outside, the rain continues to hammer the building. Marshall gives me a look that manages to be both hurt and menacing.

Though she's standing right next to me, Tina chooses to ignore not only what I've said but the obvious fear and panic in my voice. She's too busy making eyes at Sean, whom I'm guessing she just made out with.

That's it. I'm done. We are no longer friends. I don't care if her mother sees me returning Tina's spare bike by myself. I don't care if she asks me probing questions about Tina's whereabouts or what she's up to. I'll tell Mrs. Hirshberg everything.

Tina doesn't care about me. Why should I worry about getting her in trouble?

But before I can announce my departure, Tina speaks up.

"I've got an idea," Tina says, her wicked grin widening. "It'd be a shame to let all this rain go to waste."

I don't understand what she means, but Sean's eyes bulge, and his mouth parts. Whatever idea she's put into his head, he's excited about it.

"Right," he says, licking his lips. "It would be."

Tina and Sean share a knowing look. I glance around the room. Everybody else seems to have intuited what they're talking about, though I'm still at a loss. Even Marshall's expression has changed. He no longer looks disappointed.

Now he looks thrilled.

"Wet T-shirt contest!" Tina calls out.

The other girls giggle excitedly while the boys cheer. My stomach drops. It was bad enough having to kiss some random boy. Having all these guys ogle me is much, much worse. There's some chatter, but then the group begins to file toward the exit, where one of the horned-up boys has already thrown open the door, exposing himself to the slashing rain outside. As if this in any way makes up for what's about to happen, the boy strips his now-soaked shirt off, and the girls each rub his chest as they slip outside into the storm.

I grab Tina's arm before she gets very far.

"I am not *going out there."*

She shrugs out of my grip. "Stay in here, then."

There's only one word to describe what Marshall is doing right now: lurking. He occupies that awkward middle distance. Not far enough away to give us privacy. Not close enough either to officially be part of our conversation.

"I can't stay in here."

Tina rolls her eyes. "What's the matter? You've got tits."

At the mention of my boobs, I turn red-faced and angle myself away from Marshall, not wanting to give him any excuses—not that he needs them—to ogle me.

"What's the problem?" Tina asks.

I don't want to discuss the size of my breasts, or lack thereof, with this mouth breather lurking only a few feet away.

"Tina, would you stay with me?"

She laughs like I'm being childish. For as mad as I am with her, her dismissive, callous attitude still hurts. I'm not sure if this is the moment where we stop being friends, or if that moment already happened, or if it's still technically to come. I can't sort out my feelings while I'm worried about exposing my tiny boobs to a bunch of high schoolers and while creepy Marshall is just waiting for his opportunity to put his hands on me.

But the bottom line is, Tina should still care about me.

"I'm going outside." She flicks a glance over her shoulder. "You two can do whatever you want."

Tina flicks her hair back and strides toward the door. I watch her go, the whole time begging her to turn around, praying she turns back into the Tina I've known for years: the slightly rebel-

lious, little bit sassy, but ultimately kind, caring young woman I've always thought of as my best friend.

But she doesn't. Instead, Tina slips through the door. The dull gray light of a stormy afternoon swallows her. With a joyous shriek, she disappears in the hammering rain while another cheer from the oversexed boys outside sounds.

"Nelly."

Marshall has silently moved beside me. I start at the sound of his voice, but then paralysis kicks in. I want to move but find myself rooted to the spot.

"You're really hot," he says.

Bile rises in the back of my throat as Marshall moves in front of me, his eyes taking in my body.

"Wh-why don't you go out-outside?" I ask. "All the girls are—"

"I don't want to see them," he says. "I like your tits."

No boy has ever said such a thing to me before. I know that adults talk like that, but to me it's gross and off-putting. Marshall is only one step away. I can smell the stale sweat on him again, the alcohol, cigarette smoke. His teeth are yellow. I imagine him smooshed up against me, like what I see grown-ups doing in R-rated movies, and the thought sickens me.

"I'm going to—" he begins to say.

"I'm leaving!" I blurt out.

Somehow I overcome my paralysis and move away from him. I'm going in the wrong direction. The bikes are on the other side of the building. But I don't care. I need to get out. Away from him. I'll walk in the rain if I have to.

"Where are you going?" Marshall asks, coming up beside me.

I don't look at him. Nor do I answer.

"Hey, wait!"

He grabs my wrist.

"You can't leave," he says. "It's pouring out there."

"Let go of me."

I try to wrench my arm free, but he's strong. I'm terrified by his powerful grip. He might be chubby and oafish, but there's a lot of muscle under that flab. And the guy plays football. He knows how to throw people around.

If he wanted, he could...

"Let go."

Next thing I know, Marshall is pulling me in. His lips seek my mouth. I turn my head away and push hard. He doesn't budge. He leans against me, and I can't fight him. The backs of my legs collide with a desk. I lose my balance and tip over, my back landing on top of the desk. While I struggle, he wrenches my arm behind me.

Marshall leans on top of me.

Panicked, I try to push him away.

"Get off me!"

His lips are on my neck. I smack his shoulders, but this has no effect. I'm terrified. My whole body is shaking.

"Please don't do this. Please let me go."

"You want it," he says.

While I fight him, one arm pinned behind my back, I feel something pop in my wrist. Hot pain shoots up my arm, all the way to my elbow. His grip loosens, and I try to pull my hand free. But then he clutches my thumb. In the ensuing struggle, he wrenches my thumb too. More pain. It doesn't feel broken, but it hurts like it is.

Marshall quickly pulls his shorts down, exposing himself. I've only seen a penis one time before, in health class. It was weird and comical looking. But Marshall's is ugly. I scream.

"Please stop."

His lips crush mine. He tastes like beer and cigarettes, and his breath is horrible. I want to throw up. His tongue protrudes. I keep my mouth clamped shut, close my eyes, pretend like this isn't happening, all while my wrist and thumb throb terribly.

"You're going to like this," he says. "You know it."

I can feel his penis on my leg. Hard. Insistent. Then his free hand is fumbling with the button of my jean shorts. I don't know what to do. Only one of my hands is working, and the pain in the other is terrible. I can't push him off me. I can't kick or knee him from this awkward angle where I'm lying on a desk and he's on top of me. I start to cry.

"Shhhh," Marshall says, his breath stinking. "It'll be okay."

As if to reassure me, Marshall tries to kiss me again. I keep my mouth sealed tight and pretend like this isn't happening. But I know it is. This boy is going to rape me.

When his tongue probes my mouth again, the idea comes to me. Fighting my revulsion, I open my mouth. He groans as he slips his tongue inside my mouth. I wait till it's jammed far inside, and then I bite as hard as I can.

Marshall screams. I let go of his tongue. He wrenches away from me, shooting me a surprised look.

There's a foot of space between us. Just enough for me to hike a knee and kick him as hard as I can. I aim for his groin. Marshall lets out another groan, doubling over and stumbling backward.

I jump to my feet and run.

"You bitch!" he yells.

I run hard, bursting through a door on the other side of the building. I find myself in a narrow hallway, turn left, run hard down another stretch until I approach what looks to be the front entrance of this old factory. Hitting the doors hard, I burst outside into the hammering rain and don't look back.

I sprint until my legs are on fire, and my lungs feel like they could burst. By then I'm a quarter mile up the road. I dare to look back. Marshall isn't following me. Not at all sure what I'm doing, I clutch my wrist and yank hard. It seems to slip back into place. I do the same thing with my thumb. The pain is still there, but everything feels much better now.

Light hits the street in front of me. There's a car coming. It's coming really fast. I realize that the driver doesn't even see me in this weather. They whip around the corner, and I'm right there, along the roadside. Diving out of the way, I hear the car's brakes screech. I land in the ditch, hurting my wrist all over again.

(Later, the police will ask me if I injured my wrist and thumb in that fall.)

The car has stopped in the middle of the road, its windshield wipers throwing huge swathes of rainwater back and forth.

The driver is out of the car: a gray-haired woman older than Mom.

"Are you okay?"

I burst into tears.

20

THREE DAYS AGO – WEDNESDAY

Nelly opened her eyes. It was technically no longer Tuesday, but she wasn't quite ready for it to be Wednesday either.

It was four thirty in the morning. She'd had trouble falling asleep again, going over her conversation with the sheriff and driving herself crazy. Nelly worried that she'd made a mistake, regretted not mentioning her performance review by Emmett, and wondered if she could have said more or phrased things differently.

While she stared up at the ceiling, sleep refusing to come, Nelly began to wish she'd just made up a story about Emmett. She could have said he'd pulled her aside during fourth period, while they were both free and no one else was around, and blatantly threatened to hurt her—or worse—if she even thought about going to the police with her story.

It seemed like the obvious thing to do in hindsight. Though it would have been her word against Emmett's, it would probably have been enough for a judge to issue a TRO at the very least without her having to prove Emmett was Marshall. But then again, such a ploy could have easily backfired too. Her word against his—what if the judge didn't believe her? What if Emmett turned up the charm in the courtroom, using every ounce of his newfound charisma, and convinced the presiding judge that Nelly was deluded? A woman who was now making things up because traumatic events in her past had scarred her, damaged her beyond repair.

Even if the judge had issued the TRO, that would have created other problems. She imagined the subsequent drama at school. All her new colleagues, none of whom knew her very well, all talking about her behind her back while Emmett, beloved and respected member of the faculty and Overland community, was forced out on leave while the TRO applied and the sheriff conducted what would have been a very public investigation. She couldn't imagine teaching under those circumstances.

But she also couldn't imagine continuing to teach under the present scenario.

This was all academic anyway, however. Despite the fact Nelly believed Emmett deserved every bad thing coming his way, she could never have brought herself to lie. She was honest to a fault.

It must have been after one o'clock when she'd finally drifted off. Groggy, she rolled onto her other side. If this poor sleep continued, it would affect her performance. She wasn't twenty-five years old anymore, able to operate on only a few hours. Heck, she wasn't even thirty years old anymore. She was thirty-seven and, right now, feeling every minute of it.

Why was she even awake? Had something woken her?

Suddenly, she realized what had happened. She'd been too groggy a moment ago to notice.

Light was hitting her bedroom curtain once more.

Nelly sat up in bed and yanked open the drawer to her nightstand. She pulled out the switchblade knife she kept for self-defense and pushed the curtain aside.

There was no one outside.

Frowning, she peered into the darkness enveloping the area. But no shadows moved.

All the same, her heart was in her throat. The floodlights winked out, but she waited for her eyes to adjust to the darkness and kept peering out.

There was nothing moving.

But if that was the case, what had tripped the motion sensor? If it was raccoons or some other wild animal, she would have noticed them, right? Especially raccoons. Though they were nocturnal critters, they were also a bit nasty. Floodlights wouldn't immediately chase them away, especially if they were into trash and smelled food.

No wild animal had tripped the motion sensor.

Nelly knew exactly what this was.

It had to be a creature intelligent enough to trip the lights while remaining invisible. A human being.

Emmett.

Her hackles rose as she imagined him skulking about in the darkness shrouding Orville's property. She pictured him just beyond the tree line, perhaps with a pair of binoculars, or maybe even wearing night-vision goggles.

Watching her.

She shivered at the thought. What if—

Bump.

Nelly spun toward the direction of the sound and thrust her knife out.

Bump.

Nelly heard it again. It sounded like someone was on the steps to her apartment. Fear paralyzed her for a moment while she racked her brain to recall whether she'd locked the door. Of course she had. Locking a door was automatic. A habit. Something you didn't think about while you were doing it.

She forced herself to get out of bed, holding the knife out in front of her. There was nobody in her apartment. The door was closed. From here, she could tell the deadbolt was in position, but she couldn't tell if she'd locked the knob as well. Nelly hurried over to the door, her hands shaking. She'd locked the knob, thank God.

Bump.

Nelly shrieked. The sound was much louder this time, almost like someone was standing right outside her door. She put her back against the door instinctively, as if bracing for impact. Where was her phone? She didn't know. She'd found herself mindlessly scrolling while she'd had trouble falling asleep, and so hadn't left it on the nightstand to serve as endless temptation. But where—

On the kitchen table. There.

Nelly pushed away from the door and raced to snatch her phone off the table. She unlocked it and punched the call icon. But her screen went blank again.

Not now.

There was no landline in the apartment. Her only means of alerting the authorities in this situation was a cell phone that refused to work.

Nelly pushed her back against the door again, accidentally dropping the knife while she frantically tapped the phone. The screen lit up, but all the icons on her home screen were missing now.

"Please..."

Nelly fought tears as she cursed the phone, cursed John because he was the one who used to take care of their mobile plans and he'd divorced her, cursed Emmett, cursed the sheriff for not arresting the man on the spot, even cursed Tina for ever taking her to that condemned factory. Nelly often wondered how differently her life would have turned out if she'd never met Marshall Dawes. Would she and Tina have remained friends?

Her icons reappeared. Nelly dialed 9-1-1, her thumb hovering over the call icon. She forced herself to look out the peephole, fully expecting to see a menacing figure standing on her stoop, some hood obscuring their face in the darkness.

But there was no one there.

Nelly waited another minute. Her pulse eventually dropped from heart attack to panic attack. She peered out the peephole, then made a circuit through the apartment to look out her other windows.

There was no one there.

Eventually her adrenaline dipped, and she crashed. Putting her back to the door once more, Nelly slid to the floor. The T-shirt she slept in was soaked through with sweat. By the time she'd calmed down enough, it was after five o'clock. With this much nervous energy, there was no chance of her getting back to sleep before her alarm sounded in less than an hour.

Sighing, she rose on tired legs. Might as well get an early start on the day.

NELLY WAS the first to arrive at Overland that morning.

She yawned her way into the teachers' lounge, putting her lunch away. Today she'd brought soup. Rooting around in the drawer under the coffeemaker, she picked out what she thought was the strongest brew. Of course, now that she was at school, her body decided it was time to feel sleepy again. Nelly had a hard time keeping her eyes open as she hovered over the coffeemaker.

The brew was bitter but strong. She walked to her classroom. The light was harsh in the early morning darkness. Nelly sat at her desk and opened her bag. She got the terrible feeling that she'd forgotten to do something, but her brain would not tell her what it was. Nelly shrugged away the feeling, writing it off to being overtired and trying to cope with all these adjustments.

Using her laptop, she transferred her notes from yesterday into a digital file. She wasn't about to let anyone steal hard copies of her plans again. She felt much better about today's subject matter and wished Miguel could see her in action. Maybe she could ask him to audit her—

Thinking of Miguel made her remember.

She owed him a plan of action.

It had slipped her mind yesterday, with the soccer game, having to prep for today, and then meeting with the sheriff. He hadn't specified what the document should look like, but she also hadn't asked any clarifying questions. Nelly hoped a few bullet points would be enough to satisfy him.

As she opened a new Word document on her laptop, she heard someone coming down the hallway. She feared it was Miguel approaching. That would be just her luck, the principal arriving earlier than usual. She'd have to stall for time if it was him. Not a good look for her, but she simply wasn't ready.

She found herself hoping it was Emmett, as weird as that sounded. He seemed to arrive early, and his classroom was right across the hall. Perhaps she'd get lucky.

But it was neither of those men.

In fact, it wasn't a man at all.

"Good morning, Nelly."

The high heels Vanessa was wearing only served to accentuate her height, seeming to stretch those already long legs out to comic proportions. The woman's head nearly reached the top of the doorway as she stepped into Nelly's classroom before being invited. Once more, Nelly thought of Vanessa and Emmett as an odd pairing. Emmett was gregarious, totally in command of any social situation, while this woman was cold and pained by interactions.

"Do you mind if I come in?" Vanessa asked after the fact.

Nelly wondered what this woman could possibly want. She had nothing against Vanessa, but she also didn't think it wise to get close to the woman engaged to Emmett.

"Sorry, Vanessa," Nelly said, "but I'm right in the middle of—"

"I actually need your advice," Vanessa said.

Nelly was so surprised, she didn't know what to say.

"My advice?"

For once, Vanessa's typically frosty demeanor thawed. She had a vulnerable look in her eyes as she closed the door. She sat in the chair beside Nelly's desk, looking out of sorts.

Despite everything else Nelly had going on, she was genuinely concerned.

"Is everything alright, Vanessa?" Nelly asked.

Vanessa's lips thinned. She fidgeted in her chair for a moment before steeling herself to look Nelly in the eye.

"I hope you don't take this the wrong way," Vanessa said. "But word got around about you being divorced, and I, uh, I was hoping I could talk to you about that."

Nelly stiffened. It was one thing to assume that your coworkers were discussing you behind your back. But it was another thing to know it with certainty.

"Look, Vanessa," Nelly said, now feeling a bit put off, "I don't like to discuss my private life at work—"

"And believe me, I'm not one to pry," Vanessa said. "I'm a very private person myself, which makes this incredibly hard."

Nelly was at a loss.

Vanessa grimaced. "It's just...I'm getting cold feet. You know. About marrying Emmett."

Nelly tried to hide her surprise. "Oh?"

Vanessa nodded, her eyes drifting down to her restless hands. "I'm sorry. Maybe this wasn't a good idea."

She rose and headed for the door. Nelly didn't want to come across as nosy, but this was a good opportunity to learn a little more about Emmett.

"Wait," she said, motioning toward the chair once Vanessa turned back around. "I'm certainly no expert on marriage, but if I could be any help..."

Vanessa hesitated but eventually returned to the chair.

"Sometimes I feel like I don't even know him," Vanessa said, looking her deeply in the eyes for the first time. "Do you know what I mean?"

She had never felt that way about John. Until the end of their marriage.

"I think so."

Vanessa smiled, as if relieved to hear that. "Thank God. I thought I was going crazy."

"I think that's normal for most couples," Nelly said.

The other woman's smile slipped. "But it's more than that. It's..."

Nelly tried to hide her interest. But on the inside, she was bursting at the seams to hear more.

"...those times when I don't know Emmett. It's like he's this completely *other man.*"

Nelly wanted to tell Vanessa to trust her instincts. She was tempted to tell this woman everything in this unguarded moment.

"What do you mean?" she asked, keeping her voice neutral.

"I don't..." Vanessa tipped her head back and looked up at the ceiling. Nelly could tell this conversation was very difficult for her. "It's scary, sometimes. Do you know what I mean?"

Nelly had inched forward on her seat. Now she leaned in.

"Do you mean you're scared of Emmett?"

Vanessa hesitated. Just long enough.

"I'm being silly," the woman said dismissively. "It's just the jitters."

Vanessa rose quickly. "I'm sorry to put this on you. Lord knows you have enough going on without having to worry about my relationship with Emmett."

"Wait," Nelly said, also rising.

But Vanessa was already at the door.

"Vanessa," Nelly said, "if you ever need to talk to somebody—"

Vanessa's hand was on the doorknob, but she hadn't opened it yet. She turned just her head to peer back at Nelly.

"I just worry that I'm getting myself into something I'm going to regret. I've been alone for so long, and I was perfectly happy that way, to be honest."

Nelly held out her palm. "Vanessa, I have to ask you again: are you *scared* of Emmett?"

Vanessa smiled like Nelly was being silly. "No. Of course not. He'd never hurt a fly."

Nelly looked the other woman in the eye.

"Right?" Vanessa asked.

There was a pregnant pause. Before Nelly could answer, Vanessa continued speaking.

"I'm imagining things." She laughed, but it was forced. "You should have seen him last night. He was so *upset* about what happened with you yesterday. He was worried that he'd been too unfair with his feedback and that maybe he should have postponed the audit."

Nelly's eyes bulged. Emmett and Vanessa might have been engaged, but it was unprofessional and unacceptable of Emmett to have shared any details of the audit with his bride-to-be.

Vanessa caught Nelly's reaction. "He didn't go into specifics, Nelly. He would *never* do a thing like that. He's got a really high emotional intelligence. Anyway, my point was, he felt horrible last night about it, and if something like that would cause him to lose sleep, then surely he must be a good person."

Nelly was at a loss.

Vanessa brightened again. “Well, thanks for listening. Sorry this was a bit of a ramble.”

Then she was gone.

21

Nelly emailed Miguel her plan of action when fourth period started; then she locked her laptop in her drawer along with her phone. She'd hoped to squeeze in a few minutes to speak with the sheriff about last night's events, but she didn't want to keep her boss waiting. Nelly took another sip of her coffee and left the mug on her desk. She was going to need another cup to get through this day.

Emmett was leaving his room at exactly the same time as she. The man gave her an apologetic look.

"Morning, Nelly," Emmett said, looking nervous. "How are you?"

"Fine," she said, not asking him the same thing.

They were headed in the same direction.

"Listen, Nelly," he said, rubbing the back of his head sheepishly. "I was wondering if you had a minute to talk?"

She had to give it to him. The man was an exceptional actor. He came off as sorry, almost repentant. His tone carried genuine concern, even a little nervousness. His gait wasn't as certain either. He didn't quite know whether to keep up with her or give her space.

"Sorry, Emmett," she said. "I'm on my way to see Miguel."

"Maybe after?" he asked.

"I'll see," she said. "I've got some work to do before fifth period."

"I heard you were helping out with the car line today?"

He decided to match her pace. Nelly wanted nothing more than to get away from the man. But she couldn't do that without being obvious about it. She couldn't very well break into a run.

"Yes," she said. "I'm happy to do my part."

"I know you are," he said. "And we appreciate that. Do you have any plans this weekend?"

Nelly shot him an incredulous look. First of all, what were the odds she had plans when she was new to town? And second of all, assuming she *did* have plans, did this man honestly think she'd share them?

"I have a few ideas," she said vaguely.

"That's good," Emmett said. "If you ever need more, you should talk to my fiancée. Vanessa has lived in Overland her whole life and knows everything about this place. I'm helping out at the women's shelter this Saturday, if you'd care to volunteer."

Nelly pretended she hadn't heard the question.

Emmett went on. "Then Vanessa and I might head up to my cabin for a short weekend."

He went on and on about his cabin. Nelly stifled a yawn, not caring if she came across as bored by his story.

"You look like you could use a coffee," Emmett said. "I'm

just headed to the bathroom, then to the lounge. I can grab you a cup while I'm in there if you'd like."

She shook her head. The last thing she wanted was this man bringing her a drink. Who knew what he'd do with it?

"No, thank you."

"Are you sure?" he asked. "It's no bother."

"I'm sure," she said. "I've got some coffee already back in my room."

He nodded once, then picked up right where he'd left off about his cabin. "It's in this lovely private community. This time of year, the neighborhood is practically empty. The summer season is over, so the renters aren't around. Great place to be alone. You don't have to worry about anyone bothering you."

He was still talking when Nelly knocked on the principal's door, not bothering with politely ending the one-sided conversation with Emmett. As she pulled the door closed, she met Emmett's eyes. He looked genuinely offended by her behavior.

She didn't care.

"Nelly," Miguel said, looking to be in a much better mood than yesterday, "have a seat."

She took the same chair as yesterday while Miguel opened her plan of action on his laptop. "How is it going today?"

"Good," Nelly said.

Miguel nodded. "And you're still able to help out with the car line?"

"Happy to," Nelly answered.

Miguel's mouth hung open as he scanned the document she'd emailed. "This is a good start, but I'd like to see some more detail."

Nelly groaned inwardly, all the while keeping a polite smile on her face. She wanted to point out that Miguel hadn't provided any direction on this. But she kept her thoughts to herself.

"Because you're not as familiar with the material," he said, "I think you should develop lesson plans a week ahead."

It was standard practice to lesson plan only three days ahead. Sometimes you flew through material, the students absorbing everything quickly. While other times, it took you twice as long as you expected. Either way, it didn't make sense to map out the next seven days of teaching in great detail. The plan would never hold true and thus would require adjusting, only creating more work that wouldn't have been necessary in the first place.

"What are your thoughts on that?" Miguel asked.

Nelly had been drifting. Stifling a yawn, Nelly realized she wasn't in a position to push back.

"I've never planned that far out in advance, but I'm happy to try."

"Good." Miguel nodded, then reappraised her. "Are you feeling alright?"

She smiled weakly. "Having trouble sleeping."

"Is that all?" he asked. "You really don't look well."

Nelly hesitated just a bit too long. He knew something was up.

"I'm still getting adjusted," she said. "And I'm obviously not happy with how things turned out yesterday."

Miguel waved her worry away. "All you can do now is try to be better today."

She groaned inwardly. She'd been fine yesterday. Emmett had poisoned him against her.

"Right," Nelly said.

NELLY STOPPED IN THE TEACHERS' lounge and took her thermos out of the fridge. As she was doing so, her phone buzzed with a text. Nelly set her thermos down on the counter and opened the message. It was from Tina.

Nelly had asked if she could give the sheriff Tina's phone number so they could speak about Emmett and Marshall. But rather than give Nelly a simple yes or no answer, however, Tina had instead asked Nelly to call her after school let out for the day.

"Heya, Nelly," Emmett said, coming into the lounge fast.

She smiled politely at him, but couldn't muster a verbal response. He stopped in front of the fridge, coming very close to her. Nelly quickly closed out of her texts, not wanting Emmett to know she was in contact with Tina.

"Soup today?" he asked, eyeing her thermos.

"Yes," she said.

Emmett opened the fridge and collected his Tupperware. "If you're eating in here, maybe we could talk?"

"Sorry, Emmett," she said in a flat voice. "I have work to do."

She carried her steaming soup back to her classroom. Nelly sat at her desk and wondered why Tina was reluctant to speak with the sheriff. Her identification was vital to Nelly's allegations. Without Tina's support, it was Nelly's word against Emmett's, assuming the sheriff couldn't find anything.

She didn't have much of an appetite, but she forced herself to finish her soup. Her coffee was only lukewarm, but rather than risk another encounter with Emmett, she forced herself to drink it that way. Having lost its warmth only served to exaggerate its bitterness.

22

Tom Stovitch was going to be a problem. She'd heard from Beck that he'd been held back in grade school, so he was a year older than his seventh-grade peers.

More than a year, actually. Tom stood six feet tall and had already begun to fill out, looking more like a high school sophomore than someone in seventh grade. Nelly suspected he suffered from a learning difference, which she sympathized with. Many children went undiagnosed for years, slipping through the cracks of an admittedly imperfect system. She genuinely felt for these poor kids. They needed intervention. They needed to be taught differently.

At the same time, this was the third day in a row he'd been disruptive.

Nelly had made it clear on Monday that she had a zero-tolerance policy for phones during class. If she were dealing with college students, she might take a different attitude. But these were twelve- and thirteen-year-olds. They didn't know how to use their phones responsibly. The devices proved much too tempting and addictive.

Even worse, every time she noticed Tom sending what she assumed was a text, his buddy sitting in the back row would check his own phone and start cracking up. Based on the hurt looks several other students had adopted during these text exchanges, Nelly suspected Tom and his friend were making inappropriate comments about their classmates.

"Phones away, Tom," she said.

He'd been smiling, but now he adopted a serious expression.

"I'm sorry, Ms. Peaks," he said.

"That's *Peak,*" she corrected him, her face reddening.

She'd overheard another student refer jokingly to her like that in the hallway between class. It didn't take a genius to figure out the nickname was a reference to her breasts. Kids didn't realize how obvious they were sometimes. It wasn't the first time she'd heard that joke in her career. More like the ten-thousandth.

"Sorry, Ms. *Peak,*" he said, appearing contrite. "But my cousin is very sick. She has cancer, real bad. I was only texting my uncle to see how she's doing. She started chemo recently."

Nelly suppressed a look of disbelief. She might have given him the benefit of the doubt if this wasn't the first time he'd been disruptive. But so far Tom was three-for-three, causing problems every day this week.

"I'm sorry to hear that. But you can check in with your uncle between periods," she said. "Now put your phone away, or I'll confiscate it."

"You can't do that," he said, an edge to his voice. "And

why are you yelling at me? I just told you my cousin is sick. She's got *cancer*!"

He was the one yelling, not her. Normally this disrespectful attitude didn't bother Nelly. Fifteen years of teaching middle schoolers had hardened her. But today she was in no mood. She also felt that Tom was lowering the bar for acceptable behavior, providing a bad example for others about what could be gotten away with in her classroom. She had to nip this in the bud.

She held out her hand. "Give me your phone."

Tom shot her a murderous look. "No. I'm not giving you my phone. It's *mine.* It's my property."

Nelly was close to losing her cool. She considered sending Tom to the principal's office, but she didn't want Miguel thinking she couldn't handle something this mundane herself. It would make her look weak, not exactly the message she wanted to convey to her boss right now.

So she approached Tom's desk.

The class perked up. Middle schoolers loved drama.

Tom hugged his phone and hunched over it so she couldn't reach it.

"You can't take my phone."

Nelly held her hand out, palm up.

"Give me your—"

Right when she extended her arm, Tom did something very strange. He flailed in his chair. His shoulder briefly, inadvertently—and gently—came into contact with her hand.

"Ow," he said. "What are you doing? You can't *hit* me."

Nelly rolled her eyes. "Come on, Tom, you moved into me."

He shook his head.

Nelly groaned inwardly. She had no choice but to involve Miguel now.

"Give me your phone, or take it with you to the principal's office," she said.

"Fine," Tom said. "I'll tell him you hit me."

"Tom," she said, losing her cool, "don't be ridiculous."

"I saw you," Tom's buddy in the back said.

"Yeah," another boy said, "I saw you too."

Nelly felt the situation spiraling out of control. While Miguel probably wouldn't have taken Tom Stovitch at his word, if several *other* students misrepresented her behavior, there might be a problem.

"Is everything okay in here?"

Nelly's head whipped around at the sound of Emmett's voice. He had opened her door and stuck his head in the room. The unexpected sight of him threw Nelly for a loop.

"I heard shouting," he said. "I wanted to make sure everything was alright."

Nelly's face was burning. Several of her students were in hysterics, while Tom and his buddy began screeching. Nelly had to raise her voice over the din.

"Everything is fine," she said. "I am taking Tom to see Miguel."

"Why don't you let me do that?" Emmett frowned, giving the rest of her students a tentative look. "I think you'd better stay in here."

Nelly glared at him. She knew he was going to use this moment as an opportunity to further undermine her. While dropping Tom at the principal's office, he'd surely mention her class was out of control. The way he'd tell it, Emmett would make it sound like a full-scale riot.

"Aren't you..."

A sharp pain ripped through her. Nelly clutched her belly as her stomach growled embarrassingly.

"Are you okay?" Emmett asked.

She nodded, pretending like there was no pain in her stomach. For whatever reason, the soup she'd had for lunch was disagreeing with her. Wonderful timing.

"Aren't *you* teaching a class right now?" Nelly asked him. "It will only take me a moment to walk Tom down."

Emmett shook his head. "My students are focused on their work. Everything's fine in my classroom."

He couldn't keep the smugness entirely out of his voice. He had control over his students. She did not.

Her class picked up on it as well, not missing a beat. Her students gave each other knowing looks, many of them enjoying watching her squirm.

"Come on, Tom," Emmett said. "Let's you and I have a little talk. Why don't you let me have your phone?"

Tom gave Nelly an offended look, as if she'd wronged him somehow, before turning to Emmett gratefully. As they left her classroom, Emmett took the phone and shot Nelly one last meaningful look before disappearing behind the door.

NELLY STOOD outside in the surprisingly hot afternoon behind the gymnasium in the area designated for the car line. She'd been expecting to make use of a school app for the procedure, but during her free time in seventh period, Megan had instead brought out a clipboard with several pieces of paper attached.

"You don't have an app?" Nelly asked, incredulous.

"Hopefully next term," Megan said.

The administrator explained the process. She was to ask for the student's name and compare it to the information on the master document, which included parents' names, vehicle types, and license plate numbers. It had seemed straightforward while Megan explained everything, herself in a hurry to get out the door. She explained that she had to take her ailing mother for a doctor's appointment this week.

But now that Nelly stood behind the gymnasium, shielding her eyes from the glare of the sun, the procedure didn't seem so straightforward. Car line was the only non-instructional duty she'd never performed before in her fifteen years of teaching.

And she wasn't feeling great.

After speaking with Megan, Nelly had spent most of the remainder of seventh period in the bathroom. When she emerged, with only minutes to spare before her final class, her skin was pale, and she was covered in sweat. She'd never had food poisoning before and wondered if this was what it felt like: sharp stabbing pains and nearly constant nausea.

She'd managed to get through eighth period. Barely. As soon as the bell sounded, she was the first out the door, racing to the bathroom. She had to work the car line in only a few minutes. By the time she realized this was going to be a problem, it was too late to ask someone else to take over. Even if there had been, that would not be a good look for Nelly. After all, yesterday she'd volunteered to help out. She couldn't back out of the task literally a day later.

Once she was done getting sick, Nelly quickly splashed some water on her face. As she headed for the door to enter the hallway, her stomach lurched. The nausea had come storming back. Nelly was torn. If she didn't get outside in the next minute, everyone would start to wonder what the problem was.

She gritted her teeth, feeling the nausea ebb. She'd just gotten sick. Surely she could manage for the next fifteen minutes or so.

Nelly hurried back to her classroom, grabbed the clipboard, and made her way to the gymnasium. A bunch of students were horsing around near the door where they'd be dismissed for car line. There must have been fifty, maybe sixty, kids in here waiting for her. This was going to take longer than fifteen minutes.

The students bunched up as she approached the door. Nelly asked them to move back before she propped it open. The warm sun on her skin brought on another wave of nausea. Nelly ignored it and peered out. A long line of cars snaked through the parking lot.

The first vehicle moved forward, the passenger window sliding down. The driver called out the name of her son. One of the children, a short boy, was already making his way toward the vehicle. Nelly consulted the clipboard, ticking off the child's name. More children came forward, eager to get home for the day. Nelly checked them out one by one, but her nausea was getting worse.

"How's it going, Nelly?"

It was Emmett. He must have walked around the exterior of the gymnasium to meet her outside like this.

She gritted her teeth against another wave of nausea. "Fine. I'm fine."

"You don't look well," Emmett said.

Truth was, she didn't think she'd manage to sign out all these kids before she had to sprint to the bathroom. Her stomach felt like it was being ripped apart.

"Do you need me to take over?" he asked.

"No," Nelly said. "I can do it."

She might have been ready to get sick everywhere, but she would not accept this man's help. He'd only use it as another way to undermine her later with Miguel.

"You really don't look well," he said, giving her a meaningful look.

Through her agony, Nelly realized what must have happened.

This wasn't food poisoning.

Emmett had slipped something into her food. No, in her coffee. He wanted her feeling like she had to run to the bathroom and be sick during class. And he knew she was scheduled for car line this afternoon.

"Really, Nelly," Emmett said, "if you need help, you need to tell someone."

"I..."

But she didn't have the ability to put up a fight in this moment. Bile was creeping up her throat. Without another word, she stuck the clipboard in Emmett's chest and hurried away, the children bursting into laughter at her antics.

At least she made it to the bathroom on time.

YET ANOTHER BAD day came to a close. As she was packing her things up, another aftershock of nausea hit Nelly. Feeling weak, she feared she'd have to run to the bathroom once more, but the feeling mercifully passed. All she wanted to do at this point was avoid her colleagues and boss and sneak out of school. If Miguel had something to say about Tom

Stovitch, she'd listen tomorrow. But she wanted today to be over.

Nelly locked her desk drawer and then turned out the lights. Proceeding down the hall, the sight of Miguel's closed door brought a smile to her face. She could get out of here without another difficult conversation. Tomorrow she could start over. Tomorrow would be better.

It certainly couldn't get any worse.

Before she reached the front desk, however, Miguel's door opened.

"Nelly," Miguel said in a neutral tone, "have you got a moment?"

23

"Nelly," he began, "I'm concerned."

She swallowed hard. Hoping this would be a short conversation, she'd kept her jacket on and sat with her bags in her lap. Now she put those bags on the floor and unbuttoned her jacket. This was going to take more than a few minutes. She also wanted to send a clear message: she was receptive to whatever he had to say and was in no rush to get anywhere until she heard it.

"Tom Stovitch claims you hit him in class," Miguel said. "Now then, Tom can be a handful, so I'm not inclined to believe him. But apparently there are other students backing up his story."

"His friends," Nelly said.

"Be that as it may," Miguel went on, "I have yet to speak to someone taking your side here."

Her life had turned into an absolute nightmare. Though she didn't believe in karma, Nelly wondered what she could have possibly done to deserve any of this. As soon as she asked herself the question, she realized how childish she was being. There was no such thing as deserve. The universe didn't dole out punishments or rewards.

Things happened.

Marshall Dawes had been attracted to her and, due to some bad combination of nature and nurture, had tried to rape her.

John had loved her for many years. She knew that for a fact. But then things had changed. She'd done nothing wrong in the marriage. She also knew that for a fact. She'd been loving, faithful, thoughtful. He'd changed, or she'd changed, or they'd both changed. One day he'd woken up and was no longer in love with her.

Things just happened.

"Have you had an opportunity to speak to everyone in the class?" Nelly said, trying to gather her wits. She felt like she was under siege in this town. Trapped behind rings of walls as the enemy closed on all sides. "Because I'm certain if you talk to a student who's not friends with Tom, you'll get a different story."

"Not yet," Miguel allowed. "But any time a student makes a serious accusation like this, I'm forced to take it seriously. It doesn't help that Tom's father is the mayor."

Nelly closed her eyes. Any more bad luck, and she was going to turn into a full-fledged fatalist.

"Who his father is has no bearing on the truth," she said.

It was true, or should have been.

And she knew it wasn't.

Miguel grew thoughtful. "I'm becoming concerned here, Nelly."

He'd already said that. It was code for *I don't think you're cut out for this job.*

Nelly grew desperate. "Tom has the markings of a bully. I

think he was texting a friend in class and making fun of people. Other students might not feel safe speaking out against him."

"That's also true." Miguel nodded. "But at this point, I'm afraid I have to put you on review."

Nelly froze. Performance reviews usually ended in one of two ways. A quitting or a firing. Rarely did someone ever successfully rehabilitate their reputation.

"Now then, let's talk about car line," Miguel said. "Why don't you tell me what happened?"

Nelly frowned. She didn't want to go into detail about her sudden illness, but Miguel apparently wanted more information. In generic terms, Nelly quickly went over what happened.

"I think it was food poisoning," Nelly said.

"I'm sorry that happened," he said. "But if you need help, Nelly, you have to ask for it."

"I thought I'd be fine," she said.

"I see." He did not sound like he believed her. "Well, I'm afraid there was a mix-up. You marked someone as gone on the form, but then Emmett saw their parent pull up. Naturally, we were worried an unauthorized individual had picked them up—"

"Wait a minute," Nelly said, unable to help herself. "Which child did I mark as already gone?"

"Christina Woodward," Miguel said.

Nelly shook her head. "No, that's not right."

She thought back. Though the nausea and stomach pains had been a horrible distraction, she had only checked out a handful of students and did not remember that name.

"Emmett figured it out," Miguel said. "The first student

you released was Chris Woldron. Right above Christina on the car line roll."

Nelly narrowed her eyes.

She was *certain* she hadn't made that mistake. She remembered ticking the correct box for Chris Woldron.

"It's an easy mistake to make," Miguel said, "especially given how awful you were feeling. But all the same, Nelly, it's simply a mistake we cannot afford."

Nelly shook her head. This was Emmett's doing. He'd somehow made her ill and then conveniently swooped in during car line to take over. It'd be easy for him to come up with a story—with Nelly stuck in the bathroom for the duration of dismissal, she had no way to counter anything he said.

"I'm...sorry."

Miguel was not happy.

"We cannot have any more mistakes like this," Miguel said. "Or I'll be forced to take more formal action. Now I'd like to see your lesson plans tomorrow morning. That'll be all, Nelly."

She rose on unsteady legs, absently reaching for her bags. Shuffling away, she stopped in front of the door, hand hovering by the knob.

"Nelly?" Concern creeped into Miguel's voice. "Is something wrong?"

She turned to face him.

"Someone is stalking me," Nelly blurted out.

She was as surprised as Miguel was by the statement. One moment, the thought of saying such a thing hadn't crossed her mind. The next, not only had the thought occurred to her, but the words were coming out of her mouth.

"I'm...sorry to hear that." Miguel sat a little taller in his chair, his face softening. "Have you spoken to the sheriff?"

"Last night," she said.

"Gosh, Nelly, I had no idea." Miguel looked unnerved. "When did this start?"

"I'm sorry..."

Suddenly she was crying. It was all too much. She found herself back in the chair. Nelly worried that he'd see this as an act, a ploy to garner sympathy, a ready-made excuse for her subpar performance. But she couldn't help the outburst.

"There, there." Miguel came around the desk and held out a box of tissues. "Here you go."

Nelly grabbed some tissues and wiped under her eyes. When she got herself under control, she answered his previous question.

"It started when I got here," Nelly said. "But I have to be careful about what I say. Please, *please* don't tell anyone. The sheriff is looking into this quietly."

"Your secret is safe with me," Miguel said. "Is it someone you know? Has someone followed you from California?"

Nelly didn't want to answer. "I can't say anything more, I'm sorry."

"No, I understand." Miguel was shocked. "Nelly, I want you to know that this is a safe space. You can tell me anything, of course."

"Thank you," she said. "I don't mean to put this on you, but I'm telling you because I think it's affecting my performance. I can't sleep, and I'm preoccupied...I'm not trying to make excuses for anything, but it's difficult."

"Whoever they are, they had better hope I don't know them," Miguel said.

The irony. If only Miguel knew who was making her life

hell. But she couldn't tell him anything. She needed the sheriff's support before she accused Miguel's favorite teacher of criminal behavior.

Miguel filled the silence. "Is there anything I can do?"

"No," Nelly answered. "But thank you for offering."

"Do you need some time?"

"No!" she blurted out. "I want to work, Miguel. I live for teaching. I love this job."

"Are you sure?"

She wondered if he saw this as an opportunity to get her out of the building for a few days. Maybe it was the chance he needed to bring someone else in. But she dismissed the idea. Miguel seemed like a good man. She put herself in his position and had to admit she wouldn't have acted any differently.

"I'm sure."

Nelly drove home in a fog. Not a literal one, but a mental one.

One more mistake, and she was in serious trouble. While it was theoretically possible to emerge unscathed from a performance review, Nelly knew the odds were absolutely against her. The review lasted for a period of thirty days. A lot could go wrong in that time, and none of it her fault too. All it might take was for one more student to complain. She could picture it now...

Miguel would call her once more into his office. Behind closed doors, he would explain the situation to her.

"Listen, Nelly. It's not working. Right now, I don't have enough to fire you, but that's the direction we're headed. This is

your opportunity to step down. It'll be so much better for all parties involved if you do. I don't feel comfortable providing a reference, but at least this way you'll be able to say you weren't terminated. These things happen. Sometimes, it just doesn't work out. I'm very sorry."

She pulled into the parking lot of a shuttered three-store strip mall. A hobby store used to be located at one end, some of the peel-off lettering still decorating the window. The middle store was completely empty, its signage absent. At the other end sat what used to be a gas station. The pumps were gone.

That was how she felt. Hollowed out.

No longer there.

Nelly looked at herself in the rearview mirror.

"Get it together," she said. "This is your life."

Wonderful. Now she was having out-loud conversations with herself. She was losing it.

Nelly wanted to speak to Bill Van Dyke about last night. She figured the longer she went without notifying the sheriff, the fishier her story would sound, especially considering the fact she had no physical proof anyone had been near her apartment.

But she also had to connect with Tina. It'd be nice to call the sheriff with her old friend's phone number. She dialed Tina. The call went immediately to voicemail. She left Tina a message, then tried the sheriff.

"Heya, Nelly," he said. "How are you?"

"Hi, Bill," she said. "I've been meaning to call you all day. I think someone was outside my apartment last night."

She went on to describe the events. He listened without interruption. When she was done, he asked, "And what time did you say this was?"

"The floodlights woke me at four thirty."

"You're sure of that?" he asked. "Four thirty."

"Yes. I checked my phone for the time."

"And how long were you awake?"

"Like I said, I had trouble falling back asleep. I don't know when I dozed off."

"How long did you hear the noises for?"

"Well..." She thought it over. "The lights switch off if there's no motion after a minute or so. I got out of bed to make sure the door was locked, and that was when I heard what sounded like footsteps."

"Right," he said. "And how long do you think the noises went on for?"

"A few minutes," Nelly said. "They weren't constant."

"You think it was someone coming up the stairs?"

"Yes."

"But you didn't see anybody out the peephole."

"Right," she said, feeling like he didn't believe her. "But you can't see the entire set of stairs out the peephole. The person could have been near the bottom."

"Did you open the door and look?"

"There was no way I was opening that door under the circumstances."

"Right, understood," he said. "How about this morning? Did you check the area before you went to work?"

Nelly frowned. "I didn't see anything."

The sheriff let that fact float between them for a moment. "How about your friend Tina? Have you had a chance to speak to her yet?"

"We keep missing each other," Nelly said.

That wasn't exactly true.

"I see," the sheriff said. "Tell you what, I'm going to send

Deputy Sullivan out to your place to check things over. That okay?"

"That'd be great."

"If anything else happens, you know where to find me."

"Sheriff," Nelly said, "I know it's only been a day, but is there anything you can share?"

"Nelly, I appreciate your wanting answers," he said, a hint of condescension creeping into his voice, "but I've just started looking into this."

"Right," she said. "I understand."

"To be clear," he went on, "your case is important to me, and I'm going to give it all the attention and respect it deserves. But like I told you, it's going to take some time."

"Right," she said again, abashed. "I'm sorry."

"No need to apologize. I get where you're coming from. Now do me a favor, Nelly. Get in contact with your friend, alright? It'd help if I could speak with her."

"I will, Sheriff. And thank you."

24

Nelly's eyes opened. She was aware, somehow, of the fact that it was a strange time to be waking up. Having hardly slept the last several days, she'd dozed off on the couch after getting home from school. It was now almost seven thirty. With her stomach starting to feel better, she should have figured out dinner. But she also hadn't drafted her lesson plans for the next seven days yet, and that had to be done.

She realized what had woken her.

Tina was calling.

Her cell phone nearly slid off the coffee table in front of the couch. Shooting her hand out, she accidentally struck her bad wrist on the table, sending a jolt of pain up her arm. Not that she needed a reminder, but the pain called to mind that horrible day in the factory, when Marshall had wrenched her arm and dislocated her thumb as he tried to hold her down.

Nelly's phone hit the floor. Shaking her wrist, Nelly swiped the phone with her good hand.

"Hi, Tina."

"Nelly."

Her friend's voice was subdued.

"Where are you?" Nelly asked, sensing something was wrong.

"I got out of the apartment for a smoke," Tina said. "Mikey's in rare form again."

"Mikey?"

"My husband."

Nelly frowned. "I thought you two were separated."

"It's complicated," Tina said. "Listen, I'm sorry I missed your call earlier. But honestly, it's not a great time."

Nelly squeezed her eyes shut. *Don't flake out on me now, Tina. Not like you did before. And not when I need you the most.*

"What's going on?" she asked.

"It's Mikey," Tina said. "He hasn't been around, but now he's back. Maybe. Our relationship isn't great, but the thing is, I need him. My youngest wants to go to college next year, and now we've got the grandkid also."

Nelly was stunned. "I had no idea you had a third child."

"He's my stepson," Tina said. "But not with Mikey. It's a long story."

Nelly rubbed her forehead. Tina had a lot on her plate. But there was no two ways about it: she needed Tina's help.

"I'd like to pass your number along to the sheriff here. He wants to speak with you," she said. "Is that okay?"

It was the same question, in much the same language, that she'd posed in her text message. Nelly held her breath.

"I don't know, Nelly," Tina said. "Like I said, now's not really a good time for me to get involved in something like that. Mikey would throw a fit."

Apparently, Tina hadn't changed at all. She was still self-absorbed and unreliable. How could Nelly have been so stupid to think she could rely on this person?

Nelly grew angry. "All I'm asking you to do is tell the sheriff what you told me. We're talking a ten-minute conversation, tops, here."

"It's just that..." Tina lowered her voice even further. "Mikey has gotten into trouble before, and he's...he's not up to anything right now, but we have to be careful. He doesn't want me speaking to the police."

This could not be happening.

"Tina, you have no idea what I'm going through here. My life is an absolute nightmare. At school, Emmett is setting me up to fail. Outside of work, he's stalking me. He slashed my tire, and he's been sneaking around my place in the middle of the night. I'm not sleeping, and now my job is in jeopardy while this guy ruins everything. I need your help."

"I want to help," Tina said. "I really do. But..."

Nelly trembled with rage. She didn't want to resort to the nuclear option: using guilt. But she was at her wit's end.

"I know what you told the police," Nelly said.

Tina was slow to answer. "What are you talking about?"

Nelly hadn't been certain before. She'd heard rumors over the years, all hearsay upon hearsay. She'd never known if she should believe it. Part of her didn't want to. But now she knew.

It explained why Tina was feeling guilty these many years later. She hadn't just turned her back on Nelly at the worst possible time. This wasn't a case of two middle school friends no longer having anything in common, drifting apart in predictable fashion. It was much, much worse.

"You told the police I was interested in Marshall," she said. "Didn't you?"

"Nelly..."

It was true.

Good God, it was actually true.

Anger ripped through Nelly.

"That's why they didn't take me seriously," Nelly said. "While I was telling them that Marshall assaulted me, you and the others were telling the cops I'd been flirting with him."

Tina sighed. "Nelly, it was a long time ago."

You bitch. "Why would you—"

"I'm sorry. Mikey's coming. He doesn't want me talking to you. I have to go. I'm so sorry, Nelly."

As darkness fell, Nelly's anxiety grew. She searched an old toiletry bag and found some medicine her last therapist had prescribed. It had expired several months ago, but she popped one anyway. It wouldn't have its full force, but hopefully it would still blunt her jangly nerves.

Nelly pulled on a shawl and opened her door. She descended the rickety stairs as a cool breeze picked up. It was supposed to rain overnight. Perhaps the weather would deter Emmett from sneaking around and terrifying her.

Or maybe not.

She crossed the footpath and then headed up the driveway to Orville's house. The light in the living room was still on. She figured he was still awake. Nelly knocked on the front door and waited. Orville opened a moment later, wearing a pair of sweatpants and a dark robe.

"Heya, Nelly. Everything alright?"

"Do you mind if I come in for a moment?"

"Sure."

He offered her something to drink, starting with coffee and then progressing to stronger things: beer, wine. But Nelly politely declined. She didn't plan on staying long.

"I came knocking earlier," he said.

"You did?" Nelly frowned. "What time?"

"Around seven. I wanted to talk to you because the deputy was by."

Oh, right. She should have mentioned Sullivan would be coming. This was, after all, Orville's property.

"I thought I heard someone on my stairs last night," Nelly said.

"Really?"

She nodded. "Did you see anything unusual when the floodlights came on?"

He shook his head. "I sleep like the dead. I didn't even know they'd come on last night."

Nelly sighed. Hoping Orville had also seen something was a long shot. If he had noticed anything, he surely would have told her.

"I'm certain I heard someone on my stairs," she said.

He frowned. "Are you sure?"

"I'm sure. No doubt about it." Nelly caught a chill and folded her arms. "I wanted to ask if I could install some lights around the barn. I'd pay for it, of course."

Orville didn't hesitate. "I can work on that tomorrow. Now that I know how to do it, shouldn't take me long."

"Oh, no," Nelly said. "I'd hire a professional. I don't want to trouble you."

He smiled at her. "How many times do I have to tell you,

Nelly? I need things to do to keep myself sane. I should be thanking you. Now, come on, how about a glass of wine?"

She was tempted, but her sleep cycle was already off. Alcohol, even a tiny amount, would only make things worse.

"Maybe another night. Thank you so much."

She returned to her apartment. Nelly rooted herself on the couch and brought her laptop out of hibernation. Her draft lesson plans were open. She tried working on them but found it impossible to concentrate. It grew late, but she didn't feel tired. If anything, she was more on edge the later it got.

Nelly had planned out five days in advance. The number of assumptions concerning progress and timing were so many that she feared the final product was a complete fiction. She knew the next five school days would bear only a passing resemblance to what these documents suggested. Again, she grew frustrated at being forced to do pointless busywork.

Unable to focus, Nelly drifted onto the internet. She searched for Emmett and Marshall but only saw the same articles as before. Changing her search parameters to cast a wider net, Nelly looked for reports of a woman being assaulted on that college campus around the time Tina would have visited. She didn't expect to find anything.

But she did.

Buried in a long-dormant sorority forum, one member posted a story that sounded close enough: some creep who didn't even attend the university had tried to rape a junior. The post did not identify the woman by name but mentioned she was local. Then someone else, wanting to show how they were the most-informed anonymous user on the internet, just had to mention that they knew the woman.

Without naming her, they stated the victim was involved in a tutoring program that undergraduates hosted to gain credits toward their teaching certificate. Other posters complained about the university not employing enough campus security officers, and the conversation got off-subject.

Nelly was intrigued. She went to the university's website. The tutoring program was, surprisingly, still being offered. There was a generic email address at the bottom of the subpage for the program. Nelly briefly considered sending a message, but what would she say? Almost twenty years ago, an undergraduate tutor had been assaulted by a man living on or near campus? Even if the university maintained records going that far back, they certainly wouldn't release any personal information on those people. And Nelly was in no position to obtain a warrant.

Nelly was about to click away when she noticed a subheading on the toolbar that read:

in memoriam irene patselas.

Out of curiosity, she clicked on the subheading, and the website opened another page.

Near the top of the page was a black-and-white photograph of a dark-haired young woman with a bright smile. In the picture, she was wearing a T-shirt with the Greek letters lambda mu on the front and stood in front of a pillared sorority house. Intrigued, Nelly read the blurb on the page.

Thank you for visiting this site. Irene was a beautiful, smart, and above all, kind woman who dedicated her life, which was cut tragically short, to education. After graduating, Irene became a grade school teacher and went on to revive the university's tutoring program designed to help local grade schoolers with learning differences. Irene had been enrolled in the program herself when she was a child, then served as an undergraduate tutor while earning her degree, and yearned to pay it forward by helping the next generation of neurodivergent learners.

Irene loved to tell her story in the hopes of inspiring others like her. "I remember when I was twelve years old and barely reading at a fourth-grade level, and I thought I'd never be able to go to college. Fortunately, my mother had heard about the tutoring program run by the university for children like me, and the rest was history. Within a year, with the help of great students in the college, I was reading at grade level. My confidence level soared. And I started to believe in myself. Being able to read opened doors for me. It made college possible."

During her tenure at the university, Irene was a member of Lamba Mu sorority, an outstanding student athlete, an actress in the...

A list of the woman's extracurriculars and many post-graduate accomplishments followed, but Nelly scrolled back up to the picture of the young woman. She studied that oval face, the dark hair, the tiny mouth.

Nelly typed Irene's full name into a search bar. The first result was an obituary from five years ago. The poor woman had been thirty-five when she passed. The obit was vague on details, however. Nelly backtracked and found an old news article.

Irene Patselas had been murdered.

She'd been found strangled to death in a back alley not far from campus. Police had confirmed evidence consistent with sexual assault prior to the murder. Nelly searched for more information on the subsequent police investigation, but the articles were few and far between. No arrest, from what she could tell, had ever been made.

The police had never found Irene Patselas's killer.

Nelly toggled back to the In Memoriam page on the university's site for the tutoring program. She read through to the bottom. The young woman had had a bright future. She'd planned on becoming a teacher, interested in helping other children just like herself, who could not learn how to read through traditional methods.

It was all so sad.

But Nelly wasn't *just* sad.

She scrolled back up to the photograph of this young woman, whose life had ended horribly. Nelly imagined the poor woman's final moments. The last thing she must have seen was her killer's face as the person choked the air out of her. The person—no doubt in Nelly's mind that it was a man—had violated her. When he was done, Irene had stared up into the eyes of her murderer, her look pleading and fearful, and she had received no mercy.

Nelly wasn't just sad.

She was also terrified.

Because Irene Patselas resembled her.

"Come on," the boy said. "Who cares if we just met?"

He put his hand on my bad wrist, already trying to lead me upstairs. But I didn't want to go. The girls I'd come to the frat party with had disappeared, one to the basement, another to a bedroom, leaving me alone at the party. I'd been ready to leave when this guy noticed me alone and came sauntering over.

I didn't want his hand on me. And I really didn't want him pulling me somewhere.

Without thinking, I tried to wrench my hand out of his grip. But the sudden movement was too fast and hard. My wrist slipped out of place. My thumb almost did too.

"Let go!"

I screamed my head off. But it was so loud and wild in the middle of this fraternity house that nobody noticed. Dale—that was his name—was a brother here. His smile slipped when he heard me screech and saw the look of pain on my face.

"Whoa!" he said, like I was being touchy. "Take it easy!"

I gritted my teeth and clamped down on my wrist. It went out of place from time to time, one of those injuries that would stay with me forever, apparently. But I never got used to the pain.

With a quick twist, followed by a flash of more intense pain, I got it back into place.

"That. Was. Awesome!" Dale said, as if he'd just seen the coolest thing ever. "Did you just put your wrist back into place?"

I managed to keep my tears in. "Yes."

"Sorry," he said, realizing he was the proximate cause of my injury. "Uh, I didn't mean to scare you. I thought we were having a good time."

His definition of good time and mine were different. Mine did not include listening to him tell me about his workout routine and gushing over how much weight he lifted. At least the pain in my wrist was already subsiding, courtesy of the two drinks we'd had before coming to the party.

"Don't ever put your hands on me again," I said, turning to leave.

"Wait!" he called out. "Don't go. I'm sorry!"

He ran to get in front of me.

"I'm sorry!" he repeated. "Really. I feel awful. Come on. Least I could do is get you a drink or something? How about it?"

It was still early. I had nothing to do back at the dorm except sit in a room by myself and watch late-night television. And one more drink would help dull the pain.

"One drink," I said. "But that's all."

He held out a hand as if giving an oath. "I understand. Hey, one of my buddies has a pair of handcuffs—"

I shot him an incredulous look. His eyes popped.

"No! I didn't mean anything sexual! I meant, like, could you get out of them, you know? With your wrist doing that?"

I rolled my eyes. "Maybe. But I don't want to try."

"Come on," he said. "That would be the coolest thing ever."

"And also very painful."

"Oh. Right." He pulled a face. "Sorry. I'm drunk. How about I get you that drink now?"

"Sure."

The moment he was gone, I no longer wanted that drink. I took some satisfaction in imagining him returning to the living room with a beer for me and coming to the realization that I'd ghosted him.

While I walked—alone—across campus, I crossed paths with all these other students headed out for fun. I wasn't a big partier, but I had been looking forward to a night out.

"Hey! Where are you going?"

I sighed. Had this guy actually followed me out of the party with the drink? Couldn't he take the hint?

I turned to face Dale.

But it wasn't Dale.

It was Marshall.

"Did you think you could get away from me?" he asked.

Marshall seized my wrist and pulled me toward a dark alley. I screamed for help, but all the other students passing us by shot me funny looks, like this was some joke and I wasn't about to be raped.

"HELP ME!"

25

TWO DAYS AGO – THURSDAY

The alarm jarred Nelly awake the next morning. She'd barely slept again. Each noise she'd heard overnight took on a sinister quality. Several times she thought she heard someone on her stairs again, but there was never anyone there.

She had a horrible headache. It did not go away after her shower or after she drank two glasses of water. Nelly popped some aspirin and then got her things together. She was moving in slow motion. When her stomach grumbled, she realized she'd forgotten to eat dinner last night. She had no leftovers to take into school for lunch, so she quickly heated some soup again and poured it into a thermos.

It was a cold morning, the sky gray. Fog clung to the farmland Nelly passed on her way to school. She arrived later than planned after her slow start this morning. The bags under her red eyes were only getting worse. The aspirin had done little to combat the headache.

Nelly made herself coffee, never taking her eyes off the

mug, and then finally got settled in her classroom. She emailed the lesson plans to Miguel first thing so she could focus on the more important task of preparing for the day. She planned to call the sheriff during her fourth-period break from her car with the information she'd uncovered about Irene Patselas. She was just getting down to work when there was a knock at her door.

"Morning, Nelly," Vanessa said. "How are you?"

"Hanging in there. How are you?" she asked. Nelly wasn't in the best frame of mind, but she couldn't ignore the fact that Vanessa was a victim too. This poor woman had no idea whom she was about to marry—and Nelly wished she could tell her.

"Doing better," Vanessa said, offering a tentative smile. "I think I was just having a bad day the other morning."

"Vanessa, your intuition is telling you something. I think you should listen."

Vanessa adopted a fake smile and acted like Nelly hadn't just spoken. "Anyway, I was wondering if you could help me in the lounge? One of those overhead fluorescents is out. Can you hold the chair for me while I change it?"

Nelly had things to do, but changing a bulb would only take a minute. She followed Vanessa to the teachers' lounge, expecting it to be empty.

But it wasn't.

"Nelly," Emmett said, "there you are."

At first she didn't understand what was happening. Then her brain made sense of what she was seeing. The entire faculty was waiting in the lounge.

For her.

There were balloons and streamers and a welcome sign.

Surprised by the gesture and overwhelmed by the attention, Nelly blushed deeply and found herself at a loss for words.

"Welcome to the faculty!" Miguel said, leading everyone in a round of applause.

The din made her head feel like it was going to explode. Nelly did her best to hide her discomfort.

Wearing a mischievous grin, Vanessa patted her shoulder affectionately before joining the other members of the faculty in their cheering. Nelly didn't know what to make of this situation. She was literally on a performance review, and here Miguel was throwing her a welcome party, with the full staff in attendance.

Nelly didn't like being the center of attention, but she forced herself to smile. Holding up a hand and nodding gratefully, she thanked everyone.

Miguel put his hands on Emmett's shoulders.

"This was Emmett's idea," the principal said. "And it was a good one."

Emmett blushed, as if embarrassed by the compliment. At the sound of his name, several members of the faculty cheered even more loudly.

Emmett was still blushing when he stepped forward and gave Nelly a sheepish look.

"Sorry about all this," he said. "We wanted to do something nice for you. But we didn't want to throw you a party on your first day while you were still getting settled in. And we also didn't want to wait too long because that would have been strange. Tomorrow, a Friday, would have been too obvious."

Nelly hadn't been expecting anything like this. She would have been surprised either way.

"Anyway, after much deliberation, we decided that Thursday morning would be best," Emmett said. "Sorry, not sorry, if we embarrassed you."

Everyone laughed at Emmett's little joke. Nelly played along, smiling and even putting her hand over her heart to pretend like she was touched.

But on the inside, she was seething.

Two nights ago, this man had been tripping floodlights and possibly walking up her stairs, absolutely terrifying her. Three nights ago, this same man had slashed her tire. And those were only his nocturnal activities.

In the light of day, he'd stolen her lesson plans. He'd given her an unwarranted lousy performance review. He'd intervened with Tom Stovitch unnecessarily, seizing yet another opportunity to paint her as incompetent with Miguel. And he'd put something in her soup or coffee yesterday to make her sick, knowing it would make her afternoon hellish.

And yet, here he was, acting like he was her biggest fan. Her best friend.

This could not get any worse.

Or so she thought.

Because Emmett wasn't done with his theatrics.

With a huge smile, the man approached her. Nelly's skin crawled at the thought of having to embrace this man. But everyone was watching. They didn't know what she knew. She saw Mr. Hyde, but they knew him as Dr. Jekyll. After all, Emmett was the person who'd taken it upon himself to organize her welcome party in the first place.

What a great guy.

Biting back bile, Nelly went dead inside. She forced herself to feel nothing. To pretend like this wasn't happening. Like it was happening to someone else. She aspired to trick herself into having an out-of-body experience.

But it didn't work.

Nelly didn't leave her body. Nor could she ignore what was happening as the man closed in on her.

She leaned in to give Emmett a quick embrace. She was aware of his body. Of his hands. Of his arms. Of his chest and stomach pressing against her. The same way it had all those years ago. Weighing down on her. She felt one of his hips mashed against hers. His embrace was a little too much, too forceful. More of a squeeze than a hug. It was yet another subtle power play. His way of flexing. Of establishing dominance.

While everyone awwwed at their embrace, Nelly wanted to cry. She let go first. But of course, Emmett held on. He kept her in his clutches for as long as he could without the situation turning awkward. After he let go, Nelly staggered backward. She must have looked a sight. Hopefully her colleagues mistook it for her being overwhelmed by the surprise party instead of what it actually was. She had hugged Emmett.

She had just *hugged* the man who'd tried to rape her.

She felt violated all over again. She wouldn't meet anyone's eye. Someone called for a speech. She pretended not to hear. Everything was a whirlwind. Nelly couldn't seem to get a grip on any part of reality. There was no way to steady herself. Beck tapped her arm. Nelly took the cup of water the other woman was holding out for her. Their eyes met, and Beck gave her a strange look. She knew something was terribly wrong with Nelly.

"We wanted to take this opportunity to welcome you to our staff officially," Emmett said, his voice loud and commanding. "I know it hasn't been the smoothest transition for you."

Nelly shot him a murderous look, but Emmett smiled easily. She looked around to gauge other faculty members' reactions. They were all smiling too, acting like he hadn't just insulted her. Of course, Emmett had a way to spin what he'd just said.

"Going from a large city to a small town like this, moving from a huge school district to ours, it must be incredibly difficult. But we wanted you to know, Nelly, that you are appreciated here. Welcome to the Overland Middle family."

Emmett raised his cup to signal the end of his toast. Nelly went through the motions. Emmett tapped her cup with his and took a drink.

"Speech!" Vanessa said, much more insistent than before. "Speech!"

Nelly couldn't ignore the calls this time. Swallowing her outrage and bitter resentment, she adopted the phoniest smile of her life.

"I'm not one for speeches," she said. "So I'll keep this brief."

"Oh, come on!" Emmett said.

Everyone was having a laugh. Everyone except Beck. Nelly caught her new friend watching her carefully. The other woman *knew*.

"No, no," Nelly said. "We all have work to do, I'm sure. But thank you for this. You've all been so welcoming."

A few of the smiles slipped. Even Nelly had to admit her words of thanks sounded half-hearted. She needed to give them a little more.

"I really couldn't imagine..."

Emmett's eyes bored into her. He wore a devilish, almost

mocking grin. Nelly wanted to point it out to the crowd. She wanted to say, *"See! You've got this man all wrong. This is who he truly is!"*

But she knew the effort would not only be in vain, it would be career suicide. They'd turn to Emmett and see nothing but a warm, friendly smile. They'd turn back to Nelly and see a deluded individual, someone entirely out of touch with reality.

"I really couldn't imagine a nicer group of people to work with," Nelly said.

Someone *awwwed.* Emmett burst into applause. The group followed his lead. Vanessa cuffed the back of Nelly's arm, gently ushering her to the table where the food was. They had gone to a lot of trouble for her. The food looked delicious. But she couldn't imagine eating.

To be sociable, Nelly took a sesame seed bagel and marble doughnut. A few colleagues she hadn't spoken to much cornered her by the counter. She was aware of them saying things and of herself responding, but it was also like she was somewhere else. Like someone else was socializing on her behalf. All the while, she was desperate to leave. But social decorum kept her rooted to the spot. When a group of people threw a party in your honor, you could hardly be the first to leave.

Nelly absently listened to the guidance counselor. She nodded at appropriate intervals, even mustered a smile or two. But eventually, above all the other sounds in the lounge, Nelly could only hear one voice.

Emmett was talking to another group of people only a few feet away. Their eyes met. Nelly fought to maintain her bearing, but putting on a mask had become too much. The man was ruining her. Even worse, he was doing it with a smile. Subtly manipulating situations in invisible ways so that no one would believe her. What was the sheriff going to say if he found out Emmett had arranged a surprise welcome party for her? It would only serve to confirm Bill's pre-existing opinion of Emmett.

That he was a great guy.

One corner of Emmett's mouth twitched in a mocking grin. Something inside Nelly tore. The man was openly taunting her now. Right in front of all the staff.

But no one noticed.

And even if they saw that cruel smirk, they wouldn't see it for what it was.

It broke her. Nelly gave up the polite act. She dropped the fake smile and stopped pretending to be interested in what the guidance counselor was saying. She muttered a monotone apology, the best she could do, about needing to get caught up on work.

As she left the teachers' lounge, feeling the disappointed, offended looks of the entire faculty, Emmett followed her with those narrow-set eyes and same mocking grin.

WHEN SCHOOL LET OUT, Nelly didn't linger. She gathered her things and headed straight for her car. Beck called out to her from down the hallway just before she exited the building, but Nelly pretended not to hear her.

As the day had gone on, she found it increasingly difficult to focus on her job. By the time sixth period rolled around, she could not maintain her train of thought. Little things that usually did not register—a student tapping their foot, someone with a runny nose constantly sniffling, the muted chuckles from the usual troublemakers—served as major impediments. Unignorable distractions that completely derailed her at every turn. At one juncture, finding herself at a loss and simply rephrasing things she'd already made clear, Tom Stovitch had rudely asked, "Are you having an aneurysm?"

Unable to deal with the kid, Nelly had sent him back to the principal's office. But afterward, she worried that had been a mistake. Once more she was admitting to facing a problem she could not handle herself. Besides, Tom had already done his damage. He'd made a joke at her expense, undermining her in front of the students. Sending him to the principal's office wouldn't unring that bell. She should have kept him in the classroom, not given him another opportunity to discredit her with Miguel.

Rather than risk another painful conversation, Nelly hurried out of school. This couldn't go on any longer. Her life, if this could even be called a life, was unsustainable.

She drove straight to the sheriff's office.

Bill Van Dyke wasn't expecting her. So she sat once more in the tiny waiting area while Deputy Sullivan tried to contact the sheriff, making small talk in between attempts. Nelly gave one-word answers, bordering on rudeness. Eventually Val got a hold of the sheriff, who promised to be back in fifteen if Nelly could wait.

As the minutes passed, Nelly thought of all the things she *could* be doing instead of sitting in a police station. Catching up on sleep. Eating something healthy. Lesson planning. Getting the apartment together.

Or how about enjoying a walk on a warm autumn day? Making plans with Beck to grab a drink. Trying out a new yoga studio. Finding the best used-book store in the area.

Sitting in a cozy coffeeshop with her headphones on and knitting. Exploring local museums.

Meeting people.

Not so long ago, she'd taken all these activities for granted. But sitting here now, these things seemed like luxuries, pursuits that were far out of reach. It was beginning to feel like life would never go back to being normal.

Even worse, she was daydreaming when she should have been preparing for back-to-school night, which was only two hours away. Miguel had asked each faculty member to create a short slide deck, no more than three pages. Nelly had intended to do that during her seventh-period break. But instead she hadn't done much of anything. When she wasn't fighting to keep her eyes open, she was lost in thought. At one point she realized she'd been staring out the window for over ten minutes.

Under normal circumstances, Nelly could have whipped together a high-level presentation for parents quickly. She'd done this thing many times before. But she was not herself. She'd managed to get the first slide done—the easiest, of course—but struggled to flesh out any of her ideas.

Get it together, Nelly.

After moving across the country and being out of work for almost a year, she had to make this work. Thinking about losing her last job was unbearably sad. She had loved it there and had planned on teaching in sunny California for the rest of her life. But then she'd said the wrong things about the wrong, powerful man, and then the unfounded rumors had started and then—

"Hi, Nelly."

She'd been so lost in thought she hadn't heard the sheriff enter the station. His khaki uniform and dark brown hat were wet. It had started to drizzle—another thing she hadn't noticed while sitting in the waiting area.

"Hi, Bill," she said. "Do you have a minute?"

"Sure."

Once more she followed the tall, paunchy man through the station. Valerie offered Nelly a sympathetic smile as she passed the deputy's desk. In a different universe, Nelly would have asked the woman if she'd like to grab a coffee sometime. But such an idea seemed preposterous now. Having a healthy social life was pure fantasy.

Bill closed the door behind her. His office seemed even messier than last time. They took their same places as before, Bill sitting behind the desk and she in one of the two chairs facing him. She felt like they weren't starting a new conversation so much as picking up where they left off.

"I know you're very busy," Nelly said, hating how apologetic she sounded. "But I was wondering if you had any information you could share?"

The sheriff looked tired. He folded his hands and rested them on his beach-ball stomach. That thin smile slipped. There was little warmth in his expression.

"Nelly," he said, "I've told you a few times now that this sort of thing takes time."

She got the feeling he wanted her to go away.

But his answer simply wasn't good enough.

"I appreciate that," she said, trying to keep her emotions in check. "But things are escalating, and I don't know how much more of this I can take."

"Escalating how?" he asked.

She went on to explain about the disruption in her classroom yesterday and how she believed Emmett had orchestrated her being sick. The sheriff didn't even bother to hide his skepticism. Foundering, Nelly reminded him of the noises she'd heard outside her apartment two nights ago, as well as the tire slashing from three nights ago.

He was unimpressed.

"Have you gotten a chance to speak to your friend Tina?" he asked.

Nelly took a deep breath. "I have."

He arched an eyebrow. "And?"

As upset as Nelly was at Tina, she didn't want to go into detail about why her old friend was being cagey.

"She has a lot going on in her life right now," Nelly said vaguely. "I've given her your number. Hopefully she'll call."

The sheriff stared at her, unable now to hide his growing disbelief.

"Nelly," he said, "I'm going to level with you. I ran Emmett's background check three years ago when he first took a teaching job here. Absolutely nothing came up. He was perfectly clean. Glowing references from both colleges."

"Both?" Nelly asked, frowning.

"He did his first two or three years at one place and graduated somewhere else. The details escape me now, and, quite frankly, they're unimportant. He had no criminal history. No questionable behavior ever."

"But that was three years ago when you looked into him, though," Nelly said, knowing she was treading on dangerous ground now. She couldn't accuse the sheriff of doing a poor job, the one man in a position to help her. And yet... "Maybe there's something new that—"

He held out a palm. "I repeated the work. Same story. I'm afraid that from where I'm sitting, Emmett Moore is who he says he is. I have no reason to suspect otherwise. All I've got is your word that he's a fraud."

"And Tina."

"Who won't get on the phone with me, Nelly." His tone was admonishing. She felt like a student being called out by a teacher. "You must realize what this sounds like. You've got a friend who agrees with you, but this person won't get on the phone with me?"

Nelly knew exactly how it sounded.

And yet, she knew she was right.

"What about two nights ago?" she said, growing desperate. "Somebody was at my house."

"What time was that again?" the sheriff asked, pulling out his tiny notepad.

"Four thirty."

"You're sure of that?"

"Yes, I'm sure."

"Absolutely?"

"Yes." Nelly threw her hands up in frustration. "I told you, the first thing I did when I woke out of a dead sleep was check the time."

"Yeah. See, the problem with that is Emmett has an alibi."

"He has an alibi for four thirty in the morning?" Nelly asked, unable to stifle an incredulous laugh.

But the sheriff nodded. "He was on the other side of town. Emmett jogs every morning around four or four thirty."

She couldn't believe this. "That's what he told you?"

"He—"

Nelly knew she was losing her cool. But she talked right over the sheriff. "What? Did he spend the night with his fiancée? She could have been sleeping when he snuck out. Or maybe she's just lying."

"Nelly—"

"Don't tell me he's claiming someone *saw* him while he was out for a run at the crack of dawn."

"No, Nelly." The sheriff did not hide his displeasure at being interrupted. "He took cash out of an ATM on his way home from his morning jog. At 4:31 a.m. We have him on camera. Even if he jumped in his car right after, he's not getting to your place for twenty minutes."

It was a good thing Nelly was sitting down. That revelation might have sent her reeling. She couldn't think of anything to counter the evidence in the sheriff's possession.

"If somebody was outside your apartment," the sheriff said, his voice gentle again, "it couldn't have been Emmett."

"There was someone, Sheriff."

He didn't respond.

Nelly looked away. She was certain someone had been out there.

But what if she was wrong? Maybe interacting with Emmett on a daily basis had made her snap? Could she not trust herself now? It was a horrible feeling.

Then panic seized her.

"Wait...you *asked* Emmett where he was at four thirty the other night?"

The sheriff nodded. "I approached him as if my questioning were related to an early morning robbery."

Oh no. No, no, no.

"He's smarter than that," Nelly said. "Emmet is going to see right through you. He'll know I've asked you to look into his background."

The sheriff shook his head. It was a tiny gesture, but Nelly caught it all the same.

"Nelly, it wasn't him at your apartment, so why would he assume you were behind my questioning?"

Nelly had to concede the point.

"Besides," Bill added, "I had to determine the man's whereabouts. It's the only way I could rule him in or out."

She put her hands on her head and leaned forward. The walls were closing in. She was still worried that Emmett would suspect she'd put the sheriff onto him. If the man panicked, who knew what he was capable of?

"I'm telling you," Nelly said. "Emmett is Marshall."

The sheriff flipped to a different page on his notepad.

"The same man who organized your welcome party?" he asked.

Nelly was caught off guard. "It's part of his gaslighting act. He's putting on a performance for everyone so they don't suspect him of having ulterior motives."

The sheriff frowned. "But didn't he also just give you a below average performance review?"

When the two things were taken together, Emmett came across as fair-minded. He was a reasonable man, capable of being gracious but also determined to maintain the teaching standards at Overland. Nelly also regretted not telling the sheriff about this in advance. Now it looked like she'd been hiding it.

"He needs Miguel to fire me." Nelly felt trapped. "Emmett has built himself a good life here, but it's all based on a lie. I'm a threat to that. He needs to discredit and push me out."

The sheriff just looked at her.

"He has no choice," Nelly went on. She wasn't saying anything different. Her only hope was that repetition would drive the point home. "I could ruin everything for him. I'm the *last* person in the world that Emmett wants around here."

The sheriff did not respond.

As the silence stretched, Nelly's accusations sounded more and more ridiculous. While the sheriff hadn't scoffed at what she'd said, his growing impatience was becoming obvious.

"I'm telling you," Nelly said, inching all the way forward on her chair, "there must be something in his background that gives him away. You just need to find it."

"Speaking of backgrounds," the sheriff said, "I've also checked yours."

Nelly stiffened.

The sheriff's tone grew gentle, like he was preparing her for bad news.

"I want you to know that I believe you, Nelly. I'm terribly sorry about what happened when you were thirteen," he said.

"But?" she asked.

"No but," the sheriff replied. "I'm sorry, and I believe you. Full stop."

Nelly hugged herself and scooted back on her chair, stiffening.

"But there is more you have to say."

"Unfortunately," the sheriff went on, sounding like he truly regretted having to continue. "I can't ignore the fact that you were nearly sued by your ex-husband's boss for slander."

She knew if she moved at all, Nelly would completely snap. She stayed very still. Everything she felt was brimming.

"That man is a rich bully who throws his weight around

by threatening legal action," she said. "Do you know how many people he has sued or threatened to sue? Did you look into *his* background?"

"Of course I took that into account," the sheriff said, though Nelly didn't believe him. "But the thing is, Nelly, the woman you claimed he was trying to assault did not—"

"Did not corroborate my story. Yes, I know. She's a twenty-three-year-old administrative assistant, and the fifty-nine-year-old CEO is her boss's boss's boss. He has all the power in this situation. For your information, less than a month later she magically got promoted into a role she wasn't qualified for. Talk to my husband. He'll tell you the same thing. The CEO was buying her off."

Nelly realized she had slipped. For nearly fifteen years, she had referred to John as her husband. It was habit. It didn't mean anything. But the sheriff pounced.

"You mean your ex-husband?"

He just had to point it out. Make her sound like she was pining for the man. Make her sound like she was a woman scorned, someone who'd been hurt by men and was now lashing out.

"Yes, Sheriff. I meant my fucking ex-husband."

His eyes popped, but Bill quickly composed himself. "I didn't mean—"

"Sure you did," Nelly said, beginning to dislike the sheriff now. "We both knew who I was referring to, so there was no need to point it out unless you meant something by it."

He sighed. "Nelly, I don't appreciate the attitude. I've taken your allegations very seriously and looked into this myself. But there's nothing here. Emmett Moore is Emmett Moore. All I've got contradicting that is the word of a woman he's just thrown a welcome party for and given a poor performance review to."

"So that's it?" she asked.

"I will continue to look into his background," the sheriff said. "But I can't make you any promises, Nelly. As I sit here today, there is *nothing* to suggest he's living and working under an assumed name. Put yourself in my position, Nelly. This man is a beloved, model citizen."

Nelly wanted to cry. But she didn't want the sheriff to see that.

His voice grew gentle again, as if she were fragile.

"I know how difficult this must be for you," he said. "New town, new school, and seeing someone who reminds you of that boy. But it's just your mind playing tricks. Now, I think the best thing you can do is go to work tomorrow and focus on teaching. Maybe next week, once the dust has settled a bit, try talking to Emmett. If you give him a chance, I think you'll see that there's no way he could be the person you think he is. I'm not saying you need to be best friends with the guy, but if you just talk to him, it might change the way you see things."

She snorted. It was an ugly sound.

"You don't believe me," she said.

The sheriff didn't answer. But then again, he didn't need to.

"Nelly, I'm—"

She didn't even bother trying to stop the tears now. Crying silently, she shot out of her chair and hurried out of the man's office. Outside, the drizzle had turned into a slashing rain. Her feet found every puddle as she raced through the parking lot to her car.

Her vision was a blur. She started the engine, but there

was no way she could operate a motor vehicle in this state. Nelly looked at herself in the rearview mirror, seeing the red eyes and puffy cheeks and ruined makeup. She had always thought she was aging well, but now she looked old, tired.

She looked *defeated.*

The last time she had felt this low had been...

She didn't want to think about John. She really didn't want to.

26

"She said no, John. She told him to stop."

John paced back and forth. Nelly had presented him with an unpleasant fact. Now her husband had to deal with it.

"Are you sure?" he asked.

"Yes!" Nelly said, her voice loud and her ears hot.

She'd had a few drinks at the office party, but she wasn't making any of this up. She didn't like Alan Darowitz. The CEO of John's company was one of those rich bullies who seemed to get his way by simply shouting other people down. There was talk around the water cooler of his becoming involved in yet another lawsuit. The last one, over a year ago, had been brought by a twenty-something waitress he'd, ahem, allegedly harassed while on a business trip. There were many stories like that, nothing ever confirmed. There were other stories too, about former employees suing for wrongful termination, former business partners claiming breach of contract, vendors screaming about services they were never paid for.

Nelly did not like how her husband automatically defended

the man whenever these things came up. The more successful you were, John said, the more likely you'd be sued one day. He would go on to cite countless examples of prominent businessmen who seemed to spend just as much of their time in a courtroom as they did a boardroom.

Secretly, Nelly had been hoping John would move to a new company.

John stopped pacing. "Did you do something about it?"

His tie was crooked, his face red from all the stiff drinks, his hair a little out of place. They had left the party quickly after Nelly had walked into the wrong room, catching John's boss trying to force himself on a much younger woman.

Nelly was starting to get the feeling that John didn't want to believe her.

"Of course I did something," she answered, trying to keep calm. "I was standing right there. What should I have done? Walked away, acted like it was nothing?"

John went very still. His whole career was flashing before his eyes.

"What did you do?"

"I told your boss to get the hell off her," she said.

"Okay," he said. "Okay, that makes sense."

Of course it did. What didn't make sense was the fact he needed to convince himself of the fact.

"And then Christina ran out of there," Nelly said. "The moment Alan got off her, she was gone."

"She might have been embarrassed," John said, glancing away. "You walked in on them fooling around, maybe?"

He was trying to find a way out of this mess that did not involve getting his boss's boss, the owner of the company, the man who signed his paychecks, the man who decided what his salary and bonus would be, in trouble.

"John, look at me."

Her husband turned back around. Nelly was starting not to recognize him, and that scared her.

"She said no several times," Nelly said, unable to keep the tremor out of her voice. "I heard her."

Witnessing that assault had dredged up her own painful memories and shaken her. The scene had reminded Nelly how quickly things could go wrong, how sexual violence could crop up anywhere, at any time.

"I saw what I saw," she said.

John nodded then, looking glum. At the time, Nelly had thought he was worried about their future. Only later did she realize he was worried about his future.

"DID YOU KNOW ABOUT THIS?"

Nelly held up the expensive envelope, the threatening letter from Alan Darowitz's attorney sticking out of it. Flashing the paperwork in John's face, her pulse throbbed in her temple.

"Did you?" Nelly asked when he would not answer right away.

From his doorway, John looked left and right to check for neighbors.

"Come inside, would you?"

"No, John! I don't care who fucking hears me."

He cringed and held his hands out in a stopping motion. Anything to avoid a scene with the woman he was in the process of divorcing.

"Please come inside."

Nelly relented. Not for John's sake, but for her own. Despite her all-consuming anger, she realized it was better to have this very private conversation behind closed doors. So she went inside.

John had bought a new house. It was nicer than their old one, the starter home, which Nelly realized had also become their final home together.

John closed the door behind her. "Can I get you something to drink?"

She didn't feel the need to answer that. Rooting herself to the hardwood floor in his foyer, she thrust the paperwork out again.

"Did you know about this?"

He shook his head, though Nelly couldn't tell if that was a denial or an expression of regret.

"Your pig of a boss is threatening to sue me for slander!"

He held his palms out again. "Look at it from his perspective—"

"Look at it from mine, John!"

He took a sad, deep breath. "Christina did not corroborate your story."

"He's her boss," she said. "She was worried about getting fired."

"That's not true," John said, folding his arms. "She wasn't telling him to stop."

"Really?" Nelly felt like her head could explode. "Because it's the twenty-first century, and I thought no was supposed to mean no."

John pulled a face. "She meant not there, not then. But not no."

"Oh, come on." If John honestly believed that, then Nelly never knew her soon-to-be-ex-husband at all. John wasn't gullible. He was a salesman. In his line of work, he'd become great at reading people, seeing through the things they said. Only a misguided loyalty, born out of self-interest, could have blinded him to the truth. "I was there. I heard the fear in her voice."

John leveled his eyes on Nelly. He had never blown up on her before, not once. But she knew it was coming.

"Nelly, for Christ's sake...They're dating!"

His words stopped Nelly cold. Cut right through her righteous anger.

"What?"

He nodded, managed to bring himself down a notch.

"They started dating not long after the holiday party."

Nelly didn't want to believe it. But she did the math anyway: two months. Christina and Alan had been together for two months.

"That doesn't mean—"

"Nelly..." John's voice was strained. He might as well have been shaking. Nelly could tell he was doing everything in his power to contain his anger and frustration. "You have got to stop."

"Why? You're divorcing me anyway," she spat out. "This won't come back on you. You no longer have to worry about what Alan Darowitz thinks of your crazy wife."

"I'm not worried about me!" he roared. "I'm worried about you!"

Nelly was taken aback. Despite everything that had happened, and not happened, between them, she was gazing at a man who still cared. That didn't sit well with her. Nelly had cast John in the role of heartless villain in their marriage story. The cold, fickle man who'd randomly decided one day that she wasn't enough. But he wasn't that, and it confused her. In his own misguided way, John was still thinking about her.

"I never wanted to say this," John began, "but you need to hear this because this has gotten out of control. You suffered a traumatic experience when you were a girl, and that's terrible, don't get me wrong. But it's clouding your judgment now."

"How dare you."

"You had a few drinks that night, and you stumbled into the wrong room at the office party, where you saw an older man on top of a young woman. You saw a person in a position of power on top of someone half his age and much more physically attractive, right? You saw her squirming underneath him on the conference table. You heard her say no a few times—"

"It wasn't a few."

He was still speaking. "I get why you'd come away from that moment, especially after what you went through as a child, and think certain things. But I gave you the benefit of the doubt. I listened, Nelly."

"How noble of you."

He ignored her sarcasm. "But now you won't let this go, even when the woman herself explained that it was basically consensual."

Basically consensual. What a phrase.

"You were just looking for an excuse to divorce me, John."

He shook his head. "That's not fair."

"But you didn't want to be the bad guy. So you needed this."

"Nelly, stop this."

"You needed everybody to think your wife was crazy, unhinged, a troublemaker."

She could feel herself losing control.

"Do you know what you sound like?" he asked. "I heard about what happened at school, Nelly. Are you going to lose your job?"

One of Nelly's more disruptive students had complained about her "disciplinary style," using suspiciously grown-up words like harassment and toxic environment to describe it, no doubt fed those terms by parents who'd rather discredit her than face the hard reality about their child's behavioral issues. Nelly had heard about this happening to other teachers. One of her good friends, an excellent teacher with an impeccable record, had got caught up in a similar witch hunt. Though the woman had done nothing wrong, she had feared for her job. She'd been "lucky" to only be asked to undergo remedial training to address her confrontational demeanor.

Of course John had heard. Their friends were still their friends. But apparently they were more John's friends than Nelly's.

"It's bullshit," she said. "Do you know who that girl's father is good friends with? Alan Darowitz."

John's shoulders sagged. "This is insane, Nelly."

"The timing is pretty suspect, John. I have never had a complaint in all my years of teaching. Then, after I accuse that scumbag of sexual assault, one of his cronies' daughters makes up a story about my classroom."

John hung his head. "Do you hear yourself?"

She was not crazy. And she wasn't about to let this go. She wanted John to hurt. As much as she did.

"You were just waiting for something like this to happen. Your wife, the crazy one. This opportunity fell into your lap, and you took it. Now you don't have to be the bad guy. No one can blame you for divorcing me."

"No, Nelly," he said. "I'm divorcing you because I'm no longer in love with you."

She left John's new house and drove through John's posh neighborhood, wondering why his life hadn't skipped a beat while hers had been completely upended. She drove through town—what used to be their town—and passed all the places they used to go together and wondered why he got to keep all of this, why this stayed his but not hers. Why he was getting a promotion and she was in a fight for her job. Why a man who tried to rape a woman got to accuse Nelly of slander.

27

Nelly wiped away her tears. Her car was steaming up. She activated the defogger. A small hole formed on her windshield as the hot air went to work, a tiny ovoid window into the cold, rainy world outside.

She hated feeling so powerless. It reminded her of leaving John's house that day. It reminded her of resigning from her last job, still under a cloud from that student's baseless allegations of harassment. That was all resolved in her favor, of course, but by then her boss had already filled her position for the upcoming school year, and Nelly had been half out the door anyway, the damage already done.

But most of all, this feeling reminded Nelly of that day twenty-four years ago. When Marshall had forced her down onto the table. When he'd dislocated her wrist and thumb. While he'd held her there. Looked into her eyes as he'd pulled down his shorts...

No.

I will not be a victim.

Never again.

Nelly had already started her life over once. She would not do it again.

A lifetime's worth of anger filled her up. Her body shook with the rush of adrenaline brought on by sheer outrage.

She would not be victimized again. She would not show up at Overland Middle School tomorrow and pretend like everything was fine. Nor would she quietly go away. Nor would she simply do nothing while Emmett set her up to fail.

He wasn't going to ruin her life.

She was going to ruin *his.*

Nelly left her car running as she stomped through the rain-slicked parking lot. Deputy Sullivan was surprised to see her re-enter the sheriff's station. Nelly motioned toward Bill Van Dyke's office.

"I'm going to speak to him again," Nelly said.

Without waiting for approval, Nelly tromped through the station. The sheriff looked up from his computer at her through the big glass window on the side of his office. He was even more surprised to see her coming than his deputy.

Nelly opened his door without knocking.

"If you're not going to do anything about this, I will."

He was getting up, holding out a palm. "Now, Nelly, wait a minute. Don't go off doing anything—"

"I'll get you evidence," Nelly said. "Then you'll *have* to do something about this. Or I'll talk to the mayor. And he'll find someone who will."

"Nelly, hang on a second."

She didn't. Nelly strode out of the station as Bill called out, imploring her not to do anything stupid.

SHE WAS CUTTING it very close. Nelly still needed to whip together two more slides for her classroom presentation. An hour ago, that simple task had seemed impossible. But now that she was charged up, determined to take her life back, Nelly wasn't worried at all. She'd done this before and had plenty of time. Now that she'd taken action, she felt empowered.

She felt like she had agency again.

Before she returned to the school, however, Nelly had something more important to do. She pulled off the side of the road so she could focus entirely on the task at hand.

The phone rang a long time. Nelly was getting ready to leave an accusatory voicemail when Tina answered in a tentative, hushed voice.

"Hi, Nelly. How's it going?"

"Tina, I need your help." Nelly dispensed with the usual pleasantries. "Are you going to do the right thing?"

Tina was silent. Nelly wondered if the other woman was going to hang up on her. But then she heard Tina moving around.

"Give me a moment."

Nelly heard a door, then echoing footsteps in a stairwell, then another door. Finally, Tina came back on.

"Nelly, I'm really sorry about this. But—"

"Tina," Nelly interrupted, "you *owe* me."

"Mikey will kill me if I get involved."

"Do you mean that literally?" Nelly asked.

"No! Of course not. He'd never lay a hand on me. I didn't mean it like that."

"Then how did you mean it?" Nelly asked, wondering if there were any good men left on this planet.

"The thing is...this was years ago. I told him about you, about what happened. I mean, about what I thought happened at the time. And I've never since explained that I was wrong."

"So what?"

"Well, Mikey thinks you're an instigator. He's got ideas about you."

"I don't care about his ideas. I need your help."

"Nelly..."

But she could feel Tina's resolve crumbling.

"He'd never let me come see you," Tina said.

"Why do you need his permission?" Nelly asked.

"It's just...I need him right now. The kids and the grandkid..."

"Tina."

There was a long silence. Nelly waited. Normally she'd feel compelled to let a friend off the hook, tell them it was alright, don't worry about it. But not today. Nelly was tired of people letting her down.

"Okay. Look. Uh, okay." Nelly heard Tina moving around again. "I'll have to make up a story, alright? So Mikey won't know why I'm coming out there. I mean, so he won't think I'm coming out there to speak to the police."

"I don't care what you tell him," Nelly said. "So long as you come."

But Tina was hung up on this problem of hers. "I know! I'll tell him you're going through a difficult time and need a friend. Yeah, he'll believe that. It's not even a lie. Not really."

Nelly didn't care. This was Tina's problem to deal with.

Or not. It didn't matter. It didn't matter if Tina lied to a man like Mikey. He deserved it as far as Nelly could tell.

"When can you get here?"

"Well...let me think. It's already Thursday, so this week is probably out. And to be honest, I'm really busy next week, so—"

"Do you work this Saturday?" Nelly asked.

"Uh, no. But I—"

"What time do you get done tomorrow?" Nelly asked.

"Early, actually," Tina said. "I'm done at four. But I have to run some errands. Joey needs some new sweatshirts for school—"

Nelly didn't care. "You can be here by six or seven o'clock, then. If you don't feel like driving home, you can stay with me."

"I don't know, Nelly."

"Tina."

That was all Nelly said. But it worked.

"Okay. Yeah. Tomorrow works."

Nelly had an idea. "On second thought, we'd better get you a motel room. I'm pretty sure this asshole is watching my apartment. I don't want Emmett knowing you were here."

"How much do you think that's going to cost?" Tina asked. "It's just that money right now—"

"I'll pay for it," Nelly said. "Will you do it, Tina? Believe me, I wouldn't ask if it weren't absolutely necessary. This man is going to ruin me—or worse—if I don't take action."

Tina took a deep breath. "I'll be there."

"Good," Nelly said. "I'll contact the sheriff tomorrow night and set up the meet then."

NELLY MADE it back to campus with twenty-five minutes to spare. Already the parking lot was filling up, car doors opening and umbrellas budding as people hurried to get in out of the rain and wind and cold.

Nelly ran into Beck in the hallway. Her friend gave her a funny look.

"Everything okay?" Beck asked.

Nelly smiled. It was her first real smile in days. "I'm good."

"You look..." Beck gave her another once-over. "You look different. *Better.*"

Nelly nodded. She felt better. Despite the fact that everything had gone wrong at the sheriff's office, Nelly was hopeful. Bill Van Dyke might have been able to ignore her, but he couldn't *also* ignore Tina. And maybe there was something more to that house fire, or more to Irene Patselas's assault and later murder.

Nelly would look into both things when she got home. She was going to take Emmett down.

"Do you want to grab a drink this weekend?" Beck asked. "And by grab a drink, I mean try to pick up some guys?"

Nelly put her hand on Beck's shoulder. "You've been a good friend to me. I really appreciate it."

Beck was taken aback by her sincerity. "Thanks, Nelly."

"A drink would be great," Nelly said.

They agreed to make plans tomorrow night. Nelly returned to her classroom. Even though several hours had passed, it felt like she'd just left only a few minutes ago. She flicked on the lights and got down to business. She had the PowerPoint ready in ten minutes.

Miguel gave a short introduction to the evening in the gymnasium. Nelly half-listened, her eyes gravitating toward

Emmett. The man stood next to Miguel in front of the stage, nodding along with everything the principal said. Their eyes met once, but Nelly did not look away. She held his gaze, and Nelly swore that Emmett looked nervous for a moment before regaining his composure. Miguel asked him to say a few words, and it was like someone flipped a switch. Emmett was all smiles, all charm, and had the parents chuckling and looking very pleased.

After the introduction, Nelly went back to her classroom. She stuck to the bullet points on her slides, keeping her presentation short and making sure to remind the parents that it was only her fourth day here and she hadn't gotten to know all her students very well yet. For the most part, they seemed to get the message. During her first three meetings with parents of students from different classes, only one woman approached her after to ask why her son only had a 95% grade average when she thought he deserved at least a 97%.

It was all going smoothly. Nelly looked forward to the night being over so she could get back to her apartment and eat something. Along with her resolve and determination, her appetite had returned. She'd pick up overpriced takeout from a nice restaurant and gorge herself while she hunted online for more information about Emmett, Marshall, and the college house fire.

But then the mayor entered her classroom.

She already didn't like the man before she even knew who he was. He wore a smug grin and acted like the world revolved around him. Like Emmett, he said and did all the right things, but there was a theatricality to his behaviors. He made sure everyone heard that he'd just come from a very important meeting to attend the back-to-school night—he'd taken time he didn't have out of his busy schedule was the implication—and would have to run right back out to attend *another* very important meeting. She smiled politely at him, but the mayor did not return the gesture, instead giving her a tight nod while he found a place in the back of the classroom, his diminutive wife following in his wake, looking every bit like an afterthought in his life.

Nelly went through her slide deck again. The mayor surprised her by being disruptive like his son. Not more than two minutes could go by without him making some unnecessary remark, or cracking some dumb joke. The man needed to be the center of attention.

Due to all the interruptions, it took Nelly nearly twenty minutes to get through her slide deck, leaving little time for questions.

"I'm so sorry," she said. "But the next group is about to come in. Please email me with any questions you might have. I look forward to getting to know your children better."

"Hold on," the mayor said. "Don't you have time for questions?"

"I'm sorry," Nelly said, hoping she sounded sincere. "But the presentation ran long. I'm afraid we're out of time."

"Perhaps it could have been a little shorter, then," the mayor said, looking none too pleased.

Nelly looked him in the eye. "As I said, I'm happy to answer any questions you might have over email."

The bell sounded, signaling the end of this meeting time. Nelly only had one more group of parents to meet. Everyone filed out, but the mayor strode to her desk like it was his classroom.

"My son tells me you put your hands on him," the mayor said.

Nelly maintained her bearing. “That’s not what happened.”

“I see,” the mayor said. “So you’re calling Tom a liar?”

“Myron,” his wife said, looking embarrassed.

She shot Nelly a quick, apologetic look. Her husband ignored her pleading tone.

“I won’t presume to tell you what is going on inside your son’s head,” Nelly said. “But the truth is, he has been disruptive every day this week.”

The mayor shook his head. “He’s never had behavioral problems before.”

She was supposed to back down. Capitulate. Make allowances. Re-characterize Tom’s behavior in the best possible light. Promise the parents she would try harder.

But Nelly didn’t do any of those things.

“Be that as it may,” Nelly said, “he’s having them in my classroom now. If this continues, we will have to sit down with Miguel and figure out a plan of action.”

The mayor narrowed his eyes at her. “You know, Nelly, I respect Miguel a whole hell of a lot. And normally I trust his judgment. But I think he’s made a mistake hiring you. I’ve spoken to the sheriff about you and know how things turned out at your last job.”

“I left in good standing,” Nelly said. “And if you need reassurances, I’ll send you a list of my teaching awards as well as my references.”

The mayor shook his head. “I can’t believe how disrespectful and unprofessional you’ve been. Come on, hon,” he said to his wife. “Let’s go see Miguel. He and I need to have a chat.”

The mayor’s wife shot Nelly another embarrassed look on their way out the door. Nelly realized she should have been worried. No one wanted to make an enemy out of their mayor. But the truth was, she was proud of herself. She hadn't let the man's status or title cow her. She'd stood her ground. It wouldn't earn her any brownie points with Miguel, but it made her feel empowered.

She felt like she was retaking control of her life.

28

The penne vodka was delicious. Nelly ate way too much of it.

Sitting on the floor between her couch and coffee table, she checked her phone. All night long, she'd been expecting Tina to cancel her trip, but so far no texts or calls had come through. There was still a chance, obviously, that Tina would flake out tomorrow. Make up a story about something coming up, or even laying the blame at Mikey's feet. But that hadn't happened yet.

Once more Nelly searched for information on Emmett and Marshall, but she saw all the same articles she'd already reviewed multiple times. She scrolled through a search on local private detectives. None of them advertised their prices, but at this point she was prepared to pay top dollar for help. She jotted down the names of two men with extensive law enforcement experience. If the sheriff refused to take this seriously, even after Tina provided him with a statement tomorrow night, then she'd contact one of these PIs. The time for half measures was over.

Switching gears, Nelly searched for Tina's friend from college, the poor girl who had died in the house fire. She didn't have Alice's last name, but it wasn't difficult to find several stories about her and her friends, given how tragic the event was.

Alice Pembry had just turned twenty-one the day before her death. She and her roommates had been out celebrating the young woman's birthday on-campus at a college pub. The article did not identify the friends they met at the bar, but it sounded like they were meeting men. After closing the place down, the girls returned home from the bar. It was unclear whether any of the young men went with them. The article concluded with details about some of the funeral arrangements, noting that the lone survivor was still recovering in the hospital from third-degree burns.

Nelly backed out of that article and read through several more. They included much the same information. It wasn't until Nelly reached the fourth item that she found something of interest. One of their neighbors had come forward. She was a TA at the college, renting the house next door with other graduate students. Woken by the sounds of Alice and her friends coming home, the neighbor had looked out her window to see the young women entering their home. The neighbor had a partial view into the backyard of the property as well. She had tried going back to bed but had trouble falling asleep and had instead started preparing an upcoming exam for her professor. Some time later, she heard a noise and saw what looked like a young man in her neighbor's backyard. He was dressed all in black and wore a hood and winter hat as well, making identification impossible. The young man darted through the backyard, disappearing from view. Ten minutes or so later, the neighbor smelled smoke. She had immediately dialed 911, but unfortunately, it was too late by then.

Nelly read several more articles, but this was the only one that mentioned a man running through the backyard. There was no further information, or even speculation, about him anywhere. The police and fire department had not, apparently, viewed this as an act of arson either. Just an unfortunate turn of events, a bad fire in an old house, either poor, out-of-code wiring, an unstubbed cigarette, a forgotten candle. Having celebrated Alice's twenty-first birthday, the young women had gotten very drunk—multiple witnesses at the bar attesting to that—with the implication being they must have all been passed out when the fire started.

Nelly sighed. It was a sad story and didn't give her much to go on other than the names of the victims. The lone survivor was a woman—no longer young—by the name of Julia Sowers.

29

ONE DAY AGO – FRIDAY

Nelly woke with a clear head and feeling refreshed. It was the first time she'd slept well since Saturday. It was amazing what one good night's rest could do for the spirit.

She hopped out of bed and got dressed. As she pulled her socks and shoes on, Nelly realized that she'd only been in Overland for one week. Seven days. It felt much longer than that. So much had happened.

There was penne vodka left over, but Nelly decided to save that for dinner this evening. She quickly boiled some soup and dumped it into her thermos and hit the road.

It was a bright, blue day. Megan wasn't at her desk yet, and Miguel's door was closed. Nelly proceeded down the hall, her step lighter than it had been all week. She stopped in the teachers' lounge to make a coffee before heading to her classroom. Sitting at her desk, she allowed herself a moment to look out the window.

You will not only get through this, you will emerge triumphant.

"Morning, Nelly."

She turned in her chair. Emmett stepped into her room and closed the door behind him.

"Excuse me," she said, instantly on guard. "What do you think you're doing?"

He came over to her desk and sat in the chair beside it. With a big sigh, Emmett crossed one leg over the other and folded his hands.

"Nelly," he said, his voice sounding a little weary, "I think it's time you and I had an honest conversation."

She didn't think he'd attack her. Not right here, first thing in the morning, when there were other people in the building. But with this guy, who knew? Nelly pushed her swivel chair away from her desk to put space between them.

Despite her anxiety, Nelly didn't clam up. Whatever he planned to say, she would not make this conversation easy for him.

"You mean you haven't been honest with me before now?" she asked.

Emmett's smirk turned nasty. "No, Nelly, I was being *polite* before."

"Could you make this quick?" she asked. "I have work to do."

"This conversation will be as long as it needs to be." Emmett sat a little taller in his chair. "The mayor and I spoke. He's a close personal friend."

Nelly's stomach did a little somersault. She was still proud of herself for standing up to the mayor last night, but now she feared it was coming back to bite her.

"You were rude to the man and dismissive of his concerns," Emmett said.

"His son is disruptive and disrespectful," Nelly said.

Emmett shrugged. "It's my understanding that no students have backed up your story. As a matter of fact, the only students speaking up are supporting Tom's account."

Nelly folded her arms. "You mean Tom's friends are backing him up? I'm shocked."

Emmett shook his head like she was being childish. "I can see I'm not going to get anywhere with you on the subject of Tom."

"You're right," Nelly said. "So was that all?"

"Miguel is going to retire soon," Emmett said. "Probably after this school year. I'm next in line."

Nelly said nothing.

"I was willing to give you the benefit of the doubt on a lot of things, Nelly," Emmett said as if he were being magnanimous. "But after I spoke with the mayor last night, I did some soul-searching. And unfortunately, I don't think you're a good fit here."

He let that sink in before continuing, "In a bigger district, like the one you came from, you had clearly defined responsibilities and could hide among the large staff. But you can't get away with that in a smaller school like Overland. Teachers here must wear many hats and be able to multitask a variety of non-instructional duties."

"I wasn't able to hide anywhere. And if you took a moment to review my CV, you'd know immediately that I wore many hats in my last job and voluntarily took on a host of other responsibilities, including several extracurriculars."

He went on like she hadn't spoken. "To be frank, you have poor organizational skills for someone with fifteen years of experience, misplacing those lesson plans on only your second day at school. And after giving it more thought, I was fair in my assessment of your classroom management, especially in light of the fact that you've apparently handled classes of thirty-plus students before. And in terms of non-instructional duties, you've had problems with those already."

"Someone took my lesson plans," Nelly said, gritting her teeth. "And under the circumstances, I did a good job. As for the car line—"

"I don't want to hear any more excuses." He took a deep breath as if it pained him to say this. "I'm sorry, Nelly, but this just isn't working out."

"Is this coming from you?" She kept her cool. "Or did Miguel ask you to deliver this message through channels?"

He palmed his chest. "This is coming from me. I don't see any value in pretending like everything is fine, essentially leading you on. Bottom line: Miguel has his doubts, and if and when I'm principal of this school, you will not be a part of this faculty."

It took all her willpower to maintain her composure. "I thought you said you were going to be honest with me."

He narrowed his eyes.

Nelly added, "Is that *all* you have to say?"

"No, Nelly. It's not. But I'm trying to keep this civil."

She ignored that. "You've been out to get me since I got here."

"Come on, really?" His smile was irritating. "I threw you a welcome party yesterday."

"It's the truth. And you know it."

"No, Nelly, here's the truth, and it's pretty simple. You can leave on your own terms now. Or you can eventually be shown the door."

"You're telling me to resign."

"I think that's for the best."

"Best for who?"

"For everyone," Emmett said. "Be reasonable, Nelly."

Her whole body was charged, like there was an electrical current passing through her. Nelly felt like she could float out of her chair. There seemed to be no point holding back anymore. Emmett had made his intentions clear.

"You have had it out for me ever since I got here," Nelly said. "You've manipulated all these situations to make me look bad."

He palmed his chest and adopted an offended expression. "Are you accusing me of something?"

"In case that wasn't clear: yes. I am. You moved my lesson plans and set me up with the car line. I think you've been stalking me too, showing up at my apartment in the middle of the night to harass me."

"Oh, I see now." He snapped his fingers, as if the idea had just occurred to him. "That's why the sheriff was so interested in my whereabouts at four thirty in the morning, whatever night it was."

Whatever night it was. Like he didn't know exactly which night they were talking about.

"It had nothing to do with that supposed robbery, then," Emmett said. "Really, Nelly. Did you tell the sheriff I was *stalking* you?"

"You are," Nelly said. "You're trying to intimidate me. But it won't work."

He grew sober. "Those are *serious* accusations, Nelly. Why on earth would I ever do those things to you?"

"I know who you are, Emmett."

He arched an eyebrow, unable to keep the hint of a smile from appearing. "Who I am?"

"Yes. And I know *what* you are."

There was an irksome playfulness about his expression now, as if he were entertaining the absurd notions of a crackpot conspiracy theorist.

"And what am I?"

"You're not going to get away with this," she said. "I won't let you ruin me."

"This is getting ridiculous, Nelly." He rose and went to the door. "No one is out to get you. I'm not *stalking* you. I didn't move your lesson plans. You screwed up the car line. You can't control your classroom. Do you hear yourself? This is insane."

Nelly forced herself to rise also. Though her stomach was churning, and though this man terrified her, she found her courage.

"I'm going to get you. Do you hear me?"

He looked at her like she was crazy.

"I was doing you a favor, Nelly, coming in here and offering you the opportunity to resign rather than risk being fired. But I can see now that was a fool's errand. You should hear yourself. You sound deluded and, for reasons I can't fathom, spiteful toward me. Why is that?"

She looked him in the eye, refusing to be cowed.

He gave her another irritating smirk. "Did some guy treat you poorly in the past? Are you one of those women who takes a prior bad experience out on every new man she meets?"

She was outraged. Nelly trembled with anger. "I don't hate men. Just certain ones."

"Well, you literally just threatened me," Emmett said, adopting a professional air once more. "I'm afraid I'll have to bring this to Miguel's attention. I know this is probably a waste of time on my part, but I must say that whatever you're planning to do to me, you should reconsider. You've already dug a hole for yourself. You don't want to make things worse, do you? Whatever your plans are, they'll probably only end badly."

They held each other's gaze for another moment; then Emmett left her classroom.

Come see me at the end of the day

THAT WAS the subject line of Miguel's email to Nelly. There was no text in the body itself. Just that simple command. She knew she was in trouble.

Nelly replayed the conversation with Emmett over and over in her mind while her sixth-period class took their test and while she sat, alone, in her classroom during her seventh-period break. Emmett had spoken out of turn by telling her she would be unwelcome back to school if and when he became principal, but other than that, he'd hadn't given himself away. He'd vehemently denied her accusations and presented an otherwise reasonable façade.

Nelly, on the other hand, had made serious allegations against him.

And then threatened him.

I'm going to get you.

It was enough to get her fired.

Her last class of the day filtered into the room. Nelly went through the motions of teaching, but her heart wasn't in it, and her mind was elsewhere. When the final bell of the day sounded, her heart was heavy. Once the students were gone, she gathered her things and took a look around. This room had just started to feel like it was hers.

But now she didn't know if she'd ever be back here. She made sure to grab what few personal effects she'd brought, stuffing them into her bag, in the event she wanted to leave quickly.

She'd never been fired before.

As she headed for the door, she got a text. Her phone was still acting up. While she tried to open her messages, the screen froze, went dark briefly, then came back to life. The text was from Tina. She opened it warily, expecting a note of apology from Tina, her friend backing out of coming here.

But instead, Nelly was in for her one pleasant surprise of the day.

Tina planned to arrive in the area between six thirty and seven and was checking into the Wayfair Motel. The text provided the address and also the nightly rate. Tina asked if they could grab a quick bite to eat and maybe a drink before they met with the sheriff. Nelly figured the drink would serve as liquid courage for her friend, but that was fine. If Tina needed a little bit of alcohol before their meeting with the sheriff, then so be it.

Nelly managed a smile in this brief moment of happiness.

Nelly didn't know what was about to happen with Miguel, but at least Tina hadn't flaked out. She wondered, briefly, what she'd do if Miguel fired her. If she went on to prove that Emmett was Marshall, would she demand her job back? Or would she move on? Now that she considered the hypotheticals, she didn't know if she wanted to keep working here. She was only five days in, but there were already too many bad memories. The place was tainted.

First things first, however. She still needed to have this conversation with Miguel.

She headed down the quiet hallway. Vanessa was coming toward her, presumably going to Emmett's classroom. The other woman did not meet her eye. Nelly wanted to pull her aside and tell her everything, tell her to leave Emmett, to change the locks on her doors and change her phone number and never speak to the man again. Nelly wanted to probe Vanessa for details about Emmett. If only she could have an honest conversation with this woman, Nelly might uncover some piece of information that would expose the man.

But Vanessa would not even look at her.

Megan was not at her desk, having left early again to attend to her mother. Nelly saw Beck at the far end of the other hallway, standing on a chair to hang the latest student artwork. She considered saying goodbye to Beck. It would be nice to give her new friend, the one bright spot in this place, a big hug. But then Miguel's door opened, and the principal peered out.

"Hi, Nelly."

His voice was cold. Official sounding.

"Please come in."

She followed him into the office. When she reached for the door to close it, he held out a hand.

"Someone is joining us."

"Who?" she asked.

"Emmett is acting as my assistant principal, so—"

"That won't work." She shook her head. "I don't know what this is about, but I have some ideas. I'm assuming we'll be discussing sensitive, personal matters, and I will have to say certain things to defend myself. These involve Emmett, and it would be highly inappropriate for him to be here."

Miguel was taken aback by her tone. "I am required by school policy to have a third party join us for a discussion like this."

"Fine," Nelly said. "Then get someone else."

Miguel studied her for a moment. "Okay, Nelly. If that's how you want it."

"Thank you." She got an idea. "I saw Beck down the hallway. Could we ask her to join us?"

She knew this would be uncomfortable for Beck, but Nelly needed a friend in the room.

Miguel excused himself. She overheard him briefly speak with Emmett by Megan's desk. The principal returned a few minutes later with an anxious-looking Beck. Miguel closed the door and sat behind his desk while Beck took the other chair in the room.

"Nelly," Miguel said, "these conversations are always difficult, so I'll get right to it. I am putting you on probation as a result of your poor performance and inappropriate behavior. I am required to do so at this point, and there will be a more formal investigation into this matter. That should not take long, however, and I expect to have a final determination about your continued employment status before we return Monday morning."

Beck squirmed in her chair, clearly uncomfortable.

Miguel was still talking. "I've already spoken to you about your classroom management and organizational deficiencies, so I won't belabor those points. But other issues have cropped up since we spoke, and I am required to raise them so we have a clear record here."

He was covering his ass. Beck offered Nelly a sympathetic smile.

"I had the opportunity to speak to the mayor this morning," Miguel said. "You were disrespectful toward him and dismissive of his concerns. That is not how we are to speak to the parents of our students."

Nelly waited for her turn to speak.

"And this morning..." Miguel shook his head, his professional demeanor slipping for a moment. "This morning, you made several wild accusations against Emmett and threatened him. This is simply unacceptable behavior, Nelly."

He sat back in his chair, folding his hands on his belly.

"Is there anything you have to say before we conclude this meeting?" he asked. "This is your opportunity to speak."

Nelly took a deep breath.

If she was going down, she might as well take that son of a bitch with her.

"Emmett Moore is a fraud," Nelly said. "His real name is Marshall Dawes. Twenty-four years ago, when we were both teenagers, he tried to rape me."

Miguel's face turned white. "Nelly—"

She talked over him. She would not be stopped. Not now.

"He pinned me to a desk so hard, he dislocated my thumb." Nelly held up her left hand. "Then he forcibly removed my shorts and underwear. He slid his shorts off and was this close to putting his penis inside me, but I was able to fight him off. I haven't seen him since, but when you introduced me to Emmett on Sunday afternoon, I recognized him immediately. I contacted an old friend who knew Marshall back then as well. She took one look at a current picture of Emmett and agreed with me. She is on her way to Overland this evening and will meet with the sheriff. She is going to tell Bill Van Dyke the same thing I've already told him, that Emmett Moore is actually Marshall Dawes.

"Emmett obviously recognizes me too. He has been stalking me ever since I arrived. He slashed my tire and has been creeping around my apartment in the middle of the night to terrorize me. He's the one who moved my lesson plans. He then gave me a poor performance review even though I did a good job under the circumstances. You weren't there to see it, Miguel, so it's just my word against his. He knows that, of course. He knows you're likely to take him at his word and doubt what I tell you because you've known him for years and I'm new here.

"Emmett has been manipulating situations to make me look bad. He made it look like I marked Chris as dismissed in car line even though I hadn't. He intervened—unnecessarily—when Tom Stovitch was disruptive the other day and then was able to paint what is surely a very unflattering, and untrue, picture of my classroom management afterward. Again, it's his word against mine, and we both know whose side you're predisposed to take.

"Emmett is out to ruin me. He has to, in order to save his reputation. By discrediting me, he knows no one will take my accusations seriously, and that way he gets to go on with the perfect life he's carved out for himself here. I'm a threat to him. That's why he wants to destroy me.

"But I won't let that happen. He doesn't get to win. That man shouldn't be anywhere near children. And I'm a good teacher. I always have been. He won't ruin me."

Beck was astonished. Miguel fidgeted nervously in his chair.

"I'm sorry you had to hear this, Beck." Nelly reached into

her purse and turned back to Miguel. "I assume you want my badge."

It took Miguel a moment to find his voice. "Nelly, those are serious allegations you've just made—"

"Do you want my badge?" she asked, impatient.

"Yes, uh, under the circumstances, I think that would be best."

She tossed it onto his desk and rose.

"What about Emmett?" she asked.

Miguel was at a loss. "What about him?"

"Are you going to put him on probation and ask for his badge too?"

Miguel didn't answer.

"Since, you know, there are *two* women asserting he's a fraud, and he's currently under investigation by the sheriff?"

Miguel slowly shook his head. "This is all news to me, Nelly. I will have to look into this, obviously, before making any decisions."

"Of course," Nelly said. "You wouldn't want to rush to judgment of anyone."

30

Nelly drove around for an hour, still buzzing from her meeting with Miguel. Part of her couldn't believe she'd been put on leave and, all kidding aside, was headed for termination.

But on the other hand, it made perfect sense. How else could this have possibly ended for her? Emmett had all the power in this situation. She was the newcomer to town. He was the one—how ironic—without the checkered past, while Nelly was the woman who'd nearly been sued for slander and had chosen to leave her last job under a bit of a cloud.

She rode past St. Peter's Church where, only a few days ago, she'd come face-to-face with Emmett, and her life had taken a turn. She continued on, passing the old movie theater, taking in Main Street. Outside of town, endless cornfields whipped past her on both sides of the road.

She had time to kill before Tina arrived, so she went to a cellular store. It was situated in a two-story mall in the next county. Many of the retail shops in the place had closed down, unclothed mannequins peering out of otherwise empty windows. The death of brick-and-mortar retail brought about by Amazon. Nelly went upstairs, passing an arcade filled with some familiar-looking faces. Her handful of students plunking tokens into arcade cabinets pretended not to notice her passing by.

A bored-looking man in his twenties looked up from his phone when she entered the cellular store. “Help you?”

The young man’s eyes glazed over while Nelly described the various malfunctions. He asked to see the phone for himself, and, naturally, the device functioned perfectly while he tooled around with it.

“Give it a minute,” Nelly said. “It will—”

“I’m sure,” he said, cutting her off. “Let me check a few things.”

She watched him work. The employee tapped icons she’d never used before and scrolled through unfamiliar menus.

“What are you looking for?” she asked.

He frowned, not answering.

Nelly let him go about his work. She meandered through the store, looking at phones and cases and chargers even though she wasn’t interested in buying anything. She just wanted her phone fixed and didn’t want to be hard-sold on the latest model. It was almost six o’clock now. She didn’t want to get stuck here, giving Tina time alone in her motel room to think.

“Oh, you got a text,” he said, glancing up. “Tina says she’s early.”

“Thank you,” Nelly said. The thought of some stranger eyeing her messages creeped her out. “But please don’t read my texts next time.”

He pulled a face like she was being touchy. "Did you download any apps recently?"

Nelly moved back to his workstation. "No."

"Are you sure?"

"Yes."

He shrugged and lapsed into silence again, continuing his tinkering. Nelly waited by his desk. Several more customers entered the store at roughly the same time, queuing up behind her. Nelly wanted to send Tina a quick reply to let her know she'd be there soon, but the man was still busy fiddling with her phone.

"You're sure?" the man asked again. "You haven't downloaded anything?"

"I can't even remember the last time I downloaded an app."

He nodded, then looked up. "What do you use this for?"

"The phone?"

"Yes."

"Calls, texts, emails. The usual stuff."

"Uh-huh." He tapped a few more buttons. "Internet?"

"Sure."

"What kind of sites?"

An impatient-looking man tutted behind her in line. Nelly shot him a pointed look while he shuffled back and forth on his feet, like he'd been waiting behind her for hours.

"The usual," Nelly said. "Sometimes I listen to audiobooks. Facebook occasionally, Google."

"Uh-huh." The employee backed out of the screen he was viewing, returning to the home screen. "Nothing, uh, funny?"

"How do you mean?"

"You know." He gave Nelly a playful, overly familiar smile. "*Funny*."

When she realized what he meant, her face turned bright red. "No! I don't look at that stuff."

The man behind her tutted again. Nelly shot him another dirty look. After the week she'd had, she wasn't going to take any flak from some random guy in a cellular store who couldn't mind his own damned business.

The employee shrugged, handing her back the phone. "You picked up a couple of viruses."

"What? How?"

"Look, ma'am, these things happen." He gave her another irritating smirk. "I got rid of them, so your phone should be fine now. Just be careful about what websites you browse. It's important to practice what we call, ahem, safe computing."

Now dying of embarrassment, Nelly stuffed her phone into her purse, quickly paid the man, and hurried out of the store. When she reached her car, she read Tina's text. It included the room number where she was staying. Nelly plugged Wayfair Motel into her phone for directions. She was twenty-three minutes away.

She wrote:

Be there soon

THERE WAS AN UNEXPECTED ROAD CLOSURE. An old tree had toppled and took out some power lines. Nelly had to backtrack and change routes on her phone. Tina hadn't written her back. Nelly couldn't shake the bad feeling she was getting about her friend. Even though Tina had driven all the way out here, that didn't mean she'd actually go through with this.

It was scary to think that Nelly's entire future hinged on Tina.

Nelly reached the Wayfair Motel nearly forty minutes later. The office, situated in the middle of the complex, was lit up. From the outside, she could see the front desk was empty. There were only two other vehicles in the parking lot, one of them stationed by the office. She drove toward the other vehicle, an old sedan that had seen better days. One of its doors had been replaced, but the new door was a different color than the rest of the car.

Nelly parked beside the sedan. It wasn't easy to make out the old numbering on the motel doors. Some of the plastic numbers had been replaced by stickers. The sedan next to her was parked in front of the room where Tina was supposedly staying.

Nelly took a deep breath and checked herself in the rearview. She hadn't seen Tina in almost twenty years, and she wanted to look presentable. She couldn't give Tina any reason to doubt her or have second thoughts.

The last time they had crossed paths, they were both wearing caps and gowns for graduation. Nelly had been headed to college, while Tina had been pregnant with her first. Recalling that moment now, Nelly remembered thinking she might never see Tina again. Nelly was going to school out of state and had no plans to return to her hometown after graduation. It was the fresh start she'd been so looking forward to.

Much like coming to Overland had been.

Incredibly nervous at seeing her old friend, hoping

against hope that Tina would not go back on her word, Nelly stepped out of the car. A tractor trailer roared by on the narrow, two-lane road fronting the motel. Out of habit, Nelly checked her phone before putting it away in her purse. Despite that idiot's assurances at the cellular store, the device was still acting up. The screen froze on her again. Frustrated, Nelly stuffed it into her purse. She'd take it back to the store tomorrow and give the guy a piece of her mind.

As she approached, however, Nelly noticed that Tina's door was slightly ajar. She hadn't noticed from her car because the interior of the room was dark, and the light above Tina's door was out. Frowning, Nelly stepped up and knocked.

"Tina?" she called out. "Are you in there?"

There was no answer.

It seemed strange that Tina would not be in her room but leave the door open. But then a thought occurred to Nelly. Her friend had probably gone for ice. That was what everyone staying in a hotel did, right? She was probably right around the corner, filling up a bucket.

Nelly waited a moment for Tina to return. But as she looked around, Nelly noticed the ice machine. It stood twenty-five feet away at the end of this block of rooms.

And Tina wasn't there.

Turning back around to face the door, Nelly knocked again. Now she was getting worried.

"Tina?"

This time she knocked a little more forcefully. The door inched open. The room was completely dark inside. The hairs on the back of Nelly's neck rose. Something was terribly wrong. She knew it before she set foot inside that room.

Nelly reached in, her fingers finding a nearby light switch. An overhead light came on. The room had twin beds. The pillows of the far bed were out of place, one dangling over the side. The bedspread itself was pulled almost completely off.

"Tina?"

Nelly pushed the door open all the way. A chair was tipped over in the small area between the bed and the bathroom. One boot was in the middle of the floor on its side, looking eerily out of place. Nelly forced herself to go inside, instinctively putting her hands in her pockets. She was, she realized, already treating the room like it was a crime scene.

She found Tina wedged in the small space between the twin beds. Her childhood friend was lying on her stomach with her head turned, dirty blonde hair covering her face.

Nelly knew right away.

Tina was dead.

31

Nelly sat behind the wheel of her car on the far side of the motel parking lot. The sheriff had asked her to move her vehicle so they could process the crime scene.

Crime scene.

She had sobbed uncontrollably while she waited for Bill Van Dyke and his deputies to arrive. Her grief overwhelmed her. Though she and Tina had parted on bad terms and many years had passed since, Nelly still felt the loss of a good friend.

For a long time, during their formative years, she and Tina had been inseparable, and that deep connection had persisted through time and differences that now seemed petty. A long-forgotten memory surfaced while Nelly thought of the past. One summer night, while they chased fireflies in her best friend's backyard, giggling hysterically, Tina said the nicest thing Nelly had ever heard, before or since.

Tina had said, "We're going to be best friends forever."

Nelly had agreed.

Now she grieved for her friend, and her mind turned to Tina's children, one of them still in high school. They were much too young to have lost their mother. And then Nelly thought about the grandchild, and this brought on another tidal wave of grief. Was Tina known as grandmom? Nan? Mom-Mom? It broke Nelly's heart the more she thought about it.

Nelly felt a connection to all these people she had never met. Had they even been notified yet? Probably not. This terrible knowledge was still hers alone, as Tina's family hadn't been contacted yet.

While the police went about their business, Nelly's tears eventually dried up. She went dead inside. Staring absently out her windshield as cars whipped by, she was vaguely aware that her own life was now almost certainly ruined, but oddly enough, that realization didn't stir up much emotion. It felt both a foregone conclusion and somehow unimportant.

The sheriff had asked her to stick around for questioning. Now Bill Van Dyke made his way through the darkening parking lot as the moon rose in the east. He tapped on her passenger window and asked her to come inside with him.

"Her room?" Nelly asked.

"No," the sheriff said. "The manager is letting us use the office."

She breathed a sigh of relief. Nelly didn't think she could ever set foot in a motel room again without picturing Tina's corpse on the floor, jammed between two beds. The sheriff led her into the motel office, behind reception, and into a small room with a desk and two chairs. Bill sat on the edge of the desk, motioning at the chair for her.

"Nelly, I'm terribly sorry about what happened. I know you've had a shock, but time is of the essence in an investigation like this, so I have to ask you some questions. Is that alright?"

She nodded. Nelly reached into her purse for her emergency stash of tissues. Coming up empty, she remembered she'd used them all in the car already. She'd just have to do her best not to sob.

"I need you to take me through your conversations with Tina this week," the sheriff said.

Nelly started at the beginning. The Facebook message on Sunday. The phone calls on Tuesday and Thursday. The text exchanges today.

"And remind me," the sheriff said, "why she was coming out here?"

Nelly gave him a look like he was being thick. "I told you. She was going to meet with you to identify Emmett."

"Uh-huh. And what time were you supposed to meet her here?"

"We didn't have a specific time," Nelly explained. "She was due to get in between six and six thirty. She wanted to grab dinner first before we contacted you."

"I see. What time did you arrive here?"

Nelly hadn't been watching the clock. "I'm not sure. Probably closer to seven. There was traffic. One of the roads I had to take was closed because of downed power lines."

"Right." The sheriff was jotting notes on his pad. "And you planned on contacting me tonight?"

"Yes."

"Just out of the blue?" the sheriff asked.

Nelly frowned. Where was he going with this? "Hardly, Sheriff. You know what's going on in my life right now and why I asked Tina to come out here."

"Why didn't you call to put something on the calendar if you knew Tina would be here?"

Nelly sighed. How could this possibly matter?

"Tina was nervous about meeting with you. And she'd already tried to back out once. I didn't want to call until we were literally on our way and I could be certain she wouldn't change her mind. You already don't believe me—imagine how it would have looked if I'd arranged for you to meet Tina, only to have her back out last minute."

He slowly nodded.

Nelly said, "Can you tell me how it happened?"

The sheriff watched her reaction. "It looks like she was hit on the back of the head with something before being strangled."

Oh God.

Nelly's throat felt like it was closing. Her vision blurred with tears again.

"Just so I understand, then," the sheriff went on, "the plan was to meet here, get dinner, then call me?"

"Yes." Nelly managed to get herself under control. The sheriff was wasting his time talking to her. "Do you know where Emmett is? Have you contacted him yet?"

"I don't need to call him," the sheriff said. "Because I know where he is, Nelly."

"Well, where is he?"

"He's attending an emergency school board meeting with Miguel as we speak. He's been there since five o'clock this afternoon, prior to when Tina checked in at the motel."

Even though Nelly was on the outs at Overland Middle,

she was still surprised to be hearing about this emergency school board meeting now. Typically, a principal let his faculty know if such a thing were happening, even if they couldn't share details. It was the best way to stave off rumors and misinformation.

"Are you sure?" Nelly asked. "Because Miguel didn't notify the staff."

"He did, Nelly," the sheriff responded. "He just didn't notify *you*."

Before the sheriff went on to explain, Nelly had already put it together.

Bill said, "They were meeting to discuss your employment status and what to do about next week in the event you were terminated."

The man's words stung, and Nelly wanted to defend herself. But what was the point? The sheriff already had unflattering ideas about her, and she wouldn't convince him right now that Miguel was treating her unfairly.

Moreover, Nelly was too hung up on the fact that Emmett, once again, had the perfect alibi. His happening to withdraw cash at four thirty after an early morning jog seemed too good to be true. What were the chances that would happen at the same exact time she claimed someone was outside her apartment?

But this emergency school board meeting certainly did not feel like coincidence. It made perfect sense for Miguel and his assistant principal to scramble the proverbial jets. They had to discuss the unexpected firing of a faculty member and develop contingency plans for class next week in that event.

Nelly wondered if she had lost her grip on reality.

No one could deny the last year had been incredibly

difficult for her. When she needed her ex-husband's support the most, John had asked for a divorce. Then his boss had threatened to sue her. Then a student in her class had accused Nelly of being verbally and emotionally abusive. Any one of these things by itself was enough to upend anybody's life. But all three at the same time? That would have been too much for most to handle. Nelly had gotten through it by entering therapy and trying different medications—and she'd only barely gotten through it. It was more likely than not that amount of trauma had permanently damaged her, making Nelly paranoid, overly sensitive, defensive, forgetful, not always present. The type of teacher to misplace important lesson plans and then blame a colleague. The sort of person who would accuse the man throwing her a welcome party of trying to ruin her. The kind of woman who would hear a noise in the middle of the night and think someone was outside her apartment.

She was forgetting, of course, the trauma from twenty-four years ago. Layer more recent events on top of that, fresh scars upon old wounds that never seemed to fully heal, and what could happen to a person?

What if she was wrong?

About it all?

Emmett wasn't terrorizing her. He was just a guy who looked like Marshall who happened to have a low opinion of her teaching abilities. There was nothing sinister about that. What if *she* was the one lying, only to herself? What if her performance on Tuesday, while admittedly happening under poor circumstances, had been subpar?

Was it possible for a brain to see all these things that weren't there? Of course it was, she realized. People suffered from numerous cognitive biases. They misremembered, misinterpreted, distorted, forgot. Everyone suffered from varying levels of delusion. She was not immune to such human foibles.

Had she made all this up?

She was about to give up. Ask to leave and get in her car and drive away. She couldn't prove a damned thing, and she had to admit, she looked like the crazy one here. Not Emmett or anybody else for that matter.

But then she thought about Tina.

Without prompting or coercion, Tina had taken one look at Emmett and immediately agreed with Nelly. That man was Marshall Dawes. She'd been absolutely certain.

While it was possible that both of them could have been mistaken, Nelly didn't think it likely. And then she ran through all her interactions with Emmett, recalling all the times his words had taken on double meanings, the way he'd asked her about the MeToo movement, the way he always seemed to be fighting a smile as he toyed with her. Surely she hadn't imagined all of it.

But there was a larger problem to consider, she realized. Assuming Emmett committed this murder, how did he even know Tina was coming to town?

"He was involved somehow," Nelly said, her tone unconvincing. "There's no other explanation."

"There are a lot of other explanations, Nelly." The sheriff consulted some notes before putting his pad away. "Have you ever spoken with Tina's husband, Mikey?"

"No. Why? Do you think he had something to do with this?"

The sheriff held out a palm. "Slow down there, Nelly. I'm the one who has to ask the questions right now."

She frowned at his condescending tone.

Bill said, "I spoke with him just now."

Nelly wondered where this could be going. "What did he tell you?"

"He said you were going through a rough patch, and Tina came out here to keep you company during a difficult time." The sheriff gave her a pointed look. "Mikey didn't say a thing about Emmett."

Oh no.

Everything was slipping away from her.

"That's not true."

"You mean he's lying?" the sheriff asked.

"No, I didn't say that." Nelly was having trouble thinking clearly now. The sheriff had thrown her off her game. "That's what Tina told him."

"I don't follow," Bill said, his expression growing more skeptical.

"Tina told me that Mikey is very controlling," Nelly said, hoping it didn't sound like she was making this up on the fly. "He didn't want her getting involved in a police investigation because he's been in trouble with the law recently."

"How do you know that?" the sheriff asked.

"That's what Tina told me!"

She realized she was yelling.

"That's what Tina told me," she repeated in a softer voice. "But Tina wanted to help, so she told Mikey a story. She didn't want him to know why she was really coming."

The sheriff stared at her for a long moment. He didn't believe a word she was saying.

"Why didn't you want Tina staying at your apartment?" he asked. "I mean, if she was coming out here to see you, why not put her up on the couch?"

Nelly knew how it was going to sound, but she said it

anyway. "Emmett has been stalking me. He's come by my house. If he saw Tina at my place, he'd get suspicious. I didn't want to tip him off."

"Emmett has an alibi for the night you woke up at four thirty."

As if she needed reminding.

"What about the night before that, though?" Nelly asked. "I heard somebody then also."

The sheriff microscopically shook his head. "Nelly, did you have anything to do with this?"

"What? No! Of course not! Tina was my friend!"

"Was," he said. "A long time ago."

"This is ridiculous." She was out of the chair but barely reached the much taller man's chest. Nelly looked up at the sheriff. "Why would I do this?"

"You told me before that you and she parted on bad terms."

"Twenty years ago!"

"And you also told me that she didn't even want to come out here. Right?"

"Because of Mikey," Nelly said. "Because he—"

"Tina's husband has no criminal record," Bill said.

It was like he'd slapped her.

"What? No. That can't be. That's not what Tina said."

"First thing we do in this situation is look at the significant other," Bill told her calmly. "Now, we haven't ruled anybody out yet, but I know for a fact he has no priors."

Nelly sat back down. This could not be happening. She was telling the sheriff the truth. But everything she said later looked like a lie. Even worse, Emmett had another perfect alibi.

"This place must have cameras," Nelly said. "Somebody had to see something."

The sheriff shook his head. "Not this place. It attracts clientele who don't want to be on camera usually."

Nelly slumped back in the chair.

The sheriff bobbed his head. "Do you mind if we take a look in your car while you're here, Nelly?"

32

By the time Nelly returned to her apartment, it was almost nine thirty. She hadn't eaten again, but what little food was in her fridge looked unappealing. She nibbled on some crackers while she sat in the absolute silence of her living room.

She jumped at the sound of her phone buzzing at this late hour. Expecting it to be the sheriff, she was surprised when the caller ID flashed a number she didn't recognize and a name that was familiar: MICHAEL WALKER.

Nelly didn't want to talk to anyone, never mind Tina's controlling husband, Mikey. But she felt like she couldn't ignore the call. After all, the man's wife had just been murdered.

"Hello?"

"Is this Nelly Peak?" came a gruff voice.

"Yes, it is. Mikey?"

"Yeah."

"I'm so sor—"

"What the fuck happened up there?"

Nelly held the phone away from her ear.

"I don't know, Mikey. It's just terrible."

"Terrible? Is that all you got to say?"

Nelly took a deep breath. She didn't want to get nasty with the man whose wife had just been murdered. But she wasn't in the mood herself to be verbally abused.

"I don't know what you want me to say," she answered.

"The sheriff told me it didn't look like a robbery or a sex thing," Mikey said. "Somebody just murdered my Tina."

Nelly was tempted to share her suspicions. But what good would come of that?

"Did you fucking do it?" he asked.

Nelly closed her eyes and pinched the bridge of her nose. "No. I was the one who found her."

"Exactly," Mikey said, his voice growing even more nasty. "The person who finds the body is usually the one who did it."

"I didn't kill her!" Nelly snapped. "She was my friend."

"Was," he said. "*Was.* You were friends a long fucking time ago. She didn't even want to come out there, Nelly. She told me as much. She was only coming because she felt sorry for you. But she wasn't your friend. You put the guilt trip on her about shit that went down over twenty years ago, and she felt *obligated.*"

Nelly took a deep breath.

"You made her feel guilty so she'd shlep the two hours out to Bubblefuck, Pennsylvania, to see you. Now she's dead. What do you have to say about that?"

"I'm sorry."

"Sorry?" he scoffed. "Do you know she's a mother and a grandmother? Do you know that she helps out down at the old folks' home when she's not working? Do you know that her boy suffers from depression and was already suicidal? What do you think this is going to do to him?"

Nelly had heard enough. "It's terrible. But this wasn't my fault, Mikey. Somebody killed her."

"Yeah. Somebody. What happened, Nelly? You two get into a fight? Did you lay the guilt on her about what *allegedly* happened to you in middle school or whatever? A person can only take so much before they push back. Is that what happened? Did you two get into an argument?"

"Nothing *allegedly* happened to me in middle school. A boy tried to rape me."

"Oh, sure. Is that why Tina didn't back up your story all those years ago? Did you bring that shit up again? And when she wouldn't placate you, you snapped?"

"No—"

"I know what you were after," Mikey went on. "You wanted her to point the finger at one of your co-workers, right? I'm guessing this guy doesn't like you, so you came up with this ridiculous story to get him out of the way."

"No—"

"She was just telling you what you wanted to hear, you know. She didn't actually think this guy was Marshall or whatever."

"That's a lie."

"No, Nelly, that's what she told me."

Nelly gasped.

Tina must have said that to Mikey as part of her made-up story for visiting Nelly. She didn't want him worrying that they'd get pulled into a police investigation, so she'd lied and told him that Emmett wasn't Marshall.

That Nelly was just deluded, in other words.

And that was what Mikey had undoubtedly shared with

the police. He'd told Bill Van Dyke that Tina didn't even believe Emmett was Marshall. Now Nelly's allegations looked even more suspect. No one would ever believe her.

Nelly had had enough. "That's what she told you because you're a jealous, controlling husband who didn't want her getting involved in a police investigation."

"Don't put this on me—"

"She told me about you," Nelly said. "About how manipulative and controlling you are. I know that your marriage isn't great, but that Tina needed your support—mostly financially—to help with the family. She was *placating* you, telling you a story so she could do the right thing and help me."

"You're unbelievable."

"Don't ever call me again."

Nelly ended the call and tossed the phone onto the coffee table. Only seconds later it buzzed again, Mikey calling her back. She blocked his number.

Despite the unpleasant conversation, or perhaps because of it, Nelly felt galvanized. Full of anger and outrage again, she got up and paced the small living room while she tried to figure out her next steps. Emmett had an alibi, but she was certain he was involved in Tina's murder. It was the only explanation that made sense.

But what could she do about it?

Nelly had found nothing online suggesting Emmett was an impostor. Nothing even remotely linking him to Marshall. Tina, the one person willing to back her up, was now dead. The only other person who *might* have useful information on Marshall was that poor girl who'd survived the college house fire.

Julia Sowers.

Nelly looked her up online. Her social media was all private. Nelly modified her search, adding the name of the university the woman had attended. She expected to find Julia's name on a list of graduates somewhere, and she did, but she also found something else.

Julia Sowers worked at the university. She was a librarian.

33

TODAY – SATURDAY

The next morning, Nelly didn't so much wake up as simply get out of bed. She'd drifted off a few times but hadn't cobbled together more than three hours of sleep altogether. After quickly getting ready, she hit the road.

Overland was quiet early on a Saturday morning. She didn't pass too many cars as the sun crested the horizon. Nelly stopped for coffee and a quick bite, realizing after she ordered this was the same bakery that Vanessa had gotten the doughnuts and bagels from for Nelly's welcome party.

Back on the road, Nelly made her way to the interstate. As she was crossing into New Jersey, the sheriff called. She dumped Bill into voicemail. Nelly didn't want to answer any more questions this morning. Not until she got some answers first.

It took her another ninety minutes to reach the university. The campus library opened at ten o'clock this morning. She killed some time by driving past the site of the fire. A new home had been built there. Though the property wasn't new anymore, it still stuck out among the other houses nearby, all of which were significantly older. She wanted to knock on doors and ask if anyone remembered the fire or the young women who'd perished, but it was a long time ago, and people came and went all the time on a college campus.

Nelly found metered parking near the library. Then she hunkered down, finishing her coffee. Despite hardly sleeping, she was full of nervous energy.

At nine fifty, a woman proceeded slowly up the wide sidewalk fronting the library. She was short and wore a hat and scarf even though it wasn't that cold outside. The collar of her jacket was popped too, creating an overall effect that obscured her face. The woman stifled a yawn as she went slowly up the stairs leading to the library.

Nelly waited in the car. The woman unlocked the three sets of double doors at the entrance, then slipped inside. The interior lights winked on one by one.

At ten o'clock, Nelly checked herself in the rearview mirror once more. There was no mistaking the bags under her eyes, or the puffy, bloated look of her face. The wrinkles on her forehead were more pronounced than usual. Her skin was dry, flaking near her hairline. Her frown lines stood out.

She looked terrible.

This was not the image she wanted to project to Julia Sowers. Nelly was already in danger of coming across like some obsessed crazy person, looking for information on a man Julia had probably not seen since her college days. But other than retouching her lipstick, additional makeup wasn't going to help Nelly.

Her phone buzzed again. This time it was Deputy Sullivan reaching out. Nelly didn't know why this woman was calling her as opposed to the sheriff, but she couldn't get bogged down right now. She fed the call into voicemail.

Nelly popped out of the car. This was a fishing expedition. She had no idea where the conversation would lead, assuming it went anywhere useful.

But what else could she do?

Nelly entered the library.

It was a big, airy place with two stories. The morning sun slanted in through skylights above, landing high on the brick walls of the interior. It was quiet, the only sound the hum of electricity pumping through the overhead lighting.

As Nelly approached the front of the library, Julia Sowers stepped out of the office behind the circulation desk.

She had removed her hat, scarf, and jacket. Nelly got her first good look at Julia. Half of the woman's face was covered by old burn scars. Her bottom lip looked like plastic, and the hair near one temple was missing, the skin there an unnatural shade that contrasted with the rest of her face.

"Can I help you?" Julia asked.

Her voice was youthful and soft, at odds with her appearance.

Nelly smiled. "Are you Julia Sowers?"

The woman's look became guarded. "Yes."

She stopped in front of the desk and stuck her hand out. "My name is Nelly Peak. I came here because I wanted to talk to you."

Julia tentatively shook her hand. "What is this about?"

"I have a friend named Tina Walker." Nelly was careful not to slip into the past tense when speaking about Tina. "But back when you met her, her name was Tina Hirshberg."

"Sorry." Julia was at a loss. "I don't remember anyone by that name."

"You probably only met her once," Nelly said. "She was friends with one of your roommates, Alice?"

Julia nodded at the mention of Alice. "I knew Alice, obviously, but Tina isn't ringing any bells."

"That's okay," Nelly said. Behind her, a couple of bleary-eyed students trudged in wearing shorts and hoodies and crocs. Nelly looked past Julia. "Could we speak in your office? This is a private matter."

"I'm afraid not," Julia said. "I'm the only staff member here right now, and I have work to do. If you want to speak privately, you'd have to meet me later."

Now that Nelly had mentioned Tina's name, she did not want Julia growing curious and searching about her dead friend online. Finding out Tina had been killed would make her leery of a strange woman showing up unannounced to ask probing questions.

"It'll only take a few minutes," Nelly said, knowing it wouldn't. "Please. I wouldn't ask if it wasn't important."

"I can't leave this desk right now," Julia said. "This is the best I can do."

Nelly just had to go for it. "It's about Marshall. Do you remember him? Marshall Dawes?"

The change that suddenly came over Julia was profound. "Now there's a name I haven't heard in years."

"You remember him?"

She nodded. "What has this got to do with your friend, what was her name, Tara?"

"Tina," Nelly said. "She came out to campus one weekend to see Alice. They knew each other from work. During Christmas break, Alice temped where Tina was employed full time. And she—"

"Oh." Julia's eyes went wide. "*Tina*. Now I remember. Tall blonde, right?"

"Yes," Nelly said. Tina was dirty blonde and five feet six on a good day, but the description was close enough. "Tina was pregnant at the time and starting to show."

"Right." Julia snapped her fingers. "I remember she wasn't drinking. My God, that was so long ago. She and Marshall knew each other, if I'm remembering correctly?"

"Yes." Nelly tried to contain her budding excitement. All she'd done so far was confirm things she already knew. She still had a long way to go, and there was no guarantee Julia could even help. "Marshall came over that night. You saw the two of them together?"

"Yeah." Julia gave Nelly a knowing look. "They talked most of the night, and...they spent the party together."

Nelly nodded. "That's right."

"I'm confused," Julia said. "You said you were here about Tina, but now you seem interested in Marshall too."

"It has to do with both of them, but could I ask you about Marshall?"

"I guess." Julia's expression turned sour. "I haven't seen him in twenty years."

Nelly smelled blood in the water. "What was he like?"

"Uh..." Julia's eyes shifted right. A college student was approaching the desk. "I have to help this patron."

Nelly moved out of the way. The young man asked Julia if the library lent out video games for the Nintendo Switch, Xbox, or PlayStation. Then he asked where all the Blu-Rays were. Julia pointed him in the right direction. More groggy students, some of them appearing hungover, were entering the library now. When Julia was free, Nelly approached the desk again.

"I was asking you about Marshall," she said. "What was he like?"

Julia hesitated. It was a pregnant pause. Nelly assumed Julia had a negative opinion of the man but that she was also trying to remain polite about a person she only briefly knew many years ago.

"I didn't care for him."

"Why not?"

Julia pursed her lips. "He was creepy."

"How so?"

"He'd stand in the corner, sort of by himself. He was always *around* the party but never quite part of it."

Julia's description of Marshall's behavior reminded Nelly of that day in the factory. She recalled all the other kids getting on well, but Marshall standing off to the side by himself, making strange remarks nobody could quite hear, and ogling her creepily.

"He'd make these weird comments too. Loud enough you could sort of hear them, you know what I mean? Anyway, I didn't talk to him much," Julia said. "I didn't like his vibe. The rest of my girlfriends didn't care for him either. That's probably why he latched onto Tina. Nobody else really liked him, and he knew her from high school."

Nelly thought back to what Tina had told her, how none of the people at the party showed much interest in her. Tina had put that off to her being a pregnant, single mother not enrolled at the university. But now Nelly was beginning to think that it was Marshall's fault. Nobody wanted to talk to him, so they all stayed away from Tina.

While Nelly was silent, Julia grew curious.

"Are you a reporter?"

"No," Nelly said.

"You're not one of those people who are obsessed with unsolved crimes, are you?"

"No."

"Because over the years, a lot of strange types have approached me about what happened."

She had to be referring to the fire. Nelly decided there was no reason to be coy.

"I'm so sorry about what happened," Nelly said. "Tina told me."

Julia nodded, a sad look crossing her face. "It was a long time ago now."

"One of the articles mentioned a report of a man in your backyard."

Julia gave Nelly a steely look. She feared she'd gone too far. But then again, was there a good way of probing into the delicate subject of the house fire?

"Our neighbor saw someone," Julia said carefully.

"Did they ever identify the person?"

Julia grew uneasy. "No."

Nelly knew there was something here. "Look. I have no evidence to back this up. It's just a hunch. But I think it was Marshall."

Julia said nothing. But her eyes did a lot of talking.

Nelly palmed the counter between them and leaned forward. "You think so too, don't you?"

"It couldn't have been him," Julia said.

"Why not?" Nelly asked.

"Because he'd already left campus by then."

"How do you know that?" Nelly asked. "How can you be sure?"

"I'm sorry," Julia said, "but I really should get back to work."

"Wait—please." Nelly looked her in the eye. "I need your help."

The other woman seemed about to turn away, so Nelly tried a different tack.

"Did Marshall ever threaten you?"

Julia sighed. "A few nights before winter break, we went out to celebrate Alice's birthday and got really drunk. She was the last of us to turn twenty-one. Marshall was at the bar by himself. He tried coming over, but Alice told him we weren't interested. He was embarrassed and stormed out. Later, when we were walking home, he came out from an alley. He scared the living hell out of me. Anyway, he and Alice got into it."

"What did they argue about?"

"He was accused of assaulting a woman. Alice and she were friends. Once we heard that, none of us wanted anything to do with him."

"Irene Patselas?" Nelly asked.

Julia nodded. "So you know about that too?"

Nelly didn't explain how. She had to keep the focus on Julia. Keep the other woman talking.

"Then what happened?" she asked.

"We threatened to call campus security," Julia said. "But that didn't work right away. He followed us for a stretch."

"What finally scared him off?" Nelly asked.

"Alice." Julia smiled as her eyes got a faraway look. "She was always the fearless one in our group."

"What did she do?"

"She told him we didn't associate with rapists, and that if he kept following us, she'd dislocate *his* thumb."

Nelly couldn't stop her involuntary reaction in time. She gasped.

"Are you alright?" Julia asked.

Nelly couldn't answer immediately.

"Why did she say that?" Nelly asked, fearing she already knew the answer.

"That's what he did to her. *Allegedly,*" Julia added.

Nelly felt sick. She pictured Marshall pinning Irene down the same way he had tried with her. She felt her own arm twisted painfully behind her back, her wrist being wrenched, her thumb—

He'd done the same thing to Irene.

"Can you tell me what you know about Marshall and Irene?" Nelly asked.

"Irene accused him of rape. But the police never arrested him. Irene was really drunk that night, apparently, so her recall of the evening, especially the important details, wasn't great. Marshall, on the other hand, remembered everything. According to him, the sex had been consensual, and while she was drunk, Irene had lost her balance and fallen, accidentally dislocating her thumb in the process. He's the one who popped it back into place."

Nelly was having trouble processing this. She kept picturing sixteen-year-old Marshall on top of her. She remembered how painful it was to have her arm pinned behind her back, with his weight on top of her.

"Are you alright?" Julia asked.

"I'm fine," Nelly said. "I was just struck by what that poor woman must have gone through."

"I feel so bad for her," Julia said. "Did you know she was assaulted and murdered five years ago? It was right off campus."

Nelly nodded. "Did they ever find who did it?"

"I don't think so."

"Was that night at the bar the last time any of you saw Marshall?" Nelly asked.

"It was the last time I did," Julia said. "But Alice saw him one more time, a few nights later when winter break began."

"Where did she see him?"

Julia clammed up again. "Will you tell me what this is about?"

Nelly pulled a face. "I promise I'll tell you. But it's really important that I find out about Marshall."

Julia suddenly looked at Nelly with fresh eyes.

"Wait a minute. Are you related to Irene?" Julia asked. "Is that why you're here?"

"No," she said. "My name is Nelly Peak. I never met Irene."

"Because you two look an awful lot alike."

Nelly nodded sadly. What terrible luck for Irene Patselas, that she happened to resemble Nelly and that she happened to encounter Marshall Dawes. The universe could be such a cold place.

"I know Marshall," Nelly said, leaning in. "And I believe Irene. There's no doubt in my mind that he tried to rape her."

Julia didn't answer.

Nelly looked her in the eye. "When did Alice see him next?"

"She didn't really see him. He was driving by in his car a few nights later."

Nelly frowned. Julia had shared a lot with her. So why had the woman been wary of telling her this seemingly insignificant detail?

"On the night of the fire, do you think it was Marshall in your backyard?"

Julia looked scared again. "I don't know what to think."

"Come on," Nelly said. "I can tell you've got an opinion."

"We don't know what happened," Julia said, her voice growing sad. "And we'll probably never know. Both Alice and Janice smoked, so they could have left a burning cigarette by accident. The building was old, too. Some of the wiring wasn't up to code. That came out in the fire investigator's report."

Nelly had to press the woman. "But you don't think it was either of those things, do you?"

Julia's expression became guarded again.

"Like I said, we'll probably never know." Julia looked over her shoulder at the clock on the wall. "I really should get to work."

Nelly didn't know what to ask next. She blurted out the first thing that came to mind in the hopes she could keep the conversation going before Julia completely shut down.

"How about those guys Marshall came around with?" Nelly asked. "Did they ever mention him again after that?"

"He wasn't really friends with them," Julia answered. "And after the fire, I didn't see any of them ever again. I was in the hospital for a month; then I took a year off school. I needed time to heal. By then, those guys had graduated. But like I said, they weren't really friends with him."

"I'm confused," Nelly said. "If Marshall wasn't friends with any of the guys who were there that night, and you girls didn't like him either, how did he end up at your party with Tina?"

Julia shrugged. "Like I said, it was a friend-of-a-friend

situation. Marshall was buddies with an undergraduate here. That guy knew Alice and Irene from class."

"What was his name?" Nelly asked.

"Emmett."

34

Nelly was floored.

"Emmett?"

Julia nodded. "Yeah, Emmett."

"Emmett...*Moore*?"

"That's it," Julia said, catching her unguarded expression of shock. "Do you know him too?"

Nelly racked her brain. "But I thought Emmett graduated from Marist in upstate New York."

"Oh, is that where he ended up?" Julia asked. "I always wondered. He dropped out of school after that semester. He never came back after winter break, apparently. But yes, Emmett was a student here."

Nelly recalled the sheriff mentioning Emmett's having attended two different colleges. She tried to contain herself.

"When did he disappear?"

"He didn't *disappear,* as far as I know. He just dropped out of school. They left for winter break, and Emmett never came back."

Nelly couldn't believe her luck. She had discovered a connection between Emmett and Marshall.

"Why did he drop out of school?" Nelly asked.

"There were the usual rumors. He had a drinking problem, he got a girl back home pregnant, he found a job that didn't require a degree and paid well, that sort of thing. But nobody really knew."

"Did you believe any of the rumors?"

"To be honest, I didn't give it much thought."

"Why not?"

"By the time I found out, I was in the burn victim unit over at the hospital."

"I'm sorry," Nelly said.

Julia bit back tears. "I was in there for almost a month. When I got out, I wasn't ready to come back to school. I took a year off to heal."

Nelly understood her to mean that she needed to heal her spirit as well as her body.

"Emmett was going through a lot at the time," Julia added. "His parents had passed away before the school year started."

"Really?"

"Yeah..." Julia's eyes did a thing. "They passed in a fire also."

"*What?*"

Julia nodded. "Freaky, right? Anyway, Emmett still came to school. He *seemed* like he was doing well. But maybe he was just good at hiding it."

"And you haven't seen or spoken to Emmett since?"

Julia sighed. "I've told you a lot, but I still don't know why you're here exactly."

Nelly took a deep breath. "Like I said, it has to do with Marshall and Tina."

"Not Emmett, though?"

"Him too," Nelly said.

Julia waited. She wasn't going to say anything more without Nelly explaining herself. Nelly was pushing her luck. The longer she went without admitting that Tina was dead, the worse things would look for her if Julia found out. She knew she had to come clean at some point.

Just not yet.

Nelly took her phone out of her pocket. "I'd like to show you a picture."

Her phone gave her problems. While she waited for it to unfreeze, Julia checked books out for two students. Finally, Nelly logged on to Facebook and found the picture from the charity race. She zoomed in on the shirtless Emmett. When Julia was free again, Nelly approached with the phone.

"Would you look at this picture and tell me who you think it is?" she asked.

Nelly passed the phone to Julia. The other woman frowned down at the screen. It took her a moment to answer.

"It's difficult to say."

"But you recognize the person," Nelly said, growing anxious.

"Sure. It's either Marshall or Emmett."

Nelly's heart stopped. "What do you mean it's either Marshall or Emmett?"

Julia took another look at the picture before handing the phone back.

"You said you knew them both." Julia gave her a funny look. "So you must understand."

"Understand what?" Nelly asked.

35

"They look alike."

Nelly was thoroughly confused.

"But my friend Tina," Nelly said, trying to slow her racing thoughts, "she would have seen them both at the party. But she never mentioned the two of them resembling one another."

Julia's eyes drifted up and to the right as she thought back. "I don't think Emmett was around the weekend Tina came by."

"Are you sure?"

"It was a long time ago," Julia said. "But yes, I remember Emmett wasn't there. He called to let us know he wasn't feeling well but that Marshall might still come by. I remember all of us talking in the kitchen—none of us wanted Marshall around, and we hoped he'd just stay home with Emmett."

"They lived together?" Nelly asked.

Julia nodded.

Now Nelly couldn't get her questions out quickly

enough. "And you all thought Marshall looked like Emmett?"

"It's not that surprising. They are related."

"*What?*"

"You don't know about this?"

Julia was growing more and more suspicious.

"I knew Marshall and Tina pretty well, but I hardly know Emmett."

Julia pressed her. "But you have seen them both?"

"I guess I never realized...I last saw Marshall twenty years ago."

Julia eyed her skeptically. Nelly was afraid she'd end the conversation.

"Emmett was adopted," Julia said slowly. "After his parents died, he contacted the agency about connecting with his birth parents. His mother was already dead, and his father was unknown. But somehow he got in touch with Marshall's family. They're first cousins once removed, or second cousins. I can never remember what the difference is. But yes, they could pass for brothers. The resemblance is uncanny."

"And you're telling me the person in that photo could be either man?" Nelly asked.

Julia nodded slowly. "I haven't seen Marshall or Emmett in a long time, and I only knew them both briefly."

"But it *could* be either?"

Julia hesitated. "What is this about? You still haven't told me."

Nelly knew she couldn't hold back any longer. "My friend Tina is dead. And I think Emmett or Marshall had something to do with it."

The half of Julia's face untouched by the fire all those years ago turned white.

"Marshall I could see. But not Emmett. No way. He was wonderful," Julia said.

"How so?"

"You took one look at him and you knew right away he was a good person. The kind of guy who'd give you the shirt off his back. There wasn't a mean bone in his body. And he was so charming and charismatic. He had this way about him, this air. He could put anyone at ease."

Nelly got the sense Julia once had feelings for Emmett.

The other woman went on. "Most guys like him wouldn't have given me the time of day, but Emmett was always so kind to me. I'll never forget this trick he taught me one night..."

Julia smiled nostalgically at the memory.

She said, "I was painfully shy growing up, so one night I asked him how he always seemed so comfortable and confident. He told me about this personal development course. That's what changed his life."

Nelly gasped. "Did he share his trick about meeting someone for the first time? You pretend like they're an old friend?"

Julia's face lit up. "Yes! How did you know? Did he share it with you?"

Nelly nodded.

Julia said, "That's what I mean. He was such a good guy. Honestly, he wouldn't have had anything to do with a person like Marshall if the two of them hadn't been related."

Nelly couldn't believe her luck. With this new information, the sheriff would have to take her accusations more seriously. Though she wanted more—some piece of incontrovertible evidence.

"I want to make sure I understand," Nelly said, struggling to keep all these facts straight. "You went out to celebrate Alice's birthday. That night, Marshall accosted you on the way home. A few nights later, Alice saw him driving past the house. Everyone goes home for winter break, including Emmett, who doesn't return for the following semester. Is that right?"

Julia nodded.

"Did any of you ever hear from Marshall or Emmett again?"

"Not Emmett," Julia said.

"But you did hear from Marshall?"

Julia said nothing.

Nelly pleaded with her. "Please, Julia. I think Marshall might have murdered my friend. You have to help."

36

Nelly hurried out of the library. She paid for more time on the parking meter through the app, then hustled across the street to a campus coffee shop. She needed caffeine and she needed to think. Nelly hurried back to her car.

She wished she had brought a notebook. Nelly wanted to write everything down. Her phone would have to do. She opened a new email and started typing. Even if she forgot to send the note to herself, it would be saved as a draft in her folder.

Nelly wrote quickly, ignoring the inevitable typos that were a result of using the tiny keyboard on her phone screen. Julia had shared so many important things. When Nelly was done typing, she read over the information.

It was a lot to take in. And it definitely supported her theory that Marshall was posing as Emmett.

But was it enough?

It wasn't proof positive. Nelly felt like she needed more, but she had no idea where to go next. She toyed with the notion of hiring a detective but feared a private investigation would take too long. Her reputation had already been ruined, and she was almost certainly about to lose her job. Nelly needed to take immediate action. Perhaps it was time to force the sheriff's hand. With the information she'd just uncovered, he'd *have* to do something. At the very least, Emmett's character would be called into question. Maybe it was too late for Nelly to save herself, but she could take the bastard down with her.

Nelly pulled up the sheriff's phone number. The man hadn't proven helpful before, but she didn't know what else to do. Reluctantly, her thumb reached for the CALL icon.

Before she hit it, however, her phone buzzed, startling Nelly. It was Beck calling.

Frowning, Nelly answered.

"Hi, Beck."

"Nelly."

Her friend's voice had an urgency to it. "What's wrong?"

"Has Miguel contacted you?"

Nelly hadn't missed a call or email from him.

"No. What's going on?"

"Shit." Beck sounded despondent. "I'm so sorry, but I have bad news and some *really* bad news. He's firing you."

This didn't come as a total surprise, but all the same Nelly was angry. She put the back of her head against the headrest and closed her eyes. Things were coming to a head. Nelly had to act quickly. It might have been too late, as a matter of fact. Now that she'd been officially terminated, any wild accusations she made against Emmett would come across as the ravings of a spiteful woman who'd lost her job.

No. He cannot win. I will not let him.

"Nelly, are you there?" Beck asked.

"I'm here," Nelly said.

"I told Miguel he was going to regret it," Beck said.

Despite her dire situation, Nelly managed a smile. "You did?"

"After the official email went around, I called Miguel right away and demanded to know how he could do that to you after everything you said yesterday. But then he told me why."

Nelly's stomach dropped. "What is it?"

"This is the really bad news," Beck said. "I'm not supposed to be telling you this. So if anybody ever asks, just tell them I called to offer my condolences for getting fired."

"Beck, what is it?"

"Miguel had to fire you because the sheriff plans to arrest you."

"*What?*"

"Apparently they searched your apartment this morning," Beck said.

Nelly's heart was hammering in her chest. "I don't believe this."

"Whatever you do, don't come back to Overland," Beck said. "Bill will arrest you. According to Miguel, they found something in your apartment."

Nelly felt like crying. Where the hell else was she supposed to go?

"What did they find?"

"That's all I know," Beck said. "I'm sorry. But I had to warn you."

Nelly managed to blink away the hot tears. She stared out the windshield as students ambled past. Only a few minutes ago, she'd been worried about losing her job. That anxiety paled in comparison to what she felt now.

The sheriff was going to arrest her.

"Thank you for calling," Nelly said. "I won't tell anyone what you said, but there's still a good chance you'll get in trouble, Beck. You could lose your job too."

"I *had* to call you," Beck said.

"Why?"

Beck was quiet for a moment. "When I was eighteen, I got a part-time job at the grocery store. I didn't normally work late, but one night I offered to help stock the shelves so I could get time-and-a-half. A bunch of people who worked overnight had called out unexpectedly. There were only three of us working. The one guy went out for a smoke break, and the other...he cornered me in the bathroom. I fought as hard as I could, but I'm tiny. And he was big."

"Oh God, Beck."

"I know what it's like." Beck was getting choked up. "I know exactly what you're going through. No one believed me either."

"Why not?"

"Because I'm a flirt." Beck laughed mirthlessly. "The other asshole working that night said I was begging for it. It didn't matter that he was out in the back smoking a joint at the time when it happened. What he said was just enough for the police to doubt me."

"I'm so sorry."

Beck had to compose herself. "I *knew* you weren't lying. I could see it in your eyes, and I could hear it in your voice. I know what it's like to tell a story like that."

Nelly smiled as she teared up. "Thank you for believing me."

"Somebody has to," Beck said.

"I've got information on Emmett." Nelly took a deep breath. "I just hope it's enough."

"Nels," Beck said, "don't do anything crazy."

Nelly couldn't suppress an exasperated laugh.

"Crazy is all I've got left."

"What are you going to do?"

Nelly sighed. "If I run, I only look guiltier."

"Wait—don't tell me you're considering turning yourself in!" Beck said. "You have no idea what the sheriff found in your apartment. If it's the murder weapon—"

"I know, Beck, but I don't see another way. My only hope is this new information will open the sheriff's eyes. Once I share it with him, he'll be forced to take action."

"Nelly, you're not thinking clearly right now," Beck said. "You can't take your chances with the man looking to arrest you for murder."

Beck was right. But still, Nelly didn't see another way.

"Just take a moment," Beck said, "before you decide to do anything. Please."

Nelly smiled. "You turned out to be my favorite part of Overland, Beck."

"I think you should run," Beck said. "While you're hiding somewhere, send that information to the sheriff. Then see what happens."

"You're probably right," Nelly said, knowing full well that becoming a fugitive was no realistic option for her. "Thanks, Beck."

Beck was begging her to listen to reason when Nelly ended the call. She sat in the car, her inertia growing. If she went to Bill Van Dyke, he'd arrest her for murder. But if she ran, he'd be much less likely to take her information on Emmett seriously.

Nelly gripped the steering wheel. One way or another, she had to make a decision quickly. Or it would be made for her.

"What do I do?" she asked her reflection in the rearview mirror.

Then someone knocked on her window.

37

Nelly shrieked at the sudden motion and sound next to her head. When she got her wits about her, she was shocked to see who was standing outside her car.

It was Vanessa. The other woman was wearing jeans and a casual top under a light brown jacket. Her hair was pulled back into a ponytail. She wasn't as put together as she normally was. Nelly didn't think she was wearing any makeup.

Vanessa gave her a weak smile and waved.

Dumbfounded, Nelly powered her window down. "Hi, Vanessa."

"Hi, Nelly."

The two women regarded each other for an awkward moment. It was too big a coincidence they'd happen to be on-campus where Emmett spent his first two and a half years as an undergraduate. They both knew there was more at play here.

Vanessa hugged herself. "I think you and I need to talk."

"Why are you here?" Nelly asked.

Vanessa's face fell. "The same reason you probably are."

Nelly's heart went out to the woman. She hadn't forgotten about their two fleeting conversations, during which Vanessa had expressed doubts and fears regarding her husband-to-be. She'd been so focused on herself through all this, however, that she hadn't had the emotional bandwidth to worry about Vanessa also.

Perhaps this was an opportunity to not only correct that, but to also speak to someone who would have more details about the man himself. Information that Nelly might never be able to obtain.

Nelly opened her door.

38

They started walking and fell into step. Vanessa motioned behind them, toward the library.

"I came here to talk to Julia myself. But I lost my nerve when I saw you going inside."

"What made you come here?" Nelly asked.

They rounded a corner. Ahead, there was a small park. A mom pushed a stroller through the area, while a man walked a greyhound on a leash. Vanessa slowed when they came to a bench and sat.

"Some things Emmett has said over the years," she answered. "Some things that didn't add up."

"Like what?" Nelly asked.

Vanessa looked away. She seemed to be holding in tears.

"I've never been in love before," she said. "Well, that's not true. I've been in love before. But nobody's ever really loved me back. I know how I come across, and I can't help it. I've always been this way...I don't process emotions the same way most others do."

Nelly bit back her questions. The woman had to come to her point in her own way.

Vanessa went on. "I've been on a lot of first dates, but very few second ones. The one man I got close to before was only after my money. And when I turned forty a few years ago, I started to think I'd never find someone. I felt like that was it for me, I was going to spend the rest of my life alone.

"Then Emmett came along. He swept me off my feet. He was everything I ever wanted: handsome and witty and charming and, above all else, kind-hearted. Any woman would *kill* to find someone like that. I fell in love with him.

"The first year was incredible. We never had an argument—and everything seemed perfect. But then, as we became more involved, I started noticing these little things about him that seemed off. When I asked him questions about his past, especially high school and college, he grew cagey and sometimes gave me contradictory answers. But I was so happy, I didn't want to think he might be lying or dodging.

"But then you came along, and I could tell right away there was something between you two. Call it a woman's intuition. You know him from somewhere, don't you?"

Vanessa finally looked her in the eye.

"Emmett's real name is Marshall Dawes."

Vanessa did not react for a moment. Then her eyes slowly slid away from Nelly and focused on the ground in front of her.

"He tried to rape me when I was thirteen," Nelly said, surprised by what she was sharing. "I knew it was him when we met at the race on Sunday. And he recognized me too. Ever since then, he's been out to ruin my reputation so I have no credibility. That way, if I were to come forward and speak out against him, no one would believe me."

Vanessa looked up again. "Do you have proof?"

"I have enough that any honest police officer would have to look into Emmett's past."

"What did you find out?" Vanessa latched onto her forearm. "Please—you have to tell me. I'm about to marry this man. I have to know who he really is."

Nelly saw the fear and desperation in the other woman's eyes. She felt like she owed Vanessa the truth. The woman had, after all, given this monster several years of her life. So she told Vanessa everything, starting with her first conversation with Tina and ending with her exchange with Julia a few minutes ago.

"But here's the most damning thing," Nelly said. "The night before winter break started, Alice saw Emmett and Marshall driving past the house to leave campus. A month later, once the new semester started, Alice found out Marshall had been in a car accident that night. Only he claimed to be *the only person in the vehicle.* When Emmett basically disappeared and wouldn't return her calls or emails, she started to get suspicious. She and Marshall spoke one more time, and she pressed him on this—he made up a story about he and Emmett getting into an argument, Emmett demanding to be driven back to the apartment, and Marshall leaving campus alone, but Alice knew better. One of Emmett's neighbors later confirmed that he didn't come back that night, so Alice knew Marshall was lying. She told him she'd get to the bottom of this, and a few days later, the house fire happens."

Vanessa stared at her without expression.

Nelly sighed. "It's not proof positive of anything, but the

timing is very suspect. I think Emmett died in that car accident, and Marshall used it as his opportunity to take Emmett's place."

Vanessa shook her head. "That's too incredible to be true."

"Look at it from Marshall's perspective, though. He has nothing going for him. No career, no higher education, a checkered past. He and Emmett resemble each other so much that anyone who didn't know any better wouldn't be able to tell the difference. So he becomes his cousin. And all of a sudden, he has nearly three years' worth of college credits. *Emmett* drops out of the university where everyone knows him, takes a year off school, and transfers to a university in another state where nobody knows him. He never contacts anyone from here again."

"It's so preposterous." Vanessa looked her in the eye. "But I believe you."

"Why did you want to talk to Julia?" Nelly said. "What do you know? If you have more information, we should pool what we know and bring it to the sheriff. Emmett is a fraud and rapist—he shouldn't be anywhere near children, Vanessa, and I think you know that. So what brought you here?"

Vanessa's eyes drifted away.

"I have to show you."

"Show me what?" Nelly asked.

"It's in my car."

"What is it?"

Vanessa's eyes grew sad. "It's all the proof you need."

Without explanation, Vanessa rose and began walking. Nelly followed. They left the park and walked another block.

It was a quiet street behind the library, cars parked on one side in front of row homes.

Vanessa slowed when she got to her car. “It’s in the backseat.”

Nelly followed her onto the sidewalk. She saw a black trash bag on the passenger side in the backseat that looked filled. She had no idea what it could be.

“He kept everything,” Vanessa said, eyeing Nelly knowingly. “I guess in case he was found out. He kept all of Marshall’s records and IDs. I found them last night in his basement.”

Nelly gasped. “Can I see?”

Vanessa took her keychain out to unlock the car. Nelly noticed the woman carried a tiny self-defense zapper on it. Vanessa hit the button to unlock the vehicle. Nelly opened the rear passenger door and reached in to take the bag out.

Then she felt a terrible jolt. Her breath caught in her throat, and she couldn’t move.

Her world went dark.

39

Nelly slowly came to.

She felt groggy, as if she'd been medicated heavily. It took her vision a moment to clear, the unfamiliar room she found herself in coming into focus. The only piece of furniture in here was the uncomfortable wooden chair she sat in. Ahead of her was a bare wall that resembled concrete but looked much older; perhaps it was the foundation of whatever structure she was in. Bare walls to her left and right as well, which were constructed out of the same material.

Nelly went to stand, but she couldn't move. With budding horror, she realized she'd been immobilized somehow. Her hands were behind her back, her arms pulling her shoulders back in a painful stretched position. She tried bringing her hands forward, but she could barely move them.

Someone had handcuffed her.

She tried to stand but could only rise a few inches in an awkward, hunched posture. Not only were her wrists cuffed, but her torso was tied to the chair as well, and her legs were duct-taped at the ankles.

Trembling with fear, memory flooded her. She recalled speaking to Vanessa on the sidewalk. Remembered seeing the self-defense Taser attached to the woman's keychain and then feeling the heart-stopping jolt of electricity, her body going rigid, then her vision fading.

Nelly could only draw one conclusion from this turn of events.

Vanessa already *knew* who Emmett was. And she was willing to kidnap Nelly to protect the man.

But what else was she willing to do? Or, rather, what was she willing to allow Emmett to do to her?

Emmett had no choice. He had to kill her.

If Nelly didn't do something, she was certainly going to die. She fought the rising panic and bit back tears. She couldn't lose her mind now.

Think.

Her hands were cuffed behind her, and she was stuck in this chair. What could she do?

A door opened behind her. Light from another room poured in. She rose the few inches the chair and rope allowed and awkwardly shuffled her feet to turn around. She didn't get very far in her stuttering spin before Emmett clamped a viselike hand on her shoulder and pushed her back down to the floor. The old chair creaked as the legs hit the floor. It wouldn't take much more force to break it.

Nelly shuddered at Emmett's touch and proximity, instinctively leaning away from him in the chair. She'd at least managed to turn enough so that the door was in her periphery. Vanessa filled the doorway, her usual icy expression back in place.

"Hi, Nelly."

Emmett stood before her, and finally, the mask came off.

"Nelly Gordon," he said. "Did you ever think we'd meet again?"

She squeezed her eyes shut as tears filled them. So it was true, then. She'd known it all along. But hearing him admit to it somehow made it more real.

Emmett Moore was Marshall Dawes.

Knowing she'd been right, however, was cold comfort. Nelly was going to be killed, just like poor Tina. Being right all along wouldn't do her any good now.

"Come on," Emmett said. "You've tried to ruin my life twice now. At least have the courtesy to look me in the face."

Nelly forced her teary eyes open. "You tried to rape me!"

He shook his head. "I was sixteen, and I made a mistake, Nelly. Ever since then, I've dedicated my life to being better, to helping people, and to giving back. I've paid back whatever debt I had to society. And now here you are, dead set on ruining my life again."

Vanessa put her arm on his shoulder. "Emmett is a good man. Just look at what he's done for the community. One bad decision from over twenty years ago shouldn't undo all that."

Nelly was astonished by how Emmett had taken the woman in. Vanessa was so in love with this man, she was willing to overlook the fact he'd once tried to rape Nelly.

"You raped Irene too," Nelly said.

Emmett pulled a face. "That's a lie. She was a headcase. The police looked into her allegations. There's a reason nothing ever came of it."

"My Emmett is a good man," Vanessa said. "But you've given him no choice. He has to protect himself."

"In this day and age," Emmett said, "accusations are all it

takes. Despite all the good I've done, my life would be over. How is that fair?"

Fair? Nelly wanted to scream.

"You ca-can't kill me," Nelly said, hating how she stuttered. "You'll never get away with it."

"You've given me no choice," Emmett said. "You're deranged and dead set on telling the world I tried to rape you because I was a horny sixteen-year-old who got a little too frisky. And we both know that's not the whole truth, Nelly."

"What?"

"It's been over twenty years," he said. "Isn't it time to admit your part in this?"

"My *part*?"

"You were giving me mixed signals, Nelly."

"I did not!"

The man was a sociopath. He had managed to turn everything around in his mind so that this was all Nelly's fault, and she deserved to die. And somehow, he'd convinced Vanessa of the same.

Nelly shook her head. She fought the horror threatening to completely overwhelm her. If she gave in to this dread, she'd grow helpless. She'd give up.

"They'll find out I talked to Julia," Nelly said.

Emmett shook his head. "Nothing will come of it. According to the police report, there was only one person in the car. And Alice can't be questioned now."

"Because you killed her," Nelly said.

Emmett smiled sadly. "No, Nelly, that was a house fire. I had nothing to do with that."

Vanessa rubbed his shoulder. "He'd *never* do something like that."

Nelly couldn't believe how deluded the woman was. "Someone will figure out Vanessa was on campus today. Somebody had to see us. It was the middle of the day on a college campus."

Emmett's grin returned. "You'd be surprised at what people see—and don't."

Nelly had to keep the man talking while she figured out what to do. *Think!*

"You had your fiancée come to my house in the middle of the night, didn't you?" Nelly asked. "And had her put something in my food or drink at school while we were in the lounge, right?"

By their silence, Nelly knew she had it figured out.

"How did you know where I was this morning?" Nelly asked. "Did she follow me to campus?"

"Don't tell her anything," Vanessa said.

But Emmett ignored her for the moment. "We installed spyware on your phone, Nelly. We had no choice."

Nelly shuddered at the invasion of privacy. She felt violated. "Right. You had no choice."

"I suspected you'd start causing trouble. And I was right, wasn't I? Anyway, we've been reading all your emails, texts, and messages. I've listened to all your phone calls. We knew where you were at all times. Vanessa followed your phone."

Nelly cursed the annoying employee at the cellular store. He'd thought she'd picked up some viruses. But if he were a little better at his job, he would have found the spyware—and she could have shown that to the sheriff.

It would have saved her life.

Instead, she was stuck in this basement, probably minutes from being killed.

No! You can't panic! Think!

"Bring the gear in, would you?" Emmett said to Vanessa.

Vanessa left the room. Nelly looked up at the monster.

"What are you going to do?" she asked.

Emmett offered an apologetic smile. "Like I said, we've been reading your emails and texts and listening to your calls. So I know what you know. But I need to be sure we haven't missed anything."

He moved close to her once more. Nelly tipped the chair back again. She didn't go as far as last time. That one leg of the chair felt like it would break if she threw herself backward and slammed into the floor.

"I need to be absolutely certain you didn't find anything else out," he said, his face inches from hers again. "I know you've spoken with Tina and Julia. But have you talked to anyone else? Is there anything you *didn't* share with Vanessa this morning?"

Nelly was about to say no, but she quickly realized what she knew—or pretended to know—was the only thing that would keep her alive.

Emmett grinned. "You're easier to read than a kindergarten primer, Nelly."

She said nothing. Vanessa wheeled a metal cart into the room. Several sharp instruments were laid out on the tray on top of the cart. Some of them were knives, while others looked like things taken from a dentist's office. Regardless of their origin, however, it was clear what they were: the instruments of her torture.

"What did you do to Emmett?" she asked.

Now that she'd asked the question, Nelly could no longer think of this man as Emmett. From here on out, he was Marshall Dawes again.

"I didn't do anything," he said. "It was a car accident. He

died. I loved him like a brother, but there was nothing I could do. He was gone. And I saw a chance to start over. He would have wanted me to do exactly what I did."

"Are you fucking serious?" Nelly said, unable to hide her astonishment.

The man was truly a sociopath. He had himself convinced that the real Emmett Moore would have wanted Marshall Dawes to impersonate him in the event of his passing.

"*Emmett*," Vanessa prompted, "I said enough. Let's get this over with."

He smiled apologetically. "You're right, hon."

Vanessa pointed at her. "Find out what she knows, then be done with this."

Marshall put his hands on Vanessa's shoulders. "It will take some time. I have to be sure. *We* have to be sure."

Vanessa was not happy. She shook her head and wormed out of his grip, turning her back on her fiancé.

"You've got five minutes," she said. "Then I'm doing it myself."

Nelly went cold.

For a moment, Marshall stared at his fiancée's back as he considered his response, but then he thought better of it. He might have been the one running the show in their relationship, but it was clear he listened to what Vanessa had to say and wanted to keep her happy.

"If you're honest with me," Marshall said, turning back to Nelly, "then I'll make your death quick and painless. But if you play games, then this is not going to be pleasant. Do you understand?"

A wave of nausea hit her. She fought the urge to vomit.

Nelly knew she couldn't bargain with them. Their minds

were made up. She was going to die. Considering her limited options, quick and painless seemed like the easy choice to make.

No, a little voice sounded in her head. *You are never going to be a victim again.*

Nelly had five minutes to work out a solution. She'd use every second of it.

For now, though, Nelly played along. She wanted Marshall to think she'd given up. Nodding mutely, letting a tear escape, Nelly looked into the monster's eyes.

"Now tell me what else you know," he said.

As she struggled to come up with a plausible-sounding lie, the idea came to her. Nelly recalled one of the things she'd taught her seventh graders this week, about how European explorers played the indigenous tribes against each other, driving a wedge between peoples who should have allied against them.

That was her only chance here. While the two of them were distracted, she might be able to extricate herself from the cuffs.

Nelly looked in the other woman's direction. "Marshall knows I don't know anything else, Vanessa. But he wouldn't let you kill me. Want to know why?"

The other woman slowly turned. She frowned at Marshall.

"What is she talking about?" Vanessa asked.

"I'm the one who got away," Nelly said. "Think about it. For twenty-four years, Marshall has done nothing but pine over me. He can't let it go. He wanted this body, but he couldn't have it, and that's driven him insane. You know what that means, don't you?"

Two tiny dots of color appeared on Vanessa's cheeks.

"After all this time, Marshall still wants me."

Vanessa shot Marshall a murderous look.

"Is that true?" she asked.

Marshall came out of his crouch and went to his fiancée. "Come on, honey. Don't lose your head now. You know it isn't like that. This woman will say anything to save herself. I don't *want* to do any of this. Remember, this is just about survival."

The two of them weren't arguing yet, but Nelly felt a storm brewing. She needed to fill Vanessa's mind with more doubt.

"If it's only about survival," Nelly said, "why does he seem to be enjoying this so much? Look at him. He looks like he could get off right now."

Vanessa studied her fiancé. Marshall grew uncomfortable under her scrutiny.

"Honey, you don't actually believe this woman," he said, "do you?"

She was already lying, so Nelly decided to keep on doing it. More fuel to the fire.

"If I'm making that up, why did Marshall recommend me for the job?" Nelly asked.

Marshall went stiff. Vanessa regarded him coolly for a moment, her expression even frostier than usual.

"You *recommended* her?" Vanessa asked.

"No, that's not true!"

Vanessa's face was bright red now.

The first crack in Marshall's armor appeared.

He looked nervous.

"Tell me the truth, *Marshall*," Vanessa said.

Hearing her say his real name, the man lowered his eyes like he'd been scolded.

Marshall's swagger was gone. "Miguel made this decision without my input, Vanessa. I *swear* to you!"

"Come on," Nelly interrupted. "You and I both know that Marshall has Miguel eating out of his hand at this point. He wants us to believe Miguel didn't loop him in? Didn't ask his opinion? That's unbelievable. Marshall *knew* I was coming. He *wanted* me here."

Marshall shook his head at her, then turned back to Vanessa. "You know how Miguel works, honey. He makes all the hiring and firing decisions. You've heard him say it before: the buck stops with him. Right?"

Nelly wasn't about to let him get the final word in. "I'm the last person in the world he should want around. But your fiancé is so enamored with me, he was willing to risk his career and his life—*and your life too*—so he could get close to me one more time. Face it, Vanessa. In his own twisted way, Marshall is still in love with me."

Vanessa wanted to believe her fiancé. But she also couldn't ignore what Nelly had said. While the two of them were engaged, Nelly used the opportunity to her advantage. She gritted her teeth against the pain she knew was coming. Then, with a quick, violent wrenching motion, she dislocated her thumb. The same one Marshall had displaced all those years ago. She had always told herself that the pain she had experienced would one day be useful to her. She had never known if that was actually true, or if that was just a thing people told themselves to make sense out of the senseless.

But now she was going to use the injury against him.

The pain was terrible. But Nelly managed to extract her throbbing hand from the cuffs. She couldn't stop the hot tears from flowing, but that hardly mattered. Marshall and Vanessa would assume she was crying from fear, not pain.

Nelly kept her throbbing wrist behind her. She managed to get her thumb back in place, but she couldn't do much with the hand. Her other hand went to work on the rope tying her to the chair back.

"Vanessa," Marshall said, rubbing her arm, "I love you. Nobody else. And you don't have to worry. I'm going to take care of this."

So far she had planted seeds of doubt in Vanessa's mind regarding Marshall's true intentions toward Nelly. But the other woman wasn't quite convinced yet. Nelly had to drive her point further home.

"Baby," Marshall was saying to Vanessa, "you can't listen to a word this bitch says. She's staring death in the face."

"He told me he loved me," Nelly said, bearing down against the intense pain in her hand. "He told me I was the one as he held me down on that desk. He still feels that way."

It was a lie.

But Vanessa didn't know that.

Marshall moved away from his fiancée and brought the knife up to Nelly's face. "Shut up! That's a damned lie!"

Nelly fought through the burning pain and the fear engulfing her. She ignored the knife thrust in her face and looked over at Vanessa and played a hunch.

"I'll bet he asked to have a moment alone with me," Nelly said. "He probably told you he'd take care of everything by himself, right? But you've got your intuitions too. You didn't trust him enough to leave him alone with me. You and I both know what he really wanted."

"Shut up!" Marshall screamed.

Marshall screamed at her to shut up again, but Nelly saw in Vanessa's changing expression that she'd hit the mark. The other woman came over and slapped Marshall on the shoulder.

"Is that true, you son of a bitch?" she asked, her face for once full of color. "After everything I've done for you, did you plan on fucking her?"

"NO!" Marshall roared, his face turning purple as he rose to his full height and faced Vanessa. "I would never do that to you!"

The veins in Vanessa's neck pressed against the skin. "Then why did you ask to do this yourself?"

Though she was still tied to the chair, Nelly didn't expect to get a better opportunity than this. It was time to make her move while the two of them screamed at each other.

Nelly tipped the chair back and kicked at the knife in Marshall's hand. He wasn't expecting the sudden violent motion from her. Her foot connected with his wrist. Using the momentum from that kick, Nelly pushed herself backward as hard as she could. The chair smashed against the floor, breaking into several pieces.

Nelly's hands were free, but only one of them was working. The dislocated thumb was one big throb after another. Quickly taking stock of her situation, Nelly discovered the impact from the fall had broken the legs of the chair, but the seat was still attached to the back. And her legs remained duct-taped together at the ankles.

Marshall was kneeling on the floor beside his fiancée. Vanessa was lying on her back, her body twitching. One of her hands, covered in blood, was up around her neck.

Then Nelly saw the knife Marshall had been holding.

It was stuck in Vanessa's throat.

40

Nelly had kicked Marshall's elbow, inadvertently causing the knife to stick Vanessa in the throat.

Judging by the amount of blood pooling and how the woman's spasmodic movements were slowing down, Vanessa was going to die.

"No! No! NO!"

Marshall helplessly knelt beside his fiancée, his hands pressing against the woman's throat in a futile effort to stop her from bleeding out.

Nelly clawed at the duct-tape keeping her ankles together. She'd put her thumb back into place, but the pain in that limb was still terrible. It left her with one working hand to extricate herself from the tape and chair.

Vanessa stopped twitching.

Nelly peeled another strip of tape off, but it tore away from the main piece, leaving her to start over.

Marshall slowly turned his head to glare at her. There was murder in his eyes.

In an eerily quiet voice, he said, "I am going to kill you."

Nelly was crying again, though this time it was fear, not pain, that brought out her tears. She couldn't rip the tape off fast enough. And she was still tied to the chair back, which would prevent her from moving quickly even if her feet were free.

Marshall picked up one of the knives that had fallen off the cart and came to his full height. Nelly fumbled with the duct tape, using her one working hand, but it was no use. They had applied several layers of tape, immobilizing her ankles. And Marshall would kill her long before she stripped it all away.

Marshall towered over her for a moment, looking down with a murderous rage. The hand holding the short knife was white-knuckled. His body trembled.

Nelly looked up at him. She knew she wasn't going to get away now. This wasn't her falling victim to despair and helplessness. This was her accepting a fact about reality. He was going to kill her.

But maybe she could take him out too.

Nelly hadn't wanted to kill Vanessa, but she took some satisfaction in witnessing Marshall's pain. Her working hand groped blindly on the floor beside her for a makeshift weapon. Perhaps one of the knives had skittered over here in the crash.

"After everything, are you really just going to kill me?" she asked, a challenge in her voice. She was buying herself time. "Then you'll never get to have me."

His eyes popped.

"Come on." Nelly bobbed her head toward Vanessa. "She's dead. She'll never know."

Marshall's gaze drifted over his shoulder, to the inert

form of his now dead fiancée. A pool of blood radiated silently away from her body, turning the floor dark.

While he was distracted, Nelly tore her eyes from him. Right there. Just out of reach. One of the chair legs. It had broken into two jagged pieces, one of them long and sharp enough to do some damage.

Marshall brought his gaze back to her. A rabid look filled his eyes. He was sixteen years old again. Unpolished. Awkward. Out of control. Feral.

An animal.

"I'm going to enjoy this, Nelly. And then I'm going to kill you."

Still clutching the knife, he unzipped his pants and undid his belt. As he began to slide them down his legs, Nelly flew into action. She lunged and grabbed the wooden shard. Marshall reacted instinctively. He stopped fumbling with his underwear and moved in to kill her, thrusting with the knife.

Nelly rolled out of the way and drove the broken chair leg upward.

Into Marshall's belly.

41

Nelly quickly peeled the rest of the duct tape off, then managed to extricate herself from the broken chair.

She couldn't believe she was still alive.

Or that Marshall was dead.

It had happened quickly. After she drove the wood into his gut, he'd barely had time to register shock before he'd slumped onto the ground beside her. Clutching at his belly, Emmett had faded fast. Nelly must have hit a major artery.

The pain in her wrist had subsided, turning into more a burning sensation that ran up into her forearm and down into her hand. Emerging from the room of horrors, Nelly entered a large open space filled with old furniture, faded paintings, and dusty heirlooms. She was in a vast basement, the ceiling high overhead. Alcoves dotted one of the walls, and two hallways extended in opposite directions. Nelly remembered Beck pointing out Vanessa's large home during their drive to the sports pub, mentioning the house was old and had been part of the Underground Railroad.

She must have been in Vanessa's basement.

It took Nelly a moment to spot the staircase leading to the ground floor. Before she headed in that direction, Nelly glanced back into the room. Blood covered much of the floor. The chair she'd been in had shattered into many pieces. Vanessa's and Emmett's corpses were on opposite sides of the room.

Nelly began to pick her way through the rows of old junk, passing between rickety metal shelves that housed generational artifacts. She found stairs and emerged in a kitchen. There was a landline beside the refrigerator. Nelly dialed the sheriff.

"Hi, Vanessa," Bill Van Dyke answered.

"It's Nelly Peak," she said. "I'm here. At Vanessa's house. You'd better come get me."

She burst into tears as Bill asked her questions and told her to hold on. Nelly didn't answer any of them. Instead, she slid down against the refrigerator till she was squatting on the floor. She let go of the phone. Bill continued to speak, but she didn't hear a word he said.

She was alive.

42

MONTHS LATER

The batting helmet was a little too big for Karly's head, looking a bit comical. But the girl didn't seem to mind as she took her place in the batter's box. Her teammates cheered her on from the dugout. Nelly clapped along with Beck, who as usual was performing her "artistic interpretation" of a cheerleading routine. Beck thrust the old pom-poms this way and that and shouted cheers she half-remembered from her high school days.

Karly took a big swing at the first pitch. It would have been enough to send the ball into the outfield, but unfortunately the softball didn't even reach home plate before it hit the dirt.

"Come on, Karly!" Nelly screamed.

The girl took another big swing at a ball that had no chance of touching the plate. Strike two.

Karly stepped out of the box to gather herself. The score was...something. Nelly had lost track. It didn't really matter. Overland didn't field a competitive team. Most of the girls playing had never tried the sport before this season. They were just out there to learn the game and be part of a team.

The outcome of this game didn't matter at all.

And yet, here they were in the bottom of the ninth, and it seemed vitally important that Karly drive in the winning run. Everyone had apparently forgotten that Overland had recorded one win in their ten games so far and had no hope of making the playoffs. As a matter of fact, Nelly wasn't even sure there were playoffs to be made.

But all the same, everyone was on their feet as Karly reentered the batter's box. The pitch came, and, miraculously, it was headed in the general direction of home plate. Karly closed her eyes and chopped at the ball.

The crack of the bat was the most thrilling sound Nelly had heard in ages. The ball just cleared the outstretched glove of an infielder. The center fielder shot forward, racing to make the play, but the ball hit the ground first.

"Run, Karly!"

In her surprised excitement, the poor girl had forgotten to move. Letting go of her bat, Karly pumped her gangly legs.

Karly's foot touched the bag just before the ball popped the glove of the first base girl. Meanwhile, the Overland player on third had already come home.

Game over.

The Overland Wolf Pack were two and ten, but the team celebrated like they'd won the Little League World Series. Nelly felt a hand on her shoulder. Karly's mother looked down at her from one row back in the bleachers, a grateful smile on her face.

"Thank you," the woman said.

Karly's parents had gone through a difficult divorce

earlier this year, and Karly's grades had begun to suffer. The girl had retreated into herself, becoming depressed and anxious. Nelly had, somehow, been able to reach her. Slowly, Karly had become herself once more. And ever since then, her mother had thanked Nelly at every opportunity. Nelly squeezed the woman's hand.

"I didn't do this—Karly did."

The woman thanked her again anyway, then went to give her daughter a big hug. Beck flung the pom-poms in the air and threw her arms around Nelly.

"We should celebrate tonight," Beck said.

Nelly laughed. Beck was always looking for a reason to go to the pub on a school night. Nelly made sure to only indulge once a week, usually Thursdays. Last week while they were out, Nelly had exchanged numbers with a cute guy who worked for a local hardware company. They were supposed to go out this weekend.

As the celebration came to an end, the children collected their belongings and ran to meet their parents.

"What a game, huh, Nelly?"

Miguel appeared by her side. The principal's hair had turned completely white now. He'd aged a lot this school year.

"I'm so happy for them," Nelly said.

Miguel smiled at her. "Is now a good time for you?"

"Yes."

They hung back while the bleachers and field emptied. It was a beautiful spring day, a warm breeze in the air that teased the coming summer. Beck shot Nelly a meaningful look before she headed up the hill toward the parking lot with a gaggle of raucous students, both athletes and spectators. Beck was by far the most popular member of the faculty with the children.

Now that Emmett was gone.

When they were alone, Nelly faced Miguel. She marveled over how much their relationship had changed.

They had gotten off to such a poor start. But ever since the most harrowing, unbelievable week of Nelly's life back in late September, the two of them had become friends. Once the truth about Emmett and Vanessa came out, Miguel had acted swiftly, removing Nelly from performance review and telling her she not only had a clean slate, she'd get the benefit of any doubt moving forward.

Following that reset in their relationship, Nelly had immediately gone up in Miguel's estimation. With Emmett gone, it was like someone had removed Miguel's blinders. When he audited Nelly's class shortly after, he realized how good a teacher she was. And since then, he had spoken glowingly of her, complimenting her classroom management and pedagogy every chance he got, often to her embarrassment in faculty meetings.

Over the school year, they'd grown close. Operating without an assistant principal and down two teachers, Miguel had leaned heavily on Nelly as well as the rest of the small faculty at Overland to fill the gaps. Along the way, Miguel and Nelly had worked out some big problems together. Despite her initial feelings about the man, Nelly had grown to respect and even like Miguel. The man had dedicated his life to this community, and now all those years of commendable service would be forever tarnished because he'd employed two sociopaths. Though that was hardly his fault alone—Emmett and Vanessa had fooled everyone in the community, including the mayor and respected members of the church—Miguel did not attempt to deflect blame.

Instead, he'd owned up to his massive error in judgment when it came to both Emmett and Vanessa, often expressing his utter regret over having been taken in by Emmett's charm and made a fool of for so long. Now he was doing everything in his power to make up for it all, knowing full well he'd likely never make up for it. The man had a good heart.

And that made this conversation all the more difficult.

"My old boss reached out," Nelly said. "There's a position for seventh- and eighth-grade history opening up next year in my old school district. I've decided to accept the offer. I'll finish out this year, obviously, but I wanted you to know sooner rather than later, so you had more time to fill my position."

Miguel's face fell, but he nodded appreciatively. "I shouldn't be surprised. You're a great teacher, Nelly. In fact, I'm amazed it took him this long to ask you to come back."

She blushed, embarrassed as always by compliments.

"We got off to a rocky start," Nelly said, "but I want you to know that I consider you a friend."

"I appreciate your letting me know of your intentions for next year." Miguel smiled. "Now then, I wouldn't be doing my job if I didn't make a counter."

Nelly was caught off guard. How did Miguel plan to counter? She knew what Overland's budget was for next year, having helped out at the recent school board meetings. Miguel could not dangle any more money in front of her. And there was little they could change about the curriculum, which was mostly mandated by the state. She supposed he could offer to take away her non-instructional duties, but that hardly seemed possible either, given how small the faculty was. Everybody needed to chip in to make things go around here, and she wouldn't have felt comfortable not doing her part.

Nelly honestly couldn't think of any perks Miguel could tempt her with.

"I need an assistant principal," he said.

Nelly was floored.

It had been seven months since Patti had taken her unexpected leave of absence, and in that time Miguel had not named her replacement yet. Nelly assumed Miguel was proceeding with great caution, having been fooled so terribly by Emmett, and wanted to be absolutely certain about the next person. Of course, that had given the staff nearly the entire school year to endlessly speculate on the hiring decision.

Nelly's name came up occasionally in those water-cooler discussions, but she'd never taken the idea seriously. Nor had anyone else. Everyone assumed Miguel would appoint someone he knew well, one of the other teachers with more experience and tenure at Overland.

"Before you say no," Miguel went on, "let me say something else. I was planning to retire this year. But with everything that happened, I don't feel it'd be a good time to step down just yet. I'd like to stay for another year, maybe two, and during that time, I would show you the ropes. You're a good teacher, Nelly. And I think you'd make an even better principal."

She was at a loss. Nelly had never envisioned being part of the administration. Her only goal coming out of college had been to become a teacher and, once she was a teacher, to stay one. Leading a classroom was meaningful and fulfilling, bringing her a joy and deep contentment she had never experienced elsewhere in life.

"It's a lot to consider," Miguel said, holding up a palm. "Why don't you take the weekend and get back to me?"

"I don't know, Miguel," Nelly said. "It's a *lot*."

"Nelly," he said, giving her a wink, "don't you realize you've already been doing all the work of an assistant principal the last few months?"

She opened her mouth to protest. But Nelly realized Miguel spoke the truth. It seemed absurdly obvious now that he'd been grooming her for the role ever since he'd begged for her help with school board meetings and other high-level responsibilities. How had she missed it?

The answer that came to her a moment later was just as obvious.

Too many other things had been going on this year for her to stop and think about the big picture. After the thing with Emmett and Vanessa, and all the unwelcome attention that had drawn, Nelly had been called out to California to testify in the civil lawsuit brought against her ex-husband's former boss, and then had been asked to give a statement to authorities as they considered criminal charges as well. The chaotic school year had kept her incredibly busy also, while Miguel scrambled to fill two teaching roles and keep the extracurriculars running smoothly.

"Take the weekend," Miguel said. "I really do hope you'll say yes."

They shook hands. Nelly lingered at the softball field, marveling over everything that had happened to her this school year.

When Nelly opened her eyes, she spotted Beck along with some of her students at the top of the hill, waving at her. She felt like part of the community now. Connected. She wanted to be a good teacher for all these children. To protect them. To help them.

Nelly waved back. She'd never wanted to be a principal before.

But she had to admit the idea was intriguing.

THANK YOU FOR READING

Did you enjoy reading *The Good Teacher*? Please consider leaving a review on Amazon. Your review will help other readers to discover the novel.

ABOUT THE AUTHOR

Brian R. O'Rourke has been writing stories since he was eight years old. A lifelong, avid reader, Brian believes that fiction has the power to change the world. He is married to a wonderful woman and is the proud father of two amazing daughters.

He also writes mysteries and thrillers under the pen name Evan Ronan.

ALSO BY BRIAN R. O'ROURKE

The New Husband

The Only Son

Her Mother's Daughter

The Good Teacher

Printed in Great Britain
by Amazon